"Your mother see[ms] [beside]
herself," Mr. Lafa[yette]

Claire watched her for a few seconds. She recognized that smile, that look of fondness on her mother's face. "She's telling him about my father."

"They must have loved each other very much."

"They did." She could feel a lump growing in her throat. Would she ever know such a love? Such a partnership?

"My father is not an outdoorsman," Mr. Lafayette said, "but every Christmas Eve he takes my brothers and me into the woods to collect pine boughs and berries because he knows my mother loves the smell of them."

Claire returned his gaze. "My father did the same. Our cabin was filled with greenery."

"Then after reading the account from Scripture, my father would tell us to place our shoes in front of the fire and hurry off to bed."

"Or Père Noël would not come?"

"Yes."

She couldn't help but smile again. "I was always told the same." She wondered what sort of boy he had been. Was he affectionate and expressive like Spotted Eagle or rough and rambunctious? Somehow she suspected the latter.

"We have lived very different lives," he then said, "but I think we ourselves are not so different."

Shannon Farrington and her husband have been married for over twenty years, have two children, and are active members in their local church and community. When she isn't researching or writing, you can find Shannon visiting national parks and historical sites or at home herding her small flock of chickens through the backyard. She and her family live in Maryland.

Books by Shannon Farrington

Love Inspired Historical

Her Rebel Heart
An Unlikely Union
Second Chance Love
The Reluctant Bridegroom
Frontier Agreement

SHANNON FARRINGTON

Frontier Agreement

HARLEQUIN® LOVE INSPIRED® HISTORICAL

Recycling programs for this product may not exist in your area.

LOVE INSPIRED BOOKS

ISBN-13: 978-0-373-42517-4

Frontier Agreement

www.Harlequin.com

Printed in U.S.A.

But my God shall supply all your need according to his riches in glory by Christ Jesus.
—*Philippians* 4:19

In memory of Gandmom McCoy
See you in the morning

Chapter One

Fort Mandan
Upper Louisiana Territory
December 1804

Pierre Lafayette cast an eager eye over the vast horizon and sighed contentedly. The air of the Great Plains was cold but fresh. Here, over a thousand miles from home, he could finally breathe.

When Captain Meriwether Lewis and Captain William Clark accepted him as an oarsman for their westward expedition, he'd realized that at long last he had finally become his own man. *I was hired because of who I am. Not because of who my father is or what he may be able to do for them.*

A strong back, sharp eye and steadiness with a musket were highly valuable skills in the wilderness. At home they had been frowned upon.

The expedition, the Corps of Discovery, was to winter here on the Missouri River, just beyond the Mandan and Hidatsa Indian villages, before continuing on further westward in the spring. Fortifications had been erected around their camp for defense, but so far the local people had proved themselves to be friendly and welcoming.

Turning his eyes in the direction of the villages, Pierre noticed a trio of natives approaching—two women and a small boy. He studied them as they drew near. Visitors to the fort were nothing new. In the past six weeks since the expedition's arrival, they had received many people. Most were tribal leaders, but there had been a few curious women and children as well. Pierre didn't recall seeing these particular Indians before, however.

They approached him cautiously. One of the squaws bowed. The other curtsied. Both were dressed in buffalo robes and had long, dark braided hair. The one who had curtsied had vibrant green eyes that showed her to be of mixed blood. Although young, she carried herself with the grace and stature of a seasoned chief's wife.

Pierre thought her pretty, pretty enough to turn many a man's head, but he gave her beauty no further thought than that. If the pampered, powdered belles and wealth of New Orleans hadn't held his interest, he could hardly be captivated by a penniless Indian woman.

He drew in a long breath. His father had wanted him to become a polished gentleman of society, to marry, beget children and one day take the helm of the family shipping business. Pierre had refused. It wasn't out of disrespect for his father or unwillingness to take responsibility. *I am no rogue, and I am willing to work as hard as any other man.* But his father's life had stifled him. He'd longed for a wider scope for his ambitions—a chance to see more of the world before he settled down into just a small patch of it.

On this expedition, he had done so, and he had loved it. This adventure meant more to him than anything life back home could offer. New Orleans was a wonderful place full of culture, cuisine and comfort, but for Pierre, the harsh unknown beckoned. The winding Missouri, the distant mountains, the Pacific Ocean—these were the only siren songs he wanted to heed. Even now, they called to him. Pierre could hardly wait for the ice on the river to thaw so they could once again be on their way.

But today, there is work to be done here...

He refocused his attention on the green-eyed girl. She had come to the fort requesting an audience with Captain Lewis. Evidently the boy had some ailment. In halting English, she tried to explain, "Boy, here... sore...back..."

Pierre tried to make sense of what she was saying. "He has a sore back?" That was a complaint hardly worthy of disturbing the captain. "Perhaps if he rests—"

She shook her head adamantly. "Great pain. Days. See captain. *S'il vous plaît...*"

The *if you please* caught his attention. "You speak French?"

"Oui." A smile of relief broke on her lips, but the moment Pierre offered one in return, it disappeared. A guarded expression took its place.

"I am Claire Manette," she stated formally in French. "I am the daughter of François Manette, a trapper. My mother and I live in this village. I require Captain Lewis's medical assistance for my cousin's young son. May I present Little Flower and Spotted Eagle."

Pierre nodded politely to the Mandan woman as Mademoiselle Manette continued.

"Spotted Eagle has a large abscess on the lower part of his back. I have drained it twice, applied poultices, but to no avail."

It wasn't that uncommon to find a French-speaking woman in an Indian village. Europeans had been traveling this part of the Missouri for years, often taking wives from among the native tribes. There was already, in fact, a Frenchman in this particular village, one by the name of Toussaint Charbonneau. He had two young squaws, Otter Woman and Sacagawea.

What is uncommon, Pierre thought, *is to find a woman so educated, so obviously refined.* Were it not for the buffalo robe and braided hair, Mademoiselle Manette could easily have been conversing in a New Orleans's ballroom. Pierre suddenly felt the need to exercise his formal manners. "I am Pierre Lafayette," he said bowing, "at your service."

Her stoic gaze told him she was hardly impressed. Clearing his throat, he straightened.

"I hoped Captain Lewis might have some sort of medicine," she said.

The Mandan woman beside her evidently understood "medicine." She nodded emphatically at the word, and then showed Pierre the sack she was carrying. It was filled with dried corn.

"She is willing to pay," Mademoiselle Manette said.

While payment in dry goods was always appreciated, Pierre doubted the captain would require all that had been brought. He signaled to the guard on the catwalk above them, then led the women and the boy into the fort. Just as he had predicted, the mademoiselle turned many a soldier's head. A private on the parade field missed his step for a glance at the guests, and at the forge the blacksmith held his iron suspended above the fire momentarily before returning his attention to his task.

For a moment, the gentleman in Pierre hesitated to leave these women unattended while he sought Captain Lewis, but he told himself that was foolish. The men were disciplined soldiers. A pause, a glance was one thing, but the men would not stray from their duties.

Pierre knocked upon the officers' quarters.

"Enter," a voice said.

Stomping the snow from his moccasins, Pierre stepped into the tiny room. The light of a single candle glowed. Captain Lewis was bent over his writing desk, scrawling out reports for *his* commander, President Thomas Jefferson.

My President, Pierre thought. *In Washington*. Not that long ago, Pierre had sworn allegiance to the emperor in France, but with Bonaparte's sale of the Louisiana territory, he had become an American. *What a strange new world.*

Captain Lewis returned his quill to the inkwell, looked up. "What is it, Mr. Lafayette?" he asked.

"Pardon the disturbance, sir, but there are two women here to see you. They've brought a young boy in need of medical treatment."

As a Virginia gentleman and the son of a devout Christian mother, the captain was never one to turn away a soul in need. He immediately stood. "Show them in."

Pierre did so at once, introducing Mademoiselle Manette as a translator. Captain Lewis nodded to Spotted

Eagle and his mother, then asked Miss Manette, "What exactly ails the boy?"

Pierre spoke for her. "The lady doesn't understand much English, sir."

The *lady* quickly corrected him. "Understand? *Oui.* Speak? No."

Captain Lewis suppressed a smile as Pierre tried unsuccessfully to will the color from his face. *She's French for certain*, he thought, *for she has no trouble speaking her mind.*

Claire resisted the urge to clamp her hand over her mouth as the two men stared at her. The dark-haired Frenchman was embarrassed, the American captain somewhat bemused. Apparently the scent of smoke-saturated wool, the writing desk and small raised bed had made her forget where she was.

She had been born in a room not unlike this one, in a small cabin in Illinois. There her father used to tell her she was passionate to a fault where truth was concerned. *But he always said it with a smile*, Claire mused, *and he said he believed the quality would serve me well.*

So far it had not. Such plainspokenness did not sit well in a village where women were treated little better than pack animals. She loved her Mandan family, her mother's people, *her people*, but after six months among them, *six hard months* trying to assimilate into the culture, she still was not fully accepted. She was Mandan, but she was also *white*, and she had taken up the white man's religion.

Yet from the looks of the two men before me, I am

not quite white enough, she thought. *I'm a curious creature, and no doubt they think me gullible and naive.*

She wasn't either of those things, and she wouldn't be taken advantage of by any white man, be he dressed in decorated uniform or common buckskin. She had learned that lesson the hard way. She was, however, intelligent enough to recognize God's provision when she saw it. Spotted Eagle was on the verge of becoming very ill. She needed the captain's help.

Claire quickly explained her presence. The Frenchman was still staring at her, but at least he had the decency to translate her words. Thankfully, the American captain wasted no time. He examined Spotted Eagle personally.

"What have you applied as poultice?" he asked her.

"Comfrey and calendula to ease the pain," she said. "Also yarrow."

The American nodded his approval. "The yarrow has kept it from festering, but it has not treated the cause." He probed the boy's back more closely. Spotted Eagle winced.

"It will be over soon," the captain promised him with a smile.

Claire appreciated the man's attempt to comfort her cousin's young son. So far, relations between the natives and the white men had been cordial. Captains Lewis and Clark had insisted the government that had sent them wished to promote peace and trade. From what Claire had observed, the trade had been fair. She hoped it would remain that way. The white man's presence could be an opportunity to reflect the light of God's love.

Or it could detract from it, she thought, for Claire

had met men before who claimed to love God but did not extend the same care to His people.

The Frenchman was still staring.

What are you looking at, sir? she wanted to say, but she already knew the answer.

Feeling more uncomfortable by the moment, Claire returned her gaze to the captain. Her eyes followed his every move. He applied a poultice, then gave Spotted Eagle a pill to swallow. After several repeated sips of water, the very large object finally went down.

"Keep on with the poultices for a few more days," the captain told Claire.

The doctoring now finished, Little Flower presented her sack of corn to him. Claire was pleasantly surprised that he took only half.

"Please tell her that her payment is more than adequate," he said.

Claire nodded, then delivered the message in Mandan. Little Flower was most pleased. After reclaiming her sack, she bowed several times to the captain. Then she did the same to the Frenchman beside him. The men bowed formally in return.

Claire curtsied. *"Merci,"* she said.

Eager to be on her way, she then reached for Spotted Eagle's hand. The Frenchman opened the door.

A cold blast of wind stung her face. Stepping outside, Claire could feel the eyes of the men around her. One particular soldier grinned. Little Flower returned his look, but Claire, drawing her buffalo robe closer, kept her eyes down as she tramped steadily back toward the village. The snow crunched beneath her moccasins. Already it was deep, and there was much more winter still to come.

Spotted Eagle trudged along quietly, but Little Flower chatted excitedly. She seemed confident the excursion to the fort had proven worth their effort. "White men have great power," she proclaimed. "Strong medicine."

"The power does not come from white men," Claire corrected her gently. "If the American captain's medicine heals Spotted Eagle, it will be because the God of Heaven, the true Great Spirit, ordains it so."

To that, Little Flower said nothing.

Open their eyes, Lord, please.

It was a prayer Claire had offered numerous times as she and her mother labored to be a light for the Lord in this village. More than anything she wished for the salvation of her cousins, her uncle Running Wolf and the rest of the Mandan people. But were their efforts really accomplishing anything, or were their "curious ways," as her uncle put it, their refusal to participate in certain tribal customs, only further alienating the kinsmen they so desperately wished to see come to Christ?

Running Wolf had taken them in because Claire's mother was his own flesh and blood and because her husband had been a friend to the Mandan people, but more than once he had stated he would not worship François Manette's supposed all-powerful God or His son, Jesus. "I will not become like white men."

Neither Claire nor her mother wished their Mandan family to forget their heritage. All they wanted was for their tribe to know the true creator, to experience His life, the life He intended, free from superstitious fear, free from disease propagated by sin.

But truth be told, there was another reason Claire was desperate for the conversion of her family. She was of marriageable age—well beyond it, in fact, by tribal standards. Upon her arrival in the village, her uncle had given her one year to mourn her father. "After that, you will be given to a husband."

Claire inwardly sighed. She, like any young woman her age, wanted a home and a family of her own. *But how am I to wed a man who does not share my faith? Without such, there can be no true union of heart or mind or spirit.* Her parents had shared such a love. She wanted the same.

If Running Wolf were to come to faith in Christ, he would understand that. Then he would not insist I wed an unbeliever.

"Perhaps, Bright Star," Little Flower said, referring to Claire by her Mandan name, "you will find a husband among the white men of the fort."

Claire felt herself flush in spite of the cold. Little Flower hadn't known Claire's thoughts, but the subject of her eligibility was obviously on her cousin's mind. Had Running Wolf enlisted her for help? Was that why she had smiled at so many of the men at the fort?

Little Flower then giggled. "You must admit, they are handsome. Especially the one who speaks in your tongue."

Claire flushed even further. She was thankful for the harsh wind. Its sting concealed the true reason for the fire in her face. Yes, she had noticed the Frenchman and yes, he was handsome. Broad shoulders, raven-black hair, eyes the color of charcoal. He had noticed her, as well, and had apparently liked what he saw. *Which is all the more reason to avoid him.*

"I do not seek a handsome man alone, Little Flower, but one who worships my God."

"Perhaps he does, Bright Star."

As intriguing as the possibility of that thought was, Claire quickly dismissed it. Even if Mr. Lafayette was a Christian, even if he did take an *honorable* interest in her, what good could possibly come of it? Marriage still wouldn't be possible between them since the expedition would be leaving in the spring.

The best Claire could hope for was that his conduct, and that of his comrades, would not snuff out any light she and her mother were trying to kindle.

Two days later, having just returned from Captain Clark's hunting excursion, Pierre stepped into the fort. He arrived just in time to see Toussaint Charbonneau storming out of it. The Frenchman was clearly angry about something, angry enough to ignore Pierre's greeting, angry enough to outpace his heavily pregnant teenage wife.

Sacagawea struggled to catch him. Pierre couldn't help but feel sorry for her. He doffed his cap at her. She offered him a sweet smile and hurried on.

Captain Lewis was standing at the entrance to his quarters, arms folded across his chest, looking rather miffed himself. *He and the trapper must have quarreled over something*, Pierre thought. *Again.*

As Pierre approached, the obvious frown on the captain's face shifted to its customary stoic expression.

"I see Captain Clark's party has returned," Lewis said. "Was the hunt successful?"

"Indeed, sir. Ten buffalo. They are being brought in by sled as we speak."

Lewis nodded pensively. "Has the captain determined what is to be done with them?"

"Yes, sir. He thought it best to take them to the main Mandan village first since it was a joint hunting party."

Lewis nodded again. "Tell Captain Clark that the men should return when the delivery of meat is complete."

"Yes, sir," Pierre replied. He started to turn.

"The woman," Lewis then said, "the one who came in search of medical assistance. What is she called?"

"Claire Manette, sir."

"She is fluent in French?" Captain Lewis asked.

"I believe so, sir."

"When you go to the village, see if she would be kind enough to assist us with our vocabulary, since Charbonneau is unable to cooperate or agree with anyone."

So that was the cause of the argument. The captains had eagerly accepted Charbonneau as an interpreter because Sacagawea could speak not only the local language but also that of the mountain tribe where the expedition was headed in the spring. She dictated vocabulary to her husband, and he translated her language into French. Then, with the help of Pierre or one of the other Frenchmen, his words were translated into English for the captains.

It was a tedious process, and Charbonneau had a tendency to argue pronunciation and the nuance of every French word rather than convey the basic messages necessary for maintaining friendly relations with the current tribe. Evidently Captain Lewis's patience was wearing thin, and he was prepared to replace the disagreeable Frenchman if he could.

"Ask Miss Manette to come to the fort," Lewis told Pierre.

The memory of her sharply spoken insistence that she could indeed understand English crossed his mind. For one split second, he grinned.

"You find that assignment agreeable, Mr. Lafayette?" Captain Lewis said.

"No, sir," Pierre said quickly, feeling himself redden. What exactly had made him grin? "That is, yes, sir. At your command, sir."

Dismissed, Pierre instantly turned for the front gate. *Make a fool of yourself, why don't you, Lafayette?*

Trekking across the snow-covered ground, Pierre recalled the adventure from which he had just returned. They had been hunting buffalo—huge, hot-breathing, massive, hairy beasts—and *he* had been the one to fire the shots that had brought not one but *two* of the animals to their knees. Pierre clutched his musket. A feeling of pride, of accomplishment surged through him. God had blessed him with a hunter's prowess, and he was making the most of it.

And I am determined to continue to do so. Of all the animals he had hunted thus far, there was one he wanted above all others—the great brown bear.

The Indians insisted the creature was like no other, a massive grizzly beast with claws strong enough to mortally wound a man in one swipe, or break him in half with a single bite. Yet as dangerous as the bear seemed, every man on the expedition wanted to see one. Pierre was determined to be the first man to bring one down.

And then, when I return from doing so with a deed for a land grant in hand, property of my own and plenty of stories of grand accomplishments to share, my father won't think my adventures a waste of time.

At the riverbank, Pierre climbed into a waiting

pirogue. The small boat carried him toward the opposite shore. He navigated the water carefully, for the
Missouri was teeming with floating chunks of ice.
Soon it would close completely, and he'd be able to
walk across the frozen water.

The smell of cooking fires and sound of excitement
was discernible as he neared the main Mandan village.
A ditch and a walled embankment of clay surrounded
the Indian dwellings. Pierre had never seen anything
quite like them before. The lodges, made of timber,
were partly sunk into the ground and then covered
with a thick layer of earth. He imagined they were
quite warm inside.

They'd have to be, he thought. *For who could survive winter after winter in this harsh landscape if not?*
That was one thing to which he had not yet become
accustomed. Upper Louisiana was much colder than
Lower Louisiana.

Following the sounds of chatter, he walked toward
the center of the village, to a plaza of sorts. There,
beneath a large tree, stood Captain Clark and Chief
Black Cat. The ten slain buffalo lay before them. The
remainder of the hunting party and the rest of the village were there, as well.

Chief Black Cat was waving his arms toward the
sky while speaking loudly in Mandan. Pierre had no
idea what was being said, but he guessed that the chief
was thanking the spirits for a good hunt. Pierre glanced
about the crowd. Someone else was giving thanks, as
well. Amid a cluster of females, two women had bowed
their heads and folded their hands.

Are there Christians in this village? he wondered.
Pierre watched for a moment. When the women raised

their heads, he recognized one of them. *Mademoiselle Manette*. The woman beside her was older but of similar features. *That must be her mother.*

Pierre lingered for a moment where he stood, watching the pair of them. Then, thinking better of what he was doing, he moved toward Captain Clark.

"Ah, young Lafayette," the buckskin-clad American said. "I presume you have a message."

"Yes, sir. Captain Lewis wishes for our men to return to the fort."

Clark nodded.

Chief Black Cat's ceremony now finished, the women of the tribe came forward to carve the buffalo. Miss Manette and her mother were among them.

Captain Clark instructed his men to take their five buffalo back to the fort. Yet the moment the soldiers moved to do so, Chief Black Cat waved his arm in a sign of obvious disagreement. He gestured toward the women, then the buffalo, then back to Captain Clark. The American did not understand.

Neither did Pierre. Was the Mandan chief insisting all ten buffalo remain in the village? Pierre felt his muscles tense. He saw Captain Clark's jaw tighten as well, apparently reaching the same conclusion—and no happier with it than Pierre was. They were *hungry*. It had been a joint hunting party. They would stand for no less than an equal share of the meat.

The chief continued gesturing toward his women, speaking louder, more emphatically. Noting the suspicious gazes of the surrounding warriors, Pierre gripped his musket tighter. Something lightly touched his arm. Jerking to the side, he found Miss Manette before him.

"Chief Black Cat is offering you assistance," she said.

"What type of assistance?" Pierre asked warily.

"He says the women will prepare your share of the buffalo for you."

"Our share?"

"Yes."

So the chief hadn't intended to claim the entire kill. Pierre quickly relayed the message to Captain Clark. The American's face softened immediately. He bowed respectfully to the chief, then looked back at Pierre. "Please tell Black Cat that while his offer is greatly appreciated, it is Captain Lewis's wish for the men to return at once to the fort. We will butcher the animals there."

Pierre relayed the instructions to Miss Manette, but she cut him off mid-message with a perturbed look. Then, turning, she spoke most respectfully to her chief.

Pierre remembered her words. *"Understand English? Oui. Speak? No."*

Black Cat forthwith dismissed the women surrounding the soldiers' portion of the kill, and the men carried off the animals. Before turning to go, Chief Black Cat made one final remark to the American captain. Clark nodded and smiled. Miss Manette chuckled softly.

"What did he say?" Pierre asked,

She suddenly looked very uncomfortable, and Pierre couldn't resist teasing her just a bit.

"Go on," he nudged. "I know it was more than a wish for pleasant dreams."

A hint of a smile tugged at her mouth, one she looked like she was trying desperately to keep hidden. *Does she think I am amusing?* he wondered.

"The chief said the white men are powerful hunters—"

"Thank you," Pierre replied, his chest swelling just a bit.

"—but that you insist on doing women's work."

So much for his pride. Irritation took its place, for the look in her eyes seemed to say that she enjoyed taking him down a peg. "I see," he said, curtly. "Thank you for relaying the message."

She nodded brusquely, then added, "Black Cat says he does not understand your ways."

And that brought Pierre directly to his next order of business. Understanding each other's ways, and words, were the keys to peace. "Which is why Captain Lewis requests your presence at the fort."

The smug look instantly vanished. Her eyes widened. Pierre couldn't help but notice again what a lovely shade of green they were. Before he could tell her exactly why the captain had requested her, the mademoiselle's mother approached.

Pierre removed his cap, bowed. "Madame," he said.

The older woman seemed more at ease with him than did her daughter. She smiled broadly.

"This is my mother," Miss Manette said guardedly. "Her name is Evening Sky."

Madame Manette then said something to her daughter in Mandan.

"Oui," the mademoiselle responded.

"Your mother speaks French, as well?" he asked.

"She understands but cannot speak with ease."

"I see," Pierre said once more.

"My mother asked if you were one of the soldiers who helped Spotted Eagle. I told her yes."

"How is the boy?" Pierre asked.

"Much better, *merci*. Please express my thanks to Captain Lewis."

"You can tell him yourself. He asks that you come to the fort and assist us with understanding your language, help us compile a list of words, an explanation of your tribal customs."

Mother and daughter exchanged glances. "But Sacagawea—" the younger woman then said.

"Evidently there has been some sort of disagreement."

"Oh."

There was a long pause. Pierre could clearly see her hesitancy. Did she think the captain would command her service without payment?

"You would be rewarded for your service," he told her.

Her eyes flashed angrily. "I've no need for useless trinkets."

So vain baubles didn't appeal to her. He respected that, but he wasn't about to tell her so. It irritated him that she had so quickly assumed she'd be paid in *useless trinkets*. What did she think he and the other men were? A pack of scoundrels looking to trick or take advantage of the native tribes? *We are here to explore the land, foster good relations between the tribes, promote fair trade for all.* "You would have to discuss payment with Captain Lewis," he said.

Her mother touched her lightly on the sleeve, spoke again to her in Mandan. The cross look on the daughter's face softened slightly, but her expression toward him remained anything but friendly. "Tomorrow," Miss Manette then said to him.

"Tomorrow?"

"Please tell Captain Lewis that I will pray about his offer and give you my answer tomorrow."

Pierre squinted. Pray about it? While he respected her faith, this was hardly a life-or-death decision. What exactly was there to pray about? It was a few days' work at most. Knowing Charbonneau, he'd come crawling back as soon as he realized the captains could do without him.

"The work is only temporary," Pierre told her.

"I understand," she said. "Still…tomorrow."

Pierre couldn't help but feel a measure of disappointment, but why, he did not know. He certainly didn't enjoy conversing with this woman. Was he disappointed in his ability to perform his duties in persuading her to comply? Did he fear his captain would think him a failure if he didn't bring her to the fort immediately?

Across the way, an Indian, a powerful-looking man with eagle plumes in his hair and arms the size of trees, was staring at Pierre. Who was he? A relative? Did he distrust the men at the fort as much as Mademoiselle Manette obviously did? *Is he the cause of her delay?* Whoever he was, Pierre instantly recognized he was not one to be trifled with.

"Very well, mademoiselle," Pierre said. "I shall relay your message to Captain Lewis." He tipped his cap to her and her mother, then returned to the fort.

After the meat had been carved and equally distributed among the tribe, Claire and her mother returned to their lodge. A comforting fire was glowing, smoke curling toward the small hole in the center of the roof. Claire was glad for its warmth. Although her mother did not complain, Evening Sky was walking slowly today. The cold made the older woman's bones ache. Claire helped settle her mother in the spot against the wall, then piled the buffalo skins around her.

They shared this dwelling with twenty other family members—Running Wolf and his wife, their children, their spouses and several grandchildren, as well. It was within these walls that Claire's Mandan family told their stories, tales of spirits and souls.

Claire loved and respected her aunt and uncle, her cousins and her cousins' children. She wanted to believe they cared for and respected her, too. After all, Running Wolf had thought enough of her judgment to have her accompany Little Flower to the fort to seek help for Spotted Eagle. He'd even praised her for her ability to communicate effectively with Captain Lewis.

"You speak to a man of powerful medicine," he'd said, "and he has honored you."

She breathed a silent sigh at the memory. If she could continue to please him in ways like this, if she could prove that she could contribute to the tribe as an unmarried woman, then perhaps Running Wolf would not be so eager to see her wed.

She'd thanked her uncle for the honor he paid *her*, but gave credit to where it was ultimately due. "I had nothing to do with Spotted Eagle's healing. It was my God who made your grandson well. He used Captain Lewis to do it."

Running Wolf had dismissed her claim of God's providence with a sniff, just like he did whenever she spoke words from her father's Bible. To him, the stories of sin and sacrifice, of life resurrected from the grave, were simply fanciful tales, products of a white man's imagination.

But I know they are true. "For God so loved the world that he gave his only begotten son..."

Her uncle, her chief and the warriors of the tribe might be formidable men, but she was determined to be a light in the darkness and pray for their salvation.

Her mother, now settled, reached for the pair of moccasins she was crafting, a gift for Running Wolf.

"You are intrigued by the invitation to work at the fort," she said knowingly.

Claire drew in a breath. Her mother knew what she was thinking. She always did. Claire *was* intrigued, but she was not certain she was interested for the right reason. She'd seen today just how quickly a simple misunderstanding over meat could turn into a disaster. Captain Clark had gotten angry. Black Cat was offended and, eyeing them both, Mr. Lafayette had laid his hand on his musket.

It was his response she remembered most vividly. Quick to assume the worst, ready to take action, just like the white men of Illinois. *And yet he seemed most relieved when I then explained Black Cat's true intentions, as though he did not enjoy the possibility of confrontation.*

The man was a mystery. A mystery with a charming smile.

He'd offered her the opportunity to help the American captains better understand her people. Would she be able to help? Could she make a difference? She supposed that even if this position provided nothing else, it could certainly be an opportunity to recapture a glimpse of her father's culture. She hadn't realized how much she missed it until now. His staring aside, the dark-haired Frenchman spoke to her with courtesy, bowed to her as though he was a Quebec gentleman asking a lady for a dance.

But Mr. Lafayette is no gentleman, she reminded herself, *and this is no palatial ballroom. This is the wilderness—cold, barren, hard. This is a place where survival depends upon good hunting and strong bodies. Men here do not pursue women for dancing or concern themselves with matters of courtship.*

Taking the pot of snow she had previously collected, Claire placed it on the fire. As it melted, she added herbs for tea. Her uncle would soon arrive, and he would be expecting his drink.

Running Wolf came into the lodge just as the tea had finished steeping. He sat down on his pile of skins. Claire brought the steaming liquid to him.

"Your tea, uncle," she said.

After he had accepted it, Claire started to move back. However, he motioned for her to stay. After taking a long draft of the tea, he then spoke. "You spoke words to the white hunter and the angry white chief then looked pleased. What did you say ?"

She told him about the misunderstanding with the meat. Running Wolf frowned slightly.

"Mandans take no more meat than needed. Did you tell all the white men this?"

Evening Sky looked up from her work. "She has an opportunity to tell them that and more, brother."

"How?"

Claire's mother then told him of the request from Captain Lewis. Running Wolf gathered his knees to his broad chest and thought for a moment, then said,

"If the white chief with the three-corner hat wishes for it, then she must obey. The white chief has great power. Perhaps he is willing to share that power with the Mandan."

"He will send his messenger for her in the morning," Evening Sky said.

Running Wolf nodded. "Then it is decided."

Decided? Claire looked at her mother, then her uncle and then back at her mother again. She knew why Running Wolf was eager to send her, but why her mother? She'd told Mr. Lafayette she'd pray about this. She hadn't even had the opportunity to do so yet. The American captains appeared to be honorable men in search of peace, but what if they were not?

She wanted to protest the decision being made for her when she was still unsure—but she knew better than to speak her mind. Running Wolf would see it as a challenge to his authority, and the likelihood of him ever listening to her on spiritual matters thereafter would be nil.

So she held her tongue, but it was hard to do so. Claire moved about the lodge at a busy pace. She stoked the fire. She cleaned the cooking pot. Soon her cousins and the rest of her family would be arriving and it would be time to prepare the evening meal.

Her mother must have recognized her distress, for when Running Wolf finished his tea and left to visit the elders, she said to her, "All will be well, child. The Lord will supply all we need." With those simple words, she returned to her beading.

There were times when Claire was envious of her mother's strong faith. She had a prevailing sense of peace, one that had held despite losing her husband, her relocation to such a hard land and their uncertain future.

Such surety must come with age, Claire thought, but she prayed that God would grant her a little of that peace now.

Chapter Two

Claire stepped from the lodge the following morning to find Mr. Lafayette waiting for her. The air was so cold that his nose and his cheeks above his black beard were as red as a choke cherry. The beard lifted with the hint of a smile the moment they locked eyes.

"Good morning, Miss Manette," he said. "Have you come to a decision?"

"I have, Mr. Lafayette," she said with much more confidence than she actually felt. Was her nervousness due to the fact that she'd actually had little say in coming to this conclusion or the unsettled feeling his smile provoked in her? Her cousin was right. He was a pleasant-looking man. Claire couldn't deny that. "I will accept your captain's invitation," she said.

His smile broadened but quickly faded the moment her uncle stepped from the lodge. Arms crossed, eagle feathers in his hair, Running Wolf nodded curtly to the white man.

Mr. Lafayette responded the same way.

"My uncle will accompany us to the fort," Claire explained, "to offer his greetings to your captains."

"As you wish," Mr. Lafayette said, and with that, he turned in the direction from which he had come. Claire and her uncle silently followed. After leaving the village, the only sounds were the fierce prairie wind and the snow pelting their clothing.

Whatever conversation might have been initiated by the Frenchman was discouraged by Running Wolf's presence. For that Claire was grateful. It allowed her time to study him. *What kind of man is he? Honest and authentic? Sly and deceitful?* All she could tell at this point was that he was most likely a good hunter. His feet made no sound. He walked like a Mandan.

They arrived at the fort, where imposing sentinels still stood guard. One word from Mr. Lafayette, however, and Claire and her uncle were allowed to pass. They followed the Frenchman to the captains' quarters. Once again she waited outside while he announced her arrival.

"These white men have made a small village," Running Wolf commented as he glanced about. "Yet they have no altars for incense or prayers."

"They address their Creator with words from their hearts," Claire said. Or at least, she hoped they did.

Mr. Lafayette returned, ushered them inside. Captain Lewis was again at his desk. Placing his quill in his inkwell, he stood and greeted her formally. "Miss Manette, I appreciate your willingness to come. Your knowledge will be a great help."

Mr. Lafayette introduced Running Wolf. Her uncle spoke his words to the captain.

"He says he has great respect for your power and wishes good health to you and your men," Claire said.

"He says that he hopes for continued peace between the white men and the Mandan people."

Mr. Lafayette promptly translated her words into English. Claire listened carefully to the captain's response.

"That is my wish, as well, Running Wolf, and why I appreciate your willingness to bring your niece to us. She will be well looked after and will return to you in a few days."

Claire began repeating the message for her uncle but halted at the captain's last sentence. *A few days?* So she—an unmarried woman, alone and unchaperoned—was expected to stay at the fort with all the soldiers? Her spine instinctively stiffened. *No! That will not do!*

She told Mr. Lafayette so immediately. Blinking, he stole a quick glance at his captain, then looked back at her.

"Tell him," she said in French. "I will not stay. It is not proper."

He repeated her message, but far less emphatically than how she had originally spoken. Captain Lewis looked taken aback.

Running Wolf didn't need a translator to tell him something was wrong. He crossed his arms over his chest and scowled, but when Claire explained the circumstances, he was not offended by the captain's thoughtless request. He was angry with *her.*

"Do as the white chief says," he ordered.

But this isn't proper! He wouldn't ask such if I were a white woman. Where am I to sleep? Sharing quarters with her blood relatives was one thing, a fort full of soldiers quite another.

The icy chill of fear caused her to shiver. Had her

uncle counted on this? *Is this his way of finding me a husband?*

It was then that Mr. Lafayette spoke. "Perhaps, sir," he said to Captain Lewis, "if mademoiselle's mother were to stay on at the fort as a chaperone, the lady may be more apt to remain."

The lady. Twice now he had referred to her in such a way. Was that how he saw her? Or was he simply saying what he thought she would want to hear? Mr. Granger back in Illinois had claimed to view her with respect and to care for her safety. It had been a lie.

Claire did not know what to think or whom to trust. She studied Mr. Lafayette, trying to discern the truth behind his words, but could garner little information. He had returned his gaze to his captain.

Captain Lewis blinked, and then looked chagrined, as if he'd only then realized the insensitivity of his plan. "Y-yes, of c-course," he stammered. "My apologies, Miss Manette. That *would* be only proper. Will your uncle allow your mother to come? I understand and respect the hardship it will place on the rest of your family."

Yes, it will be a hardship. There would be two fewer pairs of hands to cook, to sew, to tend to the children. Claire explained it to Running Wolf. When he frowned, she was certain he was going to tell Captain Lewis to forget the whole thing.

Good. That was what she hoped would happen.

"My sister cannot make the journey on foot," he said. "She has weak legs. You must send a good horse for her."

A good horse? Claire drew in a sharp breath. So she

would be staying, after all. Reluctantly she relayed her uncle's message.

"Yes, of course," Captain Lewis said, "and we will return the horse to you after your sister's arrival. You may have use of it until the women return home."

This pleased Running Wolf, for the use of a white chief's horse, even if only temporary, was a great honor. He nodded to the captain. "I will go now. I will bring her to you."

"Then I'll show you to your horse," Lewis said. He turned to Mr. Lafayette. "Kindly escort Miss Manette to her quarters."

The Frenchman snapped to attention. "Yes, sir."

Heart thudding, Claire watched her uncle follow the tall American outside. She reminded herself that her time here at the fort would be short, her work only temporary, and that God would be with her. She also reminded herself she'd been given an opportunity to foster peace between two cultures. *But will they listen?*

Mr. Lafayette cleared his throat. "If you'll follow me…"

Reluctantly she allowed him to lead her outside, down the row of wooden structures to a shack at the end of the line. He shoved open the door, found a candle and lit it. The area was so small that one would think it would retain heat well enough, but Claire doubted that would be the case. The hut was roughly the same size as the captains' quarters. Even with a fire, that room had been cold and drafty.

My mother will not fare well in such a place. It would be better to reside in a Mandan lodge, she thought. Why couldn't Captain Lewis simply send one of his men there to work with her on whatever translations he required?

"This was Charbonneau and Sacagawea's room," Mr. Lafayette said.

"And it is here I must remain until their return?" she asked.

"At the captain's request," he said. He paused, then added, "Please don't be angry with him. He has been away from proper society for some months now and is no longer accustomed to the needs of females."

She told herself she should have been grateful to this man for his assistance and attentiveness. He had, in a way, complimented her, but the phrase "proper society" gnawed at her. It reminded her once more just how the average white man saw the people of this land.

They think us savages, reprobates destined to remain that way. Are we not all such without the redeeming blood of Christ? She knew she should swallow back the words on the tip of her tongue, for they were hardly the attitude a Christian should display. Even so, out the biting question came. "And in your opinion, Mr. Lafayette, what constitutes a proper society?"

He looked rather confused for a moment. Then his dark eyes narrowed. Just when she was certain he was going to offer a pointed remark of his own, he visibly collected himself. "Your mother will be brought to you upon her arrival," he said simply, and with that, he turned and walked out, shutting the door forcefully behind him.

Pierre knew he had offended her. He could hear it in her tone, see it in her eyes. He hadn't meant to do so, but he also had no intent of apologizing.

No woman in New Orleans had ever spoken to him the way she did. Not that he missed shallow drivel and obvious flattery, but a little gratitude would have been appreciated. After all, he had done his best to make certain Miss Manette was properly looked after, and she hadn't even bothered to thank him. Instead she seemed intent on picking a fight. Her green eyes had flashed like prairie lightning, captivating him and infuriating him at the same time.

What was it about him that she so obviously disliked? And why did her distaste bother him?

I'm no more accustomed to having females around now than the captain. The sooner I get busy hunting or skinning or chopping firewood, the better off I will be. Ideally that would be the end of his dealings with Mademoiselle Manette. In all likelihood, Captain Lewis would assign one of the other Frenchmen, perhaps Drouillard or Jessaume, to work with her.

He wanted no part of her, or any woman. The need for freedom burned within him. He'd followed in his father's footsteps, been the dutiful, diligent, loyal son until the role had nearly suffocated him. He had found his freedom at last, and he intended to maintain it.

Pierre watched as Running Wolf mounted the captain's horse and rode from the fort. How he longed at that moment to ride toward the horizon, track the next herd of elk or buffalo, encounter a next tribe.

And he knew he wasn't the only one who felt that way. Captain Lewis was as restless as he. He was crossing the parade ground now with an impatient stride.

"I've shown Miss Manette to her quarters," Pierre reported.

"Good," Lewis said. "Give her mother time to arrive and settle, then let the younger woman begin her work. According to Charbonneau, the Mandans possess no written language. Therefore you shall have to rely on phonetic pronunciation. I've no doubt, though, you are up to the task."

I *am up to the task?* He saw where this was going. "Thank you, sir, but wouldn't one of the other men—"

Lewis stopped him with an upturned hand. He was clearly in no mood for discussion. "You have already established a relationship with both Miss Manette and her mother. You are the man for the job."

Pierre inwardly groaned. Of course he would do whatever was required of him to ensure the success of this expedition, but being confined to quarters with Miss Manette was not what he'd had in mind.

"Did you discuss payment for her services?" Lewis asked.

"No, sir. I assumed you would, but—" He stopped, thinking better before relaying the comment she had made to him while still in her village.

Lewis eyed him curiously. "If you have something to say, Mr. Lafayette, then do so."

He might as well prepare the man for the argument. "The lady won't work for trinkets, sir. She expressed as much to me earlier."

"I have no intention of giving her baubles. Perhaps a small ax or other tool to make her household tasks easier, or the corn her relation brought with her previously."

Captain Lewis turned for his quarters, but before doing so he instructed Pierre, "Wait for the mother's arrival. Then escort her to her daughter."

"Yes, sir," he said with much more enthusiasm than he actually felt.

Taking up post at the open gate, Pierre stared across the vast landscape. The Indian villages on the far side of the riverbank were not visible today due to the snow that fell like tufts of cotton from a swirling sky. During the night, the Missouri had iced completely over. For one irrational moment, he thought, *What if it never melts? What if I become trapped here? What if I never venture beyond this spot?*

If that were the case, he'd accomplish none of his goals. He would never see the great brown bear of the mountains. There would be no claim to fame for helping discover an all-water route to the Pacific Ocean. No land grant of his own on which to stake his claim.

He laughed then at his own absurdity. Spring would come. The Scriptures promised so. *"As long as the earth endureth...seed time and harvest..."* He then fortified his thoughts with the idea that his time spent with Miss Manette would be just as fleeting.

Sometime later an Indian rider emerged from the haze of white. Crossing the ice with ease, Running Wolf rode to the entrance of the fort. With one deft motion, he deposited his sister gently to the ground, then urged his horse back in the direction from which he had come.

Pierre bowed to her. The older woman did not curtsy but did, however, offer him a generous smile. *"Bonjour,"* she said proudly.

"And a good day to you, madame. Thank you for coming." Uncertain of how much French she could actually understand, Pierre cut the pleasantries short. He escorted her to her daughter. Miss Manette was watch-

ing his approach from the doorway, eyeing him again
with a look of suspicion.

"Your mother, mademoiselle," he said. "I shall gather
the supplies necessary for your task, then return shortly."

She said nothing to that, but clearly she did not like
the idea of working with him any more than he did her.
Ushering the older woman inside, she quickly closed
the door.

So *he* was coming back. *He* would be the one with
whom she must work. Claire sighed. Once again she
must endure his staring, his quips about proper society.
I would rather be assigned to the captain, she thought,
but then again, she trusted him no more than she did
Lafayette. After all, he was the one who insisted she
stay here at the fort.

She sighed once more, her thoughts at war with one
another. Yes, Captain Lewis had been kind in treating
Spotted Eagle's injury, and yes, Mr. Lafayette had spoken on her behalf to bring her mother as a chaperone.
Still, a person could be lulled into trust by a kind action or two, only to discover the kindness was just a
cover for cruelty and greed.

Was it peace these men actually sought? Is that
why they compiled their lists and studied her tribe's
customs? Or did they have something else entirely in
mind? Something far more sinister? Were they studying them to learn their weaknesses, to learn how to
defeat them?

*Lord, protect my people. Protect my mother. Pro-
tect me.*

Evening Sky scooted closer to the small fire Claire
had kindled in the stone ring in the center of the room,

but it did little to provide warmth or cheer. The ground was cold and hard, and not nearly as level as that of her own lodge. Carefully she piled buffalo skins and woolen blankets left by the previous occupants of the room, over the older woman.

"Thank you, child, but do not fret," her mother said.

"I cannot help but fret over you," Claire replied. "I love you."

Evening Sky offered her a smile. "And I you…*but trust.*"

The last word seemed to carry more meaning than just an assurance of her mother's health, and Claire's conscience was pricked. When Mr. Lafayette knocked upon the door a few moments later, a crate of supplies in hand, Claire did her best to walk the fine line between cordiality and guardedness, to be shrewd as a serpent but harmless as a dove.

While her mother watched silently from the corner of the room, beadwork in hand, Claire took her place at a rough-hewn desk and began poring over the lists the Frenchmen presented her.

"These are the words Charbonneau and Sacagawea compiled with Mr. Jessaume," he said. "They say you call yourselves the 'people of the pheasants.'" He tried to pronounce what had been written. *"See-pohs-ka-na—"*

"See-pohs-ka-nu-mah-kah-kee," Claire corrected him.

He struggled to repeat the phrase. "And is Sa-cagawea 'of the pheasant people'?"

"No," Claire explained. "She is of the west. Across the great mountains. She and Otter Woman were captives of war."

"War seems to be a way of life in this land," he said.

A land of less than proper society, you mean. "Is it not a way of life in all lands?" she replied. "Those who do not fight for territory or hunting rights fight for gold or covet their neighbor's possessions."

She could hear the terseness in her voice and a touch of self-righteousness, too. Again her conscience was pricked. *What am I doing? Why do I seek to provoke him? Will it not undermine the purpose for which I have come? Am I not here to foster peace?*

She was just about to apologize, but Mr. Lafayette had already moved on. "Captain Lewis also wishes to compile a history of your people," he said. "Charbonneau has already told us of the early history, how the tribe migrated to this land. He's told us as well of your relations with neighboring peoples, the wars and the sicknesses that have greatly reduced your numbers."

"Yes," Claire acknowledged quietly, her heart squeezing. Her people had been dying for centuries. *Dying without the truth. What am I doing to change that?*

"What about family life?" he then asked. "Marriage. Children."

His question touched upon another set of emotions, ones she was determined to keep hidden. She gave Mr. Lafayette only a minimal explanation of marital arrangements. "Marriages are most often arranged by the members of a young woman's family." *In my case, my uncle. If I do not find a proper husband before the end of spring, Running Wolf will choose one for me.* "If a man wishes to accept the prospective bride, he brings her family a gift."

"Is that part of the formal marriage ceremony?"

"There really isn't a *formal* ceremony. At least not in any way to which you would be accustomed. On a certain day, a bride is simply presented to a warrior, and t-they b-begin their life together." She stammered slightly over that last phrase, unable to keep from wondering just when that *certain day* would come for her.

"I see," he said. "And if a man is not pleased with his wife?"

She swallowed back the lump growing in her throat. "A divorce can be easily obtained." *And then he seeks another wife, and if not pleased with her, then another. And even if she does please him, she can be bartered away, or he can take a second wife.* She swallowed again. *Is this to be my lot in life? Is this to be the continued way of life for the women of my tribe?*

There was little regard for the sacredness of marriage here, and certainly no concept of what it was meant to reflect—a partnership, mutual affection and joy, such as the love Christ had for his bride, the church. *Nothing like what my mother and father had.*

"I see," he said once again. "We'd also like to learn more of your religious beliefs."

"I worship God the Father and His son, Jesus, as does my mother," Claire said without hesitation, "but my Mandan people do not."

"I suspected you did. I saw you bow your head to give thanks for the meat. I, too, am a Christian."

To that, Claire said nothing. She'd seen men claim the name of Christ before, then do the very opposite of what His holy words commanded. She cast a glance at her mother. She had seen it, as well.

Evening Sky eyed her silently, but there was no hint of anger or resentment on her face.

The Frenchman then pointed to the parchment in front of her. "In your opinion, are the vocabulary lists accurate?"

Claire perused what had been compiled so far. "With the exception of one or two minor discrepancies."

"Would you be kind enough to correct them?" He dipped the quill in the ink well, then handed it to her.

The feel of the feather, the scratch of the nub against the parchment, brought back a host of childhood memories. There had been no other children in her little Illinois community and therefore no school, but a visiting French priest had taught her the basics of reading and writing one autumn when her father was away.

Leaning closer, Mr. Lafayette perused the corrections she was making. Claire couldn't help but notice the broadness of his shoulders, the firmness of his jaw. He smelled of leather, gunpowder and coffee—strong, pleasing scents.

She shook off the thoughts as the bugle sounded. He abruptly stepped back.

"That's the call for supper," he explained.

Good, Claire thought. *Then you can be on your way.*

He rolled up the parchments, tied them with sinew. Looking then to her mother, he said, "Captain Lewis asks that you join us for the meal."

Evening Sky understood enough of his request to know hospitality had been extended. Such was commended among not only Christians but also Mandans. The older woman smiled appreciatively and nodded.

Claire, however, was not so eager.

Mr. Lafayette bowed to her mother. "Then I'll see

you both at the campfire," he said, and with that, he left the room.

"You do not like him," her mother said matter-of-factly after Claire had shut the door behind him.

"No. I do not," she admitted.

"And why is that?"

Though a thousand thoughts and fears marched through her mind, the only coherent objection Claire could voice was the comment he'd made about proper society.

"Perhaps he did not mean it the way it sounded," Evening Sky said. "Grant him grace, child, and take heed that you do not harbor unforgiveness in your heart. It is like a weed. It will strangle any good fruit you wish to cultivate."

The unforgiveness Evening Sky warned against was prompted by the memory of Phillip Granger, the man who had stolen away what rightfully belonged to her and her mother. Claire drew in a breath. She had tried to forgive the man but couldn't quite bring herself to do so, at least not with any lasting effect.

Bitterness and suspicion still darkened her heart. *Which is why I do not trust Mr. Lafayette or his captains...and it is likely the very reason I have seen no progress with my family. I am hindering the spread of the gospel.*

Her mother smiled at her tenderly. "You are a brave and conscientious daughter," she said, "and I am honored to have given birth to you and to have raised you, but you are not the Great Father. You cannot govern how others seek to treat you any more than you can restrain the rain clouds. All that you can control is your response."

And my response is crucial to peace—peace not only now but also in eternity. She wanted to be a light, but she knew she could not be one if she did not remain humble before God, if she did not walk in His ways. There was no room for suspicion, for haughtiness or hardness of heart along His path.

God, forgive me. Help me...

Evening Sky kissed her daughter's forehead. "Come," she said. "We mustn't keep our hosts waiting."

With an uneasy sigh and the whisper of another prayer, Claire assisted her mother to the door.

Chapter Three

Claire silently ate the meat that had been doled out to her. Once again she was under the scrutiny of those around her. She could feel their stares. But for the two American captains who approached her to test a few of their newly acquired words, *welcome*, *thank you*, *eat*, *peace*, Claire spoke to no one.

Mr. Lafayette watched her from across the cooking fire but did not venture any conversation. Claire's mother, however, having noticed a torn seam in his coat, got up from her place and made signs to the Frenchman. With quicker understanding this time than he had shown during Black Cat's offer of assistance, he shrugged off his coat. With a grateful smile and a *merci*, he handed it to Claire's mother.

Returning to her place beside her daughter, Evening Sky drew out a needle and a length of sinew from her deerskin pouch. At once she began mending the torn seam. The men crowded around the fire continued to stare. Claire marveled once again at her mother's quiet grace. Her words repeated through her mind. *"You cannot govern how others seek to treat you any more*

*than you can restrain the rain clouds. All that you can
control is your response."*

And these men have souls, Claire thought, *like my
Mandan family. If they do not know Christ*...then perhaps she had been placed at this fort for higher purpose
than *vocabulary.* After all, peace between the neighboring tribes and with the white men could be achieved
only if true peace came to each heart.

She wanted to walk God's path. If His path meant
assisting a fort full of soldiers, responding kindly to
their curious stares and ignorant remarks, then so be it.

Charity slowly slaked her fear. Looking to Mr. Lafayette, she said, "Please tell your men if they have
clothing that needs to be repaired, we will gladly see
to it."

He relayed the message. At once the soldiers scur-
ried to their quarters, returning with shirts, stockings
and various items of buckskin and broadcloth. As the
articles piled at her feet, Claire silently withdrew her
own needle from her pouch and set to work. Curiosity soon waned. The men stopped staring. The gentle
hum of conversation drifted about, some of it French,
some of it English. Most of it centered on hunting elk,
buffalo and the prize they all seemed to want most—
the great brown bear.

Claire couldn't help but remember her father's stories of the beast. He'd been eager to track one as well,
until the day came when one tracked *him.*

"I barely escaped with my own hide!" he'd said
with a laugh.

Though the danger had been deadly, Claire smiled
at the image of her robust father running for his life,
shedding every item he carried to hasten his speed.

"The Lord surely looks after drunks and fools," he'd said. To which her mother had playfully chided, *"Neither of which is a good thing to be."*

One of the soldiers produced a fiddle and began to play. As music filled the air, the men moved about, some to quarters, some to clean their muskets. The tensions of the day unwound to the rest of eventide. Claire felt herself beginning to settle, as well—until Mr. Lafayette approached her.

"You and your mother are very kind to take on such a duty," he said. "Most of our men are skilled tanners, but our clothing does not wear well. The river takes its toll."

"I imagine so," Claire replied.

He sat down beside her. Claire made her best attempt at a welcoming smile, then kept on with her work.

"I saw an Indian woman in a village south of here making holes in the buffalo skin with a sharp piece of bone," he said. "She then wove the sinew through with her fingers."

Claire nodded. "There are few sewing needles in this land. The women who have them have come by them by way of British or French traders."

His dark eyebrows arched. "Are there many British traders?"

Claire might have been only a woman, and one far removed from European entanglements, at that, but she recognized political wariness when she saw it. Frenchmen did not like Englishmen, and from what she remembered of life in Illinois, Americans did not like them, either.

"There are a few British," she replied evenly. "They come every now and again."

"And do your people acquire many supplies from them?"

Claire considered her words carefully. She was certain her comments would end up in a report to the captains, and she wanted to make the most of it. "The Mandans trade openly with anyone who treats them fairly and justly. My sewing implements, however, as well as my mother's, did not come from the British traders. They were gifts from my father."

He nodded. Whether in relief or approval, she did not know. "He was well-known in this village?"

"Yes, and respected by all."

A call from the sentinel on the catwalk captured Claire's attention, as well as everyone else's around her. The music and conversation stopped. A warrior was approaching. One apparently riding the captain's horse.

"It seems your uncle has come to pay you and your mother a visit," Mr. Lafayette said.

Is something amiss? "So it seems." Claire laid aside the clothing and stood. The gate opened. In rode Running Wolf, looking stately and dignified as usual. Spotted Eagle sat behind him. Noticing her at the fire, Claire's young cousin slid to the ground and immediately came running toward her. He fell upon her and her mother at once with kisses. Claire treasured every one of them, for she knew the time would soon come when he would think himself too old to display such affection.

She scooped him into her arms. "You wiggle like a bear cub," she said. "What brings you to the fort?"

"I came to wish you well in your new life."

She laughed slightly. He had thought she was leaving him. She felt bad that her supposed departure had caused him sadness, but it warmed her heart to know that she had been missed. "Silly child," she said with a laugh. "Do not fret. My work here at the fort is only for a few days. I shall return to the lodge soon."

Spotted Eagle shook his head. "Uncle said he wishes to make a trade with the captain."

Trade? The word made her breath hitch.

"What kind of trade?" Evening Sky asked.

"His horse for Claire."

Pain pierced Claire's heart like an arrow, and fear and panic quickly spread through her veins. So *this* had been her uncle's reason for sending her to the fort! He had purposed to sell her as a squaw, a slave to the American captain. She hadn't doubted his ability to consider such a thing if she'd failed to find a husband within her tribe in the time he permitted, but he had promised her a year of freedom before he would give her in marriage. She still had six months to go!

Claire could not move. In fact, she could barely breathe. Evening Sky, however, seemed infused with fire. Though she had grown weaker in the months since her husband's death, she now flew to Running Wolf with speed. Spotted Eagle quickly followed her.

Oh, God...please...please help...

Mr. Lafayette had witnessed the entire exchange with little understanding of the details, but he clearly recognized something was wrong. "What is it?" he asked. "Is there to be an attack?"

Apparently he wasn't the only one who thought that. Evening Sky was making such a commotion that Captain Clark now strode to where she and Running Wolf stood. He had his musket in hand. Captain Lewis for the moment remained at the fire, but his taut face and rigid stance told Claire he was poised to order action if necessary.

Claire was trembling, but she did her best to gather her senses. The lives of many could depend on it. "You are not in danger," she insisted. "There is no impending attack."

Mr. Lafayette quickly relayed her words to Lewis. Still, the man stood guard. "What is it, then?" the captain asked. "Why does Running Wolf come? Why is Madame Manette so angry with him?"

Claire swallowed hard. Her cheeks burned with shame. "I-it is a f-family matter," she stammered. She simply couldn't bear to tell the captain exactly *why* her uncle had come. What would he think of her people if he heard of such a plan? Worse, what if he agreed to it?

"It's obviously a very distressing family matter," Mr. Lafayette said. "You are trembling." He reached for her hand. Claire's immediate instinct was to jerk it free from his grasp, but she found she had not the strength to do so. His hand was rough and calloused, but his grip was gentle.

"Perhaps you should again sit," he said.

She did so. Kneeling before her, he still kept hold of her hand. "Tell me, how may I assist you?" he asked. "I'm at your service."

The concern in his voice circumvented her defenses. Would he somehow be able to intervene on her behalf? One glance at her mother told Claire the woman was unsuccessful in changing her brother's mind. Running Wolf was gesturing toward Claire, an adamant look on his chiseled face.

"Mademoiselle?"

With shame burning her cheeks, she told Lafayette what was taking place. The Frenchman's eyes widened in disbelief, and then they flashed in anger. "A trade? *You* for a *horse*?"

He relayed the translation at once. Captain Lewis immediately turned on his heel, strode toward Running Wolf.

Mr. Lafayette squeezed her hand. "The captain will handle this," he insisted.

No doubt he will, Claire thought, but just how and at what cost remained to be seen.

Pierre had known right away that something was terribly wrong. The vexing personality had instantly given way to a vulnerable creature in need of protection. Her small, delicate fingers trembled beneath his, and when she finally explained what was happening, he understood why. How dare her uncle seek to sell her! His father had once tried to persuade him to take a certain bride, one whose family name and fortune would benefit his own, but as a man, Pierre had the luxury to refuse.

I was able to retain my freedom, but odds are she will not be able to do so.

If she struck out on her own, she'd have little chance for finding gainful, meaningful employment. She'd probably end up the captive of some drunken fur trader or worse, a slave to the Sioux.

Standing, he made himself a shield between her and her uncle. The code of a gentleman, let alone Christian decency, would not allow him to stand by and watch such a thing take place. His captains had warned

him and the other men of the expedition not to interfere with tribal customs because doing so could upset
the delicate balance of diplomacy they had achieved.
Pierre, however, was prepared to defend her freedom
if need be even if no one else would. Though he desperately hoped such measures would not be necessary.

Madame Manette stood beside her imposing brother,
the young child Spotted Eagle protectively in her grasp.
Running Wolf was intensely gesturing to both captains.
A scowl filled his face. The Americans looked no more
cordial. Lewis stood with his arms crossed. Clark held
tightly to his musket. To their right, Pierre glimpsed
Sergeants Ordway and Gass. They were poised to take
action should either captain signal for it.

A standoff was underway. *I wanted adventure*, he
thought. *It appears I have found it.*

One of Pierre's fellow voyagers sidled up to him.
"What did you do, Lafayette?" he asked with half a
laugh. "Steal some warrior's squaw?"

"Certainly not," Pierre insisted, his teeth clenched.
"And you had better have the sense to realize the danger in doing so." The man had recently been the cause
of his own entanglement with a Mandan woman and
a jealous husband, one Captain Clark had been forced
to settle.

*Women could very well be the death of this expe-
dition*, Pierre thought. Yet he could hardly blame the
girl behind him. *She has obviously had no part in this.*

Pierre watched as Captain Lewis turned for his
quarters. After a few moments, the man returned and
presented Running Wolf with a small ax and several
other useful tools. The Mandan warrior did not look
pleased. He directed his frown toward his niece. Com-

ing again to her feet, Mademoiselle Manette stepped to Pierre's shoulder. She held her uncle's look with one of quiet strength and apparent courage, but he could hear the unevenness of her breathing. She was scared to death.

God help her, he thought. *Help us all...*

Running Wolf turned and mounted the captain's horse. Signaling for Spotted Eagle to join him, the two rode from the fort. Watching them go, Pierre knew not what to think. He'd been certain either the horse would remain or the women would depart.

What has just happened? Has Captain Lewis actually made the trade? Had his superior officer just purchased a maidservant? A wife? Pierre felt the knot in his stomach tighten. Mademoiselle Manette drew in a sharp breath but other than that made no sound or protest. She simply lowered her gaze to the ground, like a condemned prisoner accepting her fate.

The main gate now barred, Captain Lewis directed Madame Manette toward his quarters. Captain Clark escorted her. Lewis then approached the fire where Pierre and the younger woman stood. He stole another glance at her. Cheeks red, she still stared at the ground.

"Lafayette," Lewis said.

"Sir?"

"Please tell her that she has nothing to fear. Her uncle has been placated, although I had to deliver her payment to him for the services she rendered today."

So she hasn't been bought. Pierre heaved a sigh. However, as far as her uncle having been placated, the warrior had looked anything but. Pierre was certain further trouble with him loomed on the horizon. Still, Pierre moved to translate what the captain had said, forgetting once again that the mademoiselle was capable of understanding for herself. This time, though, she gave no look of annoyance.

Instead she curtsied, rather unsteadily, to both him and the captain. *"Merci,"* she replied, her voice wavering.

"What happens now, sir?" Pierre asked, for her benefit as well as his own.

"She and her mother will remain here," Lewis said. "She will finish her task." He turned on his heel, marched away without further word. Pierre supposed he couldn't fault the man for doing so. He was, after all, a soldier, one use to issuing commands and expecting them to be obeyed. Rigidity and routine were necessary, especially on such an expedition, but Pierre couldn't help but think that in this case, a bit more compassion was merited.

Did the young woman *wish* to stay? Did she wish to continue her work after what she had just witnessed? But on the other hand, if she left, then where could she go?

She was now gathering up the soldiers' clothing, the pieces she'd been mending. Pierre bent to help her. *"Merci,"* she said once more. The tremble in her voice remained.

Carrying the items, he escorted her toward her quarters. Part of him was in mind to stand guard outside her door all night, but he knew that was unnecessary. Lewis and Clark had handled the situation, at least for now, and there would be sentries posted at the gate all night.

Still, he felt the need to say something.

"I apologize for what just took place," he said, "but I am certain you will be well-protected at this fort."

She seemed to appreciate his apology, but he wasn't so certain she believed him about her safety. That look of vulnerability remained in her eyes.

"You have shown me much kindness today," she said, "and for that, I thank you."

He had tried to show her kindness from the first moment he'd met her, but she didn't seem to realize that. "Have no fear, mademoiselle," Pierre said. "Your safety and that of your mother's will be my *personal* concern."

For a moment, her green eyes held him, pinned him like a butterfly beneath glass, a creature bereft of freedom. He had little fear when it came to venturing into the wilds, but this was a frightening feeling. Still, he could not look away.

"You have already demonstrated great concern, Mr. Lafayette," she said, "and for that, again, I thank you."

As sincere as he was about protecting her, he was glad when she took the clothing from him, stepped inside her quarters and shut the door.

With dutiful resolve, Claire replaced the tallow candle that had burned down to a nub, stirred the small fire and then sorted through the soldiers' clothing. Despite what had just happened, she was determined to continue with her tasks, determined to walk the path before her with faith and courage.

If I give in to fear, to self-pity, it shows my lack of trust for the Lord. If I, who claim to know Him, cannot trust Him, then how can I expect others to do so?

Regrettably she knew she'd already given in to such fears. Her anxiety must have shown on her face or Mr.

Lafayette would not have spoken to her the way he did. He knew she was frightened. So did her mother.

The moment Evening Sky returned to the room, she laid aside the bolt of fabric she had been carrying and came to her daughter at once. Wrapping her arms around Claire, she cradled her close, rocking her as if she were still a fragile child.

"Oh, my Bright Star. How sorry I am. How sorry. Never in all my thoughts have I imagined my brother capable of breaking his word. He promised me he would never offer you to a man before a year, and even at that, not without my blessing. Forgive me. Forgive me for ever bringing you to such a place."

Yes, her mother had brought her to Running Wolf's lodge, but they'd had no choice. There was nowhere else to go. Tears spilled down Claire's cheeks, a release of pent-up emotions. "Did he say why he had changed the terms of our agreement?"

"He claims he has not."

"But he has indeed!"

"He claims that we misunderstood him, that the time of twelve moons of mourning began not at our arrival but at the time of your father's passing."

Her father had died last December. They had remained in Illinois for six months before traveling here. If Running Wolf was basing his calculations on that, then her year was complete. "Oh, Mother! What am I to do?"

Evening Sky wiped her own tears, took her daughter's hand in hers. "The Great Spirit has been our shield and defender in the past, and in Him we must continue to have faith. He provided safety for you at this fort tonight. The dark-haired Frenchman guarded you, and the American officers succeeded in sending Running Wolf away."

Claire vividly remembered the look on Mr. Lafayette's face, the feel of his fingers over hers. His hands were rough, gnarled, but they had conveyed tenderness and compassion. He'd displayed true Christian charity. He'd defended a woman he barely knew, and he had offered his assistance without command or promise of reward.

"I did not understand their words, but I could see their hearts," Evening Sky said. "The officers did not like giving your earnings to my brother. But I believe because of their willingness to do so, Running Wolf was willing to grant you a reprieve from marriage."

Hope quickened in Claire's chest. "A reprieve? For how long?"

"Until the ice on the Missouri melts and the white men go their own way."

This meant March or early April at the most.

"Much could still happen in that space of time," her mother reminded her.

"Yes," Claire replied, though barely above a whisper. She tried to have faith. Much *could* happen. A warrior of the tribe could come to salvation or her uncle could, *and then he would understand why I do not wish to marry outside my faith.*

Her mother smiled at her softly, then turned and reached for the fabric. "The officers made a gift to you," Evening Sky said. "The one with the three-corner hat said it is for *leggings,* but I think he meant to say the word *dress.*"

A dress? Claire remembered the indignation she'd felt and shown to Mr. Lafayette when he mentioned payment for her services. The Mandan part of her said dried corn or venison would have been a more useful gift, but the French side of her appreciated the gesture. The thick scarlet broadcloth was beautiful, and it had been a long time since she had worn anything besides animal skin.

"It is a kind and generous gift," Claire replied. "I will be certain to thank them."

"It reminds me of the bright berries your father used to fill our cabin with at Christmastime."

"Indeed." Claire sighed over the memory. Just a few days from now would mark the celebration of the Savior's birth, the salvation offered for all who believed. The moccasins Evening Sky was crafting were a present for her brother just for the occasion. She had hoped by offering that gift, he would better understand the gift that God had offered *him*.

"I shall make a dress for you for Christmas," Evening Sky insisted.

Claire was deeply touched but wanted to tell her not to go to the trouble. Such an article of clothing was unnecessary and certainly impractical for the life she now lived, but she could see the determination in Evening Sky's eyes, the desire to show love, to give Claire some semblance of the life she had once shared with her beloved father. She sensed how desperately Claire longed for such, especially tonight.

Running Wolf and the rest of their family would not celebrate Christmas, and now, given what had just happened, Claire wondered if her uncle would even tolerate their prayers and gifts, their lack of participation in certain tribal customs.

Heaviness weighed upon her once more. Faith battled fear, and for the moment the latter was winning. Yes, God had protected her tonight. Would He continue to do so? She had been offered up to strangers by her own flesh and blood. Mr. Lafayette and the American captains had defended her honor, but the day would come when she and her mother would have to return to the village, return to Running Wolf's lodge. The ice on the Missouri would eventually melt. What lay in store for her then?

Chapter Four

Pierre lay in the darkness, unable to sleep. It wasn't the snores filling the enlisted men's quarters that kept him awake. It was the thought of Miss Manette lying in the cabin next door. Had she fallen asleep or was she, like him, staring wide-eyed at the timber ceiling, wondering what the sunrise would bring? Was she even thinking of him at all?

Probably not, he thought, *nor should she be.* He told himself he need not think of her any further, either. His captains had acted honorably on her behalf. They had issued orders stating no soldier was to make any trade with Running Wolf. *I should leave the matter in their hands.*

But he couldn't stop himself from feeling concerned. Never in his life had Pierre felt such a kinship with another person as he had when he'd learned of her uncle's plan. Never before had he found himself praying so fervently for a person he scarcely knew.

All was calm now, but eventually Miss Manette would leave the protection of this fort. By spring the expedition would be on their way. *Then what? What of the next visitors to this land? Will her uncle seek to broker a deal with one of them?* Pierre's indignation burned. He and the rest of the men had been warned not to interfere in Indian affairs, that the consequences could be disastrous, not only to them but also to any other trader who would later venture this way. *But I will not see her returned to a man who treats her with such disregard. Upon my word, I will not, for she clearly did not wish to be bound to her uncle's plan any more than I had wished to be part of my father's. She should be given a choice in whom she would marry...if she wishes to marry at all.*

But just what he would do to encourage that, Pierre did not know. Advocating such a radical idea in New Orleans, let alone an Indian village, would surely be met with contempt.

He tossed and turned for hours. When reveille sounded, Pierre slipped from his bedding with no more rest gained than when he had entered it, and Miss Manette was no less on his mind. Shivering like his comrades, he hurried to layer on his furs and buckskin. The cold, however, still seeped through his clothing. This morning the mercury stood at twenty below.

We wanted to test our mettle, he thought. *These temperatures and trials will certainly do so.*

Puling on his last layer of clothing, Pierre pushed open the door and stepped into the snow. Despite the stinging cold, the fort was stirring to life. On the catwalk, the changing of the guard was taking place, the sentries gladly relinquishing their posts to the morning men. To Pierre's left, the blacksmith was stoking his fire. When the men were all assembled, Captain

Clark issued the orders for the day. Breakfast was then served.

Pierre kept a casual watch, but neither Miss Manette nor her mother appeared for their allotted portion of food. Were they still sleeping, or did embarrassment over last night's events keep them inside?

After swallowing the last of his breakfast, Pierre knocked upon the women's door.

It creaked open. He wasn't exactly sure what he had expected to find this morning, but gone was the trembling child from the previous night. A stoic expression filled the mademoiselle's face. Dark circles lined her eyes. She had slept as little as he.

"You are unwell," Pierre said.

She shook her head. "Not I." Slipping through the door, she shut it behind her. A gust of wind tightened her face. She pulled her buffalo robe closer about her. "It is my mother," she said. "My uncle—" She rephrased. "The events of the preceding evening were too much for her. She is exhausted."

Obviously she did not wish to relive the details that had occurred, so Pierre made no further mention of them. He felt bad for her mother. "Perhaps a little food? I could bring you both something."

"Thank you, but I am not hungry. I suggested that my mother eat, but she says she has no stomach for it."

Then she must be in a bad way, he thought. This cold made him ravenously hungry. "Shall I seek Captain Lewis? Perhaps he has a remedy—"

"No, but thank you. My mother insists all she needs is rest."

Pierre nodded. He would see to it, then, that she could do so. "I shall leave you to care for her." He bowed to her formally. "If I may be of any assistance, do not hesitate to ask."

A measure of surprise skittered across her face, followed by a look of shy pleasure. Apparently she'd expected him to insist that they complete their duties. Yes, the language study was important, but so was her mother's health. Surely the captains would understand.

"Thank you, Mr. Lafayette. You are very kind."

It was a simple expression of appreciation, genuine no doubt, but little more than that. Yet for some strange reason, Pierre was warmed by it. "Well, then…a good morning to you." He tipped his hat, started to turn.

"If I may…"

The uncharacteristic softness in her voice stopped him in his tracks. He looked back. Falling snowflakes dusted her rich, dark hair, making it look as though she was wearing a crown of diamonds.

"I shall look over the parchments from yesterday and consider what words you may wish to add."

So she desired to be of assistance to *him*. Evidently she was warming to him, as well, or at least becoming less distrustful. He was glad. Perhaps now they could work together as friends. In the long run it would certainly be beneficial to maintaining peaceful relations with the tribe and the expedition if they could do so.

And beyond that, she was an interesting woman. She was Indian, but she was also French. In some small way, she reminded him of his sister, delicate but tough. For all of his want of adventure, there were times when he missed his family.

"I would be grateful for whatever words you think beneficial," he said.

With a quick curtsy she then stepped back inside,

shut the door solidly in front of him. For some strange reason he continued to stare at it. An odd feeling of intrigue and discomfort flittered through him.

He marched to his officers' quarters. With this change of plans, perhaps Captain Lewis might now allow him to join Captain Clark's hunting party. To Pierre's disappointment, however, Clark had already departed the fort. Lewis sent him instead to split wood on the parade ground. Working within sight of Mademoiselle Manette's door did little to clear her from his mind.

"You should have let him come in," Evening Sky whispered from beneath the buffalo skins. "He has tasks to complete."

Claire laid the parchments on the desk and stirred the small fire. "I told him I would work on what I could. He did not insist on being present."

"He is a kind gentleman."

"Yes. I think so."

"I'm pleased you are letting go of your fear. Not all white men are like Mr. Granger."

Claire nodded slowly as she studied her mother's face in the candlelight. Her coloring did not look good. *This is more than the strain of last night,* she thought.

"Shall I make you some tea?" Claire offered. "Something to ward off the chill?"

Evening Sky shook her head. "No, Bright Star. Not today." She grimaced. The expression was almost imperceptible, but Claire recognized pain when she saw it.

"Where does it hurt, mother? Your legs?"

"No, child."

"Your loins?"

Evening Sky simply closed her eyes.

"The Frenchman offered to ask for a remedy from his captain. Shall I fetch him?"

"No, child. Do not bother the men." Evening Sky shifted beneath the skins, turned toward the wall. Claire understood the movement. It was a sign that her mother did not want to be questioned further. Claire would honor her wish, but she wasn't the least bit happy about doing so.

If I do not know exactly what is wrong, then how can I help her?

Whispering a prayer, she then went to the desk. She unrolled Mr. Lafayette's parchments and, after studying them for a few moments, wrote down a few more phrases of friendship and some words that would be useful in trade.

Trade. Her heart squeezed. She remembered all too vividly what Running Wolf had wished to trade last night. *How could he?* she thought. *He is my uncle. My mother's brother. My own flesh and blood.* Being given in marriage to a fellow tribesman was bad enough, but at least she could understand his reasoning. That was the way things were done here in the wilderness, and it was an arrangement that would benefit the tribe. She might not like it. She might seek to change it, but for now that was how it was done.

In a land of war, one way to assure the continued existence of the tribe was by begetting new families. *But to offer me to strangers, to men whose customs are so different from his own...?* Did he think she would be happier bound to a white man, or did he simply wish to be rid of her? Had her *curious ways*, her faith, been a thorn in his flesh for too long?

She could feel the tears pooling in her eyes but quickly steeled her resolve. There was no point thinking such things. She was safe for now. There was still time to find a Christian husband. God could do mighty things. As much as she feared being bound to a man to whom she was not well-suited, she was not against marriage. What would it be like to know love, to share a deep, abiding commitment, to experience the joy her parents had once had? What would it be like to be held tightly on cold, dark nights, have words of endearment whispered in her ear?

But I will live without such things if it means being asked to marry a man who does not serve God.

Claire cast a glance in Evening Sky's direction. She was now sleeping peacefully. Claire returned to her parchments and tried to focus on the task at hand.

Outside someone was chopping wood. Claire scratched her list in time with the rhythmic thwacking of the ax. Morning moved toward noon. There was no window in her hut, no way to mark the sun's advance across the sky, but Claire could estimate the time by the sounds. She could hear the second changing of the guard.

She kept on writing. The captains wished to learn about the Mandan's religious beliefs, so Claire gave an account of their beliefs on creation, the great flood and the story of the Lone Man. Her heart grew heavier with each paragraph, considerably as she listed out the details of the Okipa ceremony.

She had never actually seen the ceremony take place, for women were not allowed to view it, but she had witnessed the effects of it when she first arrived in the village. Hoping to gain the Great Spirit's favor, young warriors were starved and mutilated. The parents of those who did not survive the process bore their shame.

How different life would be for my people if they could come to understand that God's favor was not earned through suffering but given by grace... How different my life would be.

Claire dipped her quill in the ink. Evening Sky continued to sleep but stirred just before the call to supper. Her body was slow to rise, but her coloring had improved.

"Feeling better?" Claire asked.

"Yes." Evening Sky then said she thought she might take a little nourishment.

"I'll make you some tea and there are corn cakes keeping warm by the fire."

Evening Sky nodded.

Claire brought her one of the cakes and then prepared the tea. It didn't take long to warm the snow water and steep the herbs over the fire. As Claire brought the cup to her mother, the bugle sounded.

"Thank you, Bright Star," she said. "Now go. Take your own meal at the big fire. I'll be alright. I need nothing more."

Claire had smelled the camp food cooking for more than an hour. She was hungry for more than corn cakes indeed but did not wish to leave her mother unattended.

Thankfully she did not have to, for a knock sounded upon the door. Claire opened it to find Mr. Lafayette standing at the threshold. He'd come bearing bread, venison stew and chicory coffee.

"I know you said you were not hungry earlier, but I couldn't let you miss out on a feast such as this," he said. When he smiled, Claire suddenly found herself wondering what he would look like without the beard. She imagined him quite handsome, in a polished, gentlemanly way.

"Thank you, monsieur. You are most kind."

"How is your mother?" He asked.

"She is much improved." She took a half step to the side so that he might see Evening Sky for himself.

He smiled once more. "I am pleased to see that you are up and about, madame."

Her mother smiled back at him. He then looked at Claire. "Have either of you need of anything else?"

"No, but thank you."

He nodded but did not bid them good-night.

"I have added to your lists," Claire said.

"Oh? Wonderful. We can review them tomorrow."

"Yes." Why did she suddenly feel a sense of anticipation at that prospect? She told herself she was only lonely. Although Claire was glad for the rest her mother had gained today, she had missed her conversation. "Thank you again for your kindness, Mr. Lafayette," she said.

"I am your servant, mademoiselle." He bowed, smiled once more. She curtsied politely, and then shut the door.

The following morning, after breakfast Pierre made his way to the women's hut. Madame Manette was looking much improved this morning. She was sitting in the corner of the room, sewing on a large piece of red broadcloth.

Mademoiselle Manette received him in her usual reserved but stately way, although she had offered him the barest of smiles when she had opened the door. They moved to the desk, where she unrolled the parchments and explained what she had added.

"The grammatical forms are different for addressing a man as opposed to addressing a woman," she said. "Please, allow me to demonstrate."

"Of course…"

She ran through the list.

Pierre was struck by the ease with which she spoke. She shifted between Mandan and French effortlessly. When he tried to repeat the words, he stumbled and became hopelessly tongue-tied. She stifled a smile or two at his attempts but for the most part did her best to encourage him. Actually she was quite patient. She truly wished for him to learn the skills necessary to communicate with her people.

"Do not lose heart," she said. "You will master the words in time."

"Thank you, but I believe that will have very little to do with my efforts. Any fruit will be the result of your skilled cultivation. You are a patient teacher," he said. The compliment brought a slight blush to her cheeks and then a slight heat to *his* ears. She *was* pretty. "Have you taught others before?" he asked.

"My cousins' children have mastered a few French words, but one must be careful not to introduce too many or people assume you wish to make them white."

"And then you lose the opportunity to share with them what is most important," he said knowingly. *"Les bonnes nouvelles." The Good News.*

Her eyes flickered with a small measure of delight.

"Yes," she said. "Exactly."

"Have you had any success in sharing the gospel?"

The light in her eyes faded. "The children and some of my female cousins show interest in the *stories* from the Bible, but that is all."

"It is a start," he said.

"Yes."

"Pray, tell me, which stories do they particularly enjoy?"

"Noah and the great flood."

"Why that one?"

"They know him as the Lone Man, the one who endured a great deluge and survived, according to the Mandan legends."

Pierre marveled. Here was a tribe who knew nothing of the Scriptures, and yet bits of God light had penetrated the darkness. "And they accept that the Creator rescued him from the flood, used his family to assure the continuation of the human race?"

"Not exactly," she said. "You see, to the Mandans, there were once two rival deities, a creator and then the Lone Man. The creator brought forth the land south of the Missouri River, and the Lone Man was responsible for creating the land of the north."

"The land in which you now reside."

She nodded again.

"So he is, in a sense, a god to them?"

"Yes." A deep sadness came into her expression. He sensed the heavy burden she carried. Pierre sadly had to admit he could not completely relate to the enormity of her task. It was not that he had no burden for the lost. He did—but in reality, while growing up he had known very few people who had never heard of the Savior. Although not everyone in New Orleans served God faithfully, everyone he had ever encountered knew the basic accounts of Creation, man's fall from grace and God's redemptive plan.

What was it like for her and her mother to be the only believers in this village? What pressures did they face to conform? *No wonder she is so guarded. She has to be on guard at all times.*

"Then your tribe has no idea of Jesus?" he asked. "Of his sacrifice? Of eternal life?"

"My people believe that souls live forever, but that they continue on as stars or birds, some as spirits hovering in the village. They worship creation."

"I see."

"They honor courage, strength and bravery but without understanding where these things originate. I wrote down for you the details of the Okipa ceremony," she said.

"I've never heard of that. What is it, exactly?"

She bit her lip for the slightest of seconds. "Perhaps it would be better if you read for yourself." She handed him the parchment.

Reading it, he discovered the rite of passage that all Mandan men were expected to make. Young men were led to a hut, where their chests and shoulders were slit and wooden skewers were thrust behind the muscles. Using the skewers to support the weight of their bodies, the men were then suspended from the roof of the lodge.

Pierre was no weakling when it came to pain, yet he winced at the thought. "Why do they do this?"

"So they may gain the Great Spirit's approval."

"So they see no need for salvation, but they do seek appeasement?"

"Yes, and approval of the tribe."

He read on. Apparently a warrior hung from the rafters until he fainted. After that he was taken down and placed under the watch of one of the tribesmen until he awakened. The ordeal, however, was far from over. When the warrior woke, his little finger was severed with a hatchet, an offering to the spirit.

Pierre grimaced. "That certainly explains the high number of missing fingers I have observed among the villagers."

She nodded gravely. "After all of that, the men must endure a grueling race. They do this to determine who among them is the strongest." Pausing, she then added, "My uncle completed the ceremony twice."

And that told Pierre once again what type of man Running Wolf was—what influence he carried in his village. He was a highly honored warrior who would not take kindly to a white man's interference, especially when it came to a member of his family.

"Do the men ever suffer ill effects from this ceremony?" He realized how ridiculous his question sounded. "What I mean is—"

"I know," she said. "Yes, they often do suffer. Sometimes a warrior does not awaken, or his heart gives out during the race, or sometimes he later dies from festering wounds. If that happens, he is considered disgraced by the spirits, and his family bears a mark of shame."

He sighed. So this was the path young men were expected to take. This was the path that one day her sons would take, if she stayed with the tribe and married a Mandan.

"Why do you remain here?" he asked.

She stiffened. "Why? Where am I to go? I no longer have a father. Do you think the world south of the Missouri or east of the Mississippi will afford my mother any more protection than here? That is the reason we came after losing my father. We have learned that the behavior of white men is no more civilized than the behavior of the Mandan in this land."

He remembered the comment he'd made before about proper society. The one at which she'd taken such offense. The bite in her voice now told him something terrible had happened to her, and it was not confined to her uncle's attempts of marriage.

"I hope your distress has nothing to do with my behavior?" he said.

She blinked, then immediately looked chagrined. Tears gathered in her eyes. "No…not you…certainly not…" she said.

The look of shame did not fade, nor did the concern on her mother's face. Madame Manette said nothing, but it was clear by her expression that she was pained for her daughter, and her daughter was further pained because of it.

"Forgive me," she said to the woman, then to him. "Please forgive me for my outburst."

"It is I who should beg your forgiveness, mademoiselle. I was under the impression you had been born in this village."

"No," she said. "My mother and I arrived this summer."

"Then your father has only recently passed?"

Her jaw twitched. He saw the pain in her eyes. "Yes. He died of fever, a few days before Christmas last year."

"I was unaware of that. My condolences, mademoiselle." He turned to her mother. "Madame Manette. No doubt this is a very difficult time for you both."

No wonder she is so conflicted, so agitated. She's barely had time to grieve her father's death, and now her uncle is looking to marry her off to a stranger?

She drew in a breath, quickly wiped a tear that had trickled down her cheek. "You are very kind, monsieur."

He was tempted to ask what specific occurrence had made her so wary of white men but decided against it. Her composure at the moment was tentative at best. She was trying hard to portray propriety, but her wounds were raw. Pierre didn't want to risk pouring salt on them by asking a foolish or insensitive question.

Not knowing what else to do, he added a few sticks of wood to the fire. Tiny yellow sparks drifted toward the ceiling, sputtered, then died. He could tell the afternoon light was fading even though he could not see it. The room was growing chilly once again.

"You know, I just now realized we never stopped at noon to break bread," he said. "I apologize."

"There is no need," Claire replied. "Mother has wished for nothing more than the corn cakes I baked this morning and we have been busy with our work. I daresay we have accomplished quite a bit."

"Indeed."

There was an awkward pause. She didn't know what to say to him, and he didn't know what to say to her. *Should I stay or should I go?*

To his relief, the bugle sounded. "There's the call for supper," he said. He looked to her mother. "Shall I escort you to the meal, or would you ladies prefer to eat in private? I could fetch you something."

Madame Manette seemed to comprehend his question. She looked at her daughter and said something in

Mandan. The younger woman translated, "My mother says she does not wish to dine at the fire tonight. She wishes only for sleep."

"Then something for yourself?"

She shook her head slightly. "Thank you, but no."

He figured she'd say that since she was obviously still embarrassed by what had happened earlier. To prove he felt no offense, he decided he'd fetch them both something to eat anyway. They had to be hungry. One could not live on corn cakes and tea for very long.

Madame Manette then said something else to her daughter. The younger woman shook her head in respectful protest, but the older woman persisted. If Pierre was reading the signs correctly, the mother thought the daughter could do with a bit of fresh air.

After a nod, she then looked at him. "If your offer to escort me is still valid, then I would like to accept."

He wasn't certain she would really like to, but she *would* respect her mother's wishes. Pierre offered his arm. "Of course, mademoiselle. It would be my pleasure."

Chapter Five

Claire rolled the parchments, secured them with a piece of sinew and then hesitantly took hold of Mr. Lafayette's arm. She could feel the taut muscles beneath his sleeve. It was only her mother's command that caused Claire to leave the hut. "You go with him, Bright Star," she had said.

Claire was disinclined to do so for more reasons than one. She was foremost embarrassed by her earlier behavior toward him when he had asked why she remained in the village. Why had she snapped at him for such a simple inquiry? The answer was quite clear to her. Anger and bitterness toward Mr. Granger still blackened her heart, and until she dealt with those feelings properly, she would be a prickly thorn in Mr. Lafayette's flesh and a cause of grief to her mother. Neither of which she wanted.

Second, her mother's health made her hesitant to leave her unattended.

"Are you not going to eat, as well?" she had asked Evening Sky. "You had little more than a bit of meal this morning."

Her mother had waved off her concern. "Do not fret over me, child. I have had my fill today. Go enjoy yourself."

Enjoy myself?

How was Claire to do that when her feelings were so conflicted? She knew she must settle this issue in her heart with Mr. Granger once and for all. If she did not, there was little hope of her successfully sharing the light with her Mandan family. She could talk all she wanted about love and forgiveness, but if she was not practicing them herself...

My uncle is a smart man. Surely he senses the discrepancy. God, please help me truly to forgive Mr. Granger. Help me to let go of my anger, my fears...

And it wasn't just the future her uncle planned for her that she feared. Claire did not enjoy being in such close proximity to the handsome young Frenchman. He made her feel skittish and off balance. Mr. Lafayette had the uncanny ability to provoke her to anger at one moment with his comments and then fluster her with his compassion in the next.

"You love your family very much, don't you?" he said as they walked toward the campfire. "But you worry for their well-being, especially your mother."

"I do."

"I imagine it must be difficult for her without your father." He then added, "And difficult for you."

She nodded, but said nothing. That disconcerting feeling was rising inside her again. How could she feel the need to be so on guard with him and yet desire to open up to him at the same time?

He found her a seat on a log, a spot where the wind would not force the smoke of the fire back into her face. A nearby soldier was already tuning up his fiddle. Evidently she'd dallied so long in the hut that most of the men had eaten their venison stew and bread and were now making attempts to claim seconds. She felt bad for endangering Mr. Lafayette's chance at a meal and told him so.

"That is no matter of concern," he said with an easy smile, and then he managed to wrangle bowls of stew for them both.

"Merci," Claire said as she accepted a bowl from him. He sat down beside her.

They ate in silence for a few moments till Claire felt the overwhelming urge to apologize to him once again.

"I'm sorry," she said. "Truly, I am. My frustration and my anger are not meant for you."

He nodded. "May I ask at whom they *are* directed?"

Her jaw instantly tensed. He noticed.

"Forget that I asked that," he said. "I have no right to pry."

"No… I…" She sighed. "I have given you that right by my deplorable actions."

He looked at her with those deep charcoal eyes, not in an examining or judgmental way, but with an expression of kindness, friendship, a desire to understand.

"My anger is directed at someone very far away," she said. "A man named Phillip Granger."

"A white man?"

She nodded. "He was a friend of my father's."

He said nothing to that, but the look on his face begged her continue.

"My father had provided amply for my mother and me in the event of his death," she explained. "We were not wealthy, but we had all we needed. At the time of his death, there were money, supplies and property to support us, but the laws of Illinois did not allow such things to be passed from man to wife or father to daughter. My father had to sign his possessions over to his partner, Mr. Granger, on the promise that *he* would look after us."

A knowing look then came into Mr. Lafayette's face. "And he didn't—did he?"

His voice was most sympathetic. Claire shook her head as tears began to blur her vision. She'd never discussed this with anyone besides her mother and her uncle when they had first arrived. Running Wolf had showed little sympathy.

"Land belongs to no man," he had said. "We are but caretakers of it."

Perhaps his attitude had been the right one. Even so, the pain cut deep. "Mr. Granger honored my father's wishes for a mere sixty days, and then he told us the land, our cabin and everything inside it were his by law."

"He wanted you to leave."

"Yes. He told my mother that she was a worthless squaw and I, an ignorant half breed. He told us we were no longer welcome."

Mr. Lafayette's eyes widened as if he couldn't believe anyone would do such a thing. "So you came here." He laid his hand upon hers, like he had done the night Running Wolf had stormed into the fort. "I'm sorry," he said. "I am so sorry."

His apology was like a balm to her soul. It changed nothing of her circumstances, but emotionally, it helped to know someone understood her pain. "With no family to turn to but my mother's, we arrived here, with little more than the clothes on our back."

"I'm sorry," he said once more. "And I'm sorry for what I said earlier—for asking why you chose to remain here...and my comment about 'proper society.'"

"No. It is I who am sorry..."

"Think no more of it. I understand now why you were so wary of me, why you were so angry. I would be, as well."

She drew in a breath. "You asked me why I stayed here," she said. "That's why, but there is another reason...the task to which I hope to rise."

"These are your people," he said, "and you want them to hear the truth."

She nodded once more, tears trickling down her cheeks. "But I fear I am a poor instrument for heralding it."

"No," he said. "You understand the harsh cruelty of life better than most. Greed, betrayal, the struggle to forgive...does not your Mandan family deal with these very same issues? Broken tribal alliances, war...is this not the way of life in this land?"

"It is."

"God can help you to forgive. He can take away your fears... I'll pray for you."

"Thank you," she said.

"Do not lose faith," he said. "Darkness will not always cover this land."

"How are you so certain?"

He smiled. "You and your mother are here."

Claire appreciated his encouragement, his belief in her.

He let go of her hand, returned to his stew. After a

few moments he asked, "Will you tell me about your father?"

She told him about her life in Illinois before his passing, about her father's fiddle and the Bible from which he had read. The concepts of love, duty and sacrifice she had learned from him.

"He sounds as though he was a Godly man."

"He was." Her throat was further tightening. She hoped by shifting the subject slightly, she could gain better control of her emotions. "What about you? Do you come from a large family?"

"Not by some standards," he replied. "There are my mother and father, and I've two younger brothers and a younger sister."

"And grandparents? Aunts and uncles?" she asked.

"Yes, but they live in France." He smiled reminiscently. "Both my mother's family and my father's thought it foolish to leave Paris for the backwater of lower Louisiana, but my father believed New Orleans to be a profitable port, and he wished for adventure, the chance to make a name for himself."

"And your mother?" Claire asked.

"My mother was less enthusiastic about all of it, but she agreed to come with him." He blew out a breath. "Now history repeats itself."

"In what way?"

"When I chose to leave my father's now profitable shipping business to seek adventure and my own fortune, he said *I* was the fool."

Although she'd give anything to have her father back, she couldn't argue against Mr. Lafayette's desire to find his own path, even if it had been against his father's wishes. François Manette had done the same.

He'd left France first for Quebec, then moved on to Illinois.

"Do you miss him?" she asked.

"Yes…and it grieves me that our relationship is strained."

"It is a man's nature to strike out on his own," she said. "I suppose it is a parent's nature to wish to safeguard his child."

"Yes, but he wanted to do more than safeguard me."

"He wanted to control you?"

"In a way. He wanted me to marry."

"To marry?" Of all the possible points of conflict between a father and son, she had not expected that one.

"He wanted me to marry a girl *he* had chosen. A girl I did not love."

Claire heaved a sigh. There was another moment of silence.

"So," he then said, "while our circumstances may not be exactly the same, you and I do share a common bond. I know what it is like to feel trapped by family expectations. I know how hard it is to forgive."

"I see…"

"Shared experiences make for comradeship," he said, "or dare I hope friendship?"

Friendship. She would appreciate a friend, and she could tell based on what she had seen of his character thus far that his wish was sincere, unlike Mr. Granger's, who had pretended to be a protector, a helper, but in reality was looking to help only himself. "I would appreciate that."

He offered her a handsome smile. "May I be so impertinent, then, as to presume that if I promise to pray for you, you will pray for me?"

She returned his smile. "Of course. It would be my honor to do so."

They returned to their meal. Fiddle music drifted through the air, a somewhat melancholy tune, as if the soldier playing it was thinking of his own family.

"You know," Mr. Lafayette then said, "there was one thing for which I always respected the Spanish."

She was a bit taken aback by the sudden turn in the conversation but followed its course. "What is that?"

"When the Spanish controlled upper Louisiana, they allowed women to hold property. Unfortunately, when France laid claim, that right was taken away."

"And now this area belongs to America," she said ruefully, "and in time it will be subject to the same laws as Illinois."

"Well, perhaps that is something people like us can change," he said.

She smiled at his hopefulness. It was too late for her. The land in Illinois was gone, *but in the light of eternity...* She remembered what he had said before, that darkness would not always cover this land. *"You and your mother are here."* And now, so was *he.* "I appreciate your graciousness, Mr. Lafayette, and I appreciate your friendship."

He offered her a warm smile. "And I appreciate yours, mademoiselle."

Silence reigned between them for a few moments as they occupied themselves with their stew. Conversation and men's laughter drifted about them. The fiddle continued to play. Now it carried a livelier tune. One of the soldiers was dancing awkwardly.

"Tomorrow is Christmas Eve," Mr. Lafayette then said.

"Indeed." It was the time for prayers and carols. The time when children left their small shoes by the fire, expecting Père Noël to fill them with gifts. She wondered if Mr. Lafayette had participated as a child. *And now, being so far from home, does he long for the closeness of family?* Would he pass the holiest night of the year in prayerful vigil for them?

Will he pray for mine? She felt certain that he would, and that strengthened her.

He ate what remained of his food. Claire saved the last of hers. The men of the fort had eaten all that had been prepared. *I'll take this portion back to Mother. Perhaps she will be hungry when she wakes.*

Concern for her pushed Claire to her feet. "I should go."

"Won't you stay a little longer?" he asked.

The declaration of friendship aside, a strange feeling welled up inside her, a mixture of pleasure and pride. He wanted her to stay because he wanted to engage *her* further in conversation. He wished for her company.

She wanted to stay, as well, but her sense of duty would not allow it. "Thank you, but my mother… I do not wish to leave her alone too long." She saw the disappointment in his face, and that strange feeling grew. "And with tomorrow being Christmas Eve, I expect the captains will wish for us to gain an early start on our work."

"I suppose," he said. "Perhaps it is best to retire early."

"Yes. Good night." She started to turn.

"Mademoiselle Manette…"

"Yes?"

"Would you—" he hesitated "—would you permit me a dance?"

"A dance?"

"Tomorrow night."

She didn't know what to say to that. Her head told her it was a foolish, insensitive request. What room was there for frivolous merrymaking when both physical and eternal conditions here in the wilderness were so desperate? Yet her heart said one dance would not hurt. It was, after all, Christmas.

"Thank you, Mr. Lafayette. It would be my honor to partner with you."

"Pierre." He saw the confusion on her face. "My name is Pierre," he explained.

"Oh."

She did not give him permission to use her given name. Friends or not, it did not seem right. Thanking him, she turned for her hut. As she laid her hand to the latch, her mother's command passed through her mind. *"Go enjoy yourself."*

In spite of the awkward conversation at first, she *had* enjoyed herself tonight. She had enjoyed his company, enjoyed hearing of his family. For a few moments, she had forgotten what her uncle had done and what potential consequences awaited her upon her return to his lodge.

And now, as silly as it sounded, she found herself looking forward to tomorrow night's dance immensely.

The day before Christmas passed in the usual way. The bugler trumpeted the dawn. Men hastily dressed and assembled on the parade ground. Weapons were inspected. Sentries were changed. Immediately following breakfast, Pierre and Miss Manette began their work.

Upon entrance to their hut, Madame Manette greeted Pierre with a smile. She looked cheerful and well this morning. As she sewed, she hummed a French carol. Her daughter, however, was less lively; in fact, a near frown creased her forehead. Pierre couldn't help but wonder if he was the cause of her consternation. Had he made a mistake in asking her for a dance? In doing so, had he given her the impression that he was somehow romantically interested in her?

I'm not. Miss Manette is simply a friend. She speaks my language. She shares my faith. He marveled at the depth of her faith, respected her commitment. He remembered the look on her face when she thought she'd been bought by Captain Lewis. She'd resigned herself to the fate of servitude. She'd accepted the supposed sale without protest for the sake of family unity. *Would I be willing to sacrifice my own dreams for the sake of another?* he wondered.

Yes, she was pretty. Yes, she could at times be quite charming, but he was not interested in courting and definitely not interested in taking a wife. At that last thought, he laughed to himself. He had a habit of making more of situations than they actually were, and he knew he was doing it again right now. *I asked Miss Manette for a dance, not a kiss, not a lifetime. A dance, that's all.*

There was no risk. He had no dishonorable intentions, and she clearly had no romantic interest in him. The thought of that stung his male pride a bit, but his good sense told him that was a blessing.

We are friends, and as friends we can certainly

share a conversation, a dance or two without specu-
lation or entanglement. If she is somehow put off by
my request, I will simply withdraw it.

She never said that, however, and he didn't ask.
They simply continued their work.

Madame Manette then said something to her daughter in Mandan. Despite his language lessons, he still
couldn't understand. He thought he heard the word
night, but that was about all. He looked to the younger
woman.

"My mother asks if there will be any services tonight," she explained.

Pierre blinked. "Services?"

"Worship services."

"Oh. I don't believe so." While the captains had encouraged each man to worship according to the dictates
of his own conscience, there were rarely any formal
observances. The women looked disappointed. "I'm
certain there will be some singing of carols," Pierre
said, "and if you'd like…I could read a passage or two
of Scripture."

Miss Manette's eyes brightened, instantly remind-
ing him of the color of grass following a warm spring
rain. She immediately relayed the offer to her mother.
Evening Sky seemed just as pleased.

"Thank you, Mr. Lafayette," Miss Manette said.
"We would greatly appreciate that."

The look of consternation from earlier was now
completely gone. It pleased him that he had pleased *her*.

"It is after all, the Lord's birthday," he said. "We
should mark the occasion accordingly."

"Indeed."

They continued to compile their list. Today they were speaking of plants, of medicinal remedies.

"This root in particular my mother says is used for the cure of mad dog and snake bites."

"That's useful information to have," Pierre said. "How is it applied?"

"You crush the root and place it on the affected area twice a day."

Madame Manette then said something to her daughter. The younger woman chuckled.

"What did she say?" Pierre asked.

"She said not to chew or swallow any part of the root or there will be contrary affects."

"What kind of contrary affects?"

"You could die."

Pierre chuckled himself. "Yes, I can see where that could present a problem."

When the bugle sounded for supper, he bid the ladies a momentary farewell and returned to his quarters. *"Mark the occasion accordingly."* His own words echoed in his ears. No matter the fact that they were hundreds of miles from any church, Pierre thought he should look his best. He changed into a fresh shirt and then gave his coat a good brushing. Sergeant Ordway had a looking glass. Pierre asked to borrow it and stared long and hard at his reflection.

The captains had maintained scraped chins and cropped hair on this journey, but most of the men, including Pierre, had let their locks and beards grow. Black curls now framed his angular face, and thick bristles completely hid the slight cleft of his chin.

He chuckled to himself. If his mother and sister

were to see him now, they'd proclaim he'd gone native. Oddly, the "natives" here were always clean-shaven.

He reached for a razor. A few strokes into the task, he realized he wasn't doing it to emulate his captains, or even out of respect to Providence. He was doing it for someone else entirely.

All day long, Claire had been plagued by conflicting emotions. The anticipation she had felt last night concerning Mr. Lafayette's requested dance had been replaced by guilt. What right had she to dance when her world was in such desperate circumstances? Wouldn't the time tonight be better spent in prayer and reflection on Scripture? Mr. Lafayette *had* offered to read.

And yet Father celebrated Christmas with prayer and merrymaking. Claire remembered vividly how he had played his fiddle and how his feet hopped across the cabin floor. When she was very little, he'd sometimes laid the instrument aside, taken her hands in his. She'd climbed upon his boots, ridden his steps, giggled and laughed while his booming voice rang out.

"Christmas we sing here! Devout people, let us shout our thanks to God..."

And shout they did. Sing they did. It was not a solemn time. It was a time of hope, and now more than ever, she needed to hold on to that hope. The snow was deepening. Winter sicknesses would soon make their rounds. There were herbs and teas that sometimes brought a sufferer through the worst, and this year there was thankfully the addition of Captain Lewis's pills. Still, Claire couldn't help but wonder how many Mandans would pass into darkness before the dawn of earthly spring.

She sighed heavily. Her mother's health worried her in particular. Although her mother seemed to have regained her strength, there was something in her eyes that told Claire whatever sickness had ailed her had not been cured. It had only been lulled to sleep. How fierce would it be when it awakened?

Evening Sky snipped a thread. "I have finished it," she announced, and she held up her creation.

Claire gasped in wonder at the sight of the dress she had crafted. Her mother had always been quick and skillful with a needle, but the broadcloth dress she had fashioned over the past few days was anything but simple or ordinary.

The skirt was longer than Claire's deerskin dress. It was down to her ankles. The scooped neckline and high, gathered waist were in the style of what she'd seen from the fashion plates back in Illinois, but at the same time different. Evening Sky had taken the beaded border from her buffalo robe and stitched it onto the scarlet fabric. She had sacrificed her own ornaments to adorn her daughter. Tears collected in Claire's eyes. It was the perfect dress for her, French *and* Indian.

"Oh, Mother, it is beautiful."

"Come," Evening Sky commanded lovingly. "Put it on."

Despite her earlier misgivings, Claire would wear the dress. She would dance and she would allow herself to enjoy this evening. She would think of happy times of the past and hope for happy times in the future. *Lord, You came into a dark, weary land on that first Christmas. Most didn't recognize You at first, and yet You still changed the world. Help me to remember that. Help me to remember that my life, my mother's life and those of my people are in Your hands.*

"You will need to keep your inner tunic and leggings," her mother said, "for this fabric is not so fitted for winter on the plains."

Claire laid aside her outer articles of animal skin. The broadcloth was not as warm, but it did not matter. She could stand the chill for one evening. She ran her hands over the beading while her mother fastened the back of the gown. How she wished she had a full-length looking glass so she might see her entire image.

Evening Sky then began to undo her daughter's braids. "I'll pile your hair on top of your head," she said, "just like I used to do."

Claire smiled to herself. She had not worn her hair up since she had come to the Mandan village. It would be a wonderful change.

In a few minutes, the transformation was complete. Claire's dark locks had been fashioned into a bun. Small twigs served in place of hairpins, but they held just as securely. She'd never had need for curling papers, either. The few stands left at the sides of her face were already curling on their own.

She couldn't help but wonder what Mr. Lafayette would think when he saw her dressed this way. A flicker of excitement danced through her. Just what would he say?

Chapter Six

Pierre stood respectfully as the door to the women's hut opened. When Madame Manette stepped out dressed in her customary animal skins, minus the usual ornamentation, Pierre wondered if he had been remiss in donning his best clothing. Did the women dress even more simply this night to mark the King's birth in a humble stable?

Then he saw the mademoiselle and knew otherwise. *Enchanté*, he thought, for *enchanting* was exactly what she was. He'd been right when he'd thought she could fit in easily in a New Orleans ballroom. Her hair piled high accentuated the elegance of her neck and shoulders, and the dress she wore tonight revealed curves that her ordinary deer skin tunic did not.

She is absolutely beautiful.

He bowed formally as she approached. She curtsied and wished him a good evening. Pierre was so tongue-tied that all he could do was nod in response.

"You will be as cold tonight as I am," she said.

"Hmm?" He realized then she was referring to his absent whiskers. He rubbed his chin. It *was* cold.

"Yes…but, well, not very. Clouds are rolling in… There will be no stars tonight, therefore…the temperature… will be more moderate."

She chuckled softly. Leaving him to wonder if the response was simply inner joy or amusement at the problem he was suddenly having with his speech. Turning, he greeted her mother with a nod and a simple smile, and then offered them both a seat at the fire.

Sergeant Ordway quickly handed Miss Manette a plate of food, and Private Howard brought water. Pierre knew immediately there would be competition for mademoiselle's attention tonight, and he did not like it. Some of the men here seemed intent on cultivating romance with every pretty face they encountered. He would see to it that they kept their distance.

He shot the men a warning glare, then turned to Madame Manette. In broken Mandan, Pierre offered her something to eat. She nodded and accepted a plate with a smile, one that held a hint of impishness. Was his Mandan as poor as his French tonight, or did she realize how her daughter was affecting him? Affecting them all?

Sergeant Ordway glared at Pierre until he was summoned by Captain Clark. Before Private Howard could claim the spot beside the younger woman, Madame Manette pointed to Pierre, motioning for him to claim the place. He did not have to be asked twice.

"She is eager to have you read the Scriptures," Miss Manette said. "I read them to her, but it is different with a man."

"You have a Bible?"

"My father's. It was one item we managed to carry away with us."

"She misses him," Pierre said knowingly.

Evening Sky nodded and laid a hand over her heart.

"Very much so," her daughter said. "As I imagine you must miss your own family, especially tonight."

The sleeve of her dress was touching his arm. He wasn't thinking of his family in this moment, but he forced his mind to go there.

"Right about now they will be preparing to go to church."

"Is your church a large one?" she asked.

"I suppose," he said, "although I would scarcely consider it a cathedral."

"Does it have colorful glass in its windows?"

"Yes. Each window depicts a scene from the Bible." He saw the wonder in her face. Oddly, he had stared at such images for years and never once truly appreciated their beauty or meaning.

She smiled. "I should like to see something like that one day."

"Had you a church in Illinois?"

"No. At least, not a church *building*. We simply gathered in our cabin, and those who wished to join us did."

She nibbled daintily on her bread. Pierre couldn't help but smile at the paradox. Physically she was as strong as an ox yet at times she appeared as delicate as a hothouse flower.

"When your expedition is complete, do you expect to return to New Orleans?" she asked.

"No," he said. He'd apparently answered a little too adamantly, for the look she gave him then pricked his conscience. Evidently she couldn't imagine that anyone who had the opportunity to return to family would not immediately do so.

He tried to explain. "I care deeply for my parents, for my brothers and sister, but I have always sensed that their life, their business was not for me…that there was something else I was meant to do."

"You will be given a grant of land upon completing this expedition, will you not?"

Though land was surely a painful subject, she had said the words without any hint of animosity. "Yes," he said.

"I heard one of the other Frenchmen speaking of it. He seemed a bit jealous of you."

"I'm sorry to hear that," Pierre replied. "I suppose it is because Captain Lewis has chosen me to continue westward."

She blinked. "I thought all of you were heading west."

"Only the soldiers, myself and the interpreters. Most of the oarsmen, the Frenchmen, will return on the keel-boat to Saint Louis in the spring, as the boat is too large to navigate the northern Missouri."

"Then you were specially chosen," she said, "with honor."

"I'm not so certain it was that, exactly. There was simply an opening. One of the original soldiers will be sent home in the spring…a matter of having disobeyed a set of orders long before our arrival here. I was selected to take his place, and yes…if I complete the expedition successfully, I will receive a land grant, but I had no idea of such a gain when I signed on."

"No?"

"I am eager to explore. I want to stand on my own two feet, but there is something more to why I do this.

Something different. I don't know what exactly… I just sense it."

She smiled softly. "God has other purposes for you," she said.

He wanted to believe that. "I wish I knew what those purposes were," he said.

She nodded sympathetically. "You will know when the time is right. God will reveal His will to you."

No doubt she struggled with knowing her purpose in life, as well, or at least believing her purpose would bear fruit. "*Merci*, mademoiselle. I appreciate you saying that."

With that, he pulled his frayed Bible from his coat pocket. "And the will of the Lord is discovered in His word, is it not?"

She smiled again.

"The gospel of Matthew or Luke?" he asked.

"Both, if you please."

He returned her smile and then began to read.

Claire felt a warmth building inside her as Mr. Lafayette read through the account of the Nativity. His rich, deep voice was clear and strong, yet gentle and reassuring. He made no show of what he was doing, commanded no audience, but his simple straightforwardness drew her close, and others, as well.

His fellow French voyagers had all gathered around, and even the English-speaking men, though they could not understand the words, recognizing the holiness of Scriptures, paused in their conversations and kept silent before the Creator.

Oh, how Claire treasured this moment. How she

garnered strength from the words. "'For unto you is born this day, a savior which is Christ the Lord...'"

A savior for these men here, for the Mandan, a savior for all...

When Mr. Lafayette closed his reading, Mr. Jessaume started singing the carol *"Noël Nouvelet."* Those who could speak French joined him, Claire included. "'Soon the kings, by the bright star, to Bethlehem came one morning...'"

The singing grew. "'New Christmas! Christmas we sing here!'"

When the final stanza closed, Captain Clark, who had been watching from his hut door, called out to Mr. Jessaume, "I'm afraid I don't know that one, but here is one we sing where I come from..." Crossing the parade ground, he boisterously began, "'Joy to the world! The Lord is come...'"

There was a chuckle or two from the men. Apparently they were unaccustomed to their captain making merry, but those who could sing soon joined in.

"'Let heaven and heaven and nature sing!'"

Evening Sky leaned her head close to Claire and whispered, "French, American, Mandan...in Christ there is no difference."

How Claire prayed others would see it that way, too. If they did, the future would be glorious.

Private Cruzette tuned up his fiddle. Rising then to his feet, he started taking requests. The carols he knew he played with speed and enthusiasm. Those he didn't, he picked his way through as best as he could. There was laughter. There was joy. Claire's heart was full.

Soon the men commenced dancing. None of the steps were formal, but it did not matter. The fast stepping and knee slapping were as delightful to watch as a polished minuet. Although when Mr. Lafayette stood and held out his hand to her, Claire felt her merriment vanish. How exactly would they step together?

"I'm afraid I don't know this," she said.

"Neither do I," he admitted. "It will be alright. Just follow me. I promise we will not end up in a heap."

"As you say, sir." She took his hand. His fingers closed around hers, and a warmth enveloped her. She could see the firelight flickering in his dark eyes. He was a handsome man, considerably more so now, without his beard. His cheekbones were chiseled, and a slight cleft marked his chin. Claire's heart skipped erratically as they stepped hand in hand in time with the music.

It wasn't long before the simple fiddle became a stringed orchestra and the flickering firelight a chandelier's glow. Not that she had actually ever seen such things, but she had heard of them, and having heard of them, she could imagine them.

It was not all pomp and circumstance, however. She stepped on his foot once and he, in turn, upon hers. They laughed. They stumbled. He caught her squarely in his arms. The moment he did, Claire felt a surge of energy inside her, one she had never known before.

"I promised you we would not end up in a heap on the ground," he said.

"So you did."

Something significant passed between them then. Claire sensed it in her soul, saw it in his eyes. The intimacy frightened her. Immediately she took a step back. Confusion quickly darkened his features, but being the gentlemen he was, he let go of her.

The wind gusted. Claire looked toward her mother, fearful of how this cold air could be affecting her. Should she take leave? Escort her mother back to the hut?

Evening Sky, however, looked quite content. Captain Lewis was now sitting beside her, gesturing to her with signs, and she responded with the same to him, both doing the best to communicate with each other.

"Your mother seems to be enjoying herself," Mr. Lafayette remarked.

Claire watched her for a few seconds. She recognized that smile, that look of fondness on her mother's face. "She's telling him about my father."

"They must have loved each other very much."

"They did." She could feel a lump growing in her throat. Would she ever know such a love? Such a partnership?

"My father is not an outdoorsman," Mr. Lafayette said, "but every Christmas Eve he takes my brothers and me into the woods to collect pine boughs and berries because he knows my mother loves the smell of them."

Claire returned his gaze. "My father did the same. Our cabin was filled with greenery."

"And a crèche?"

She smiled. "Yes. My father carved the figures of Mary, Joseph and the infant Jesus himself."

"Ours were porcelain, and they came from a shop in Paris. We placed them on our parlor mantel. Then, after reading the account from Scripture, my father would tell us to place our shoes in front of the fire and hurry off to bed—"

"Or Père Noël would not come?"

"Yes."

She couldn't help but smile again. "I was always told the same."

"What was your favorite gift?"

"A doll, not one made of corn husk, but porcelain. She had dark hair and painted green eyes."

He smiled.

"And yours?" she asked.

"A toy musket, although I was rather disappointed when I learned it wouldn't actually fire."

She laughed slightly, wondering what sort of boy he had been. Was he affectionate and expressive like Spotted Eagle or rough and rambunctious? Somehow she suspected the latter.

"We have lived very different lives," he then said, "but I think we ourselves are not so different."

She could feel that strange, frightful sensation inside her once more. She glanced again at her mother.

"Will you help me with something?" he asked.

She wanted to say yes, but prudence warned her to be cautious. He hadn't told her what that something was yet.

"It won't take long," he promised, "but first…well, I had better speak to Captain Clark."

Now he had her curious indeed. He strode away confidently before she could any questions. The music was still playing, and one of the soldiers came to her and requested a dance. Claire politely obliged him, but her thoughts were far from her new partner. Just what was Mr. Lafayette up to?

Thankfully the fiddle soon stopped. Private Cruzette reached for a drink, then began another tune.

Mr. Lafayette returned before another soldier could claim her.

He was carrying a lantern and a hatchet. Captain Clark was on his heels. He was carrying a musket. "The captain agreed with my idea," Mr. Lafayette said.

"What idea?" she asked.

"Gathering Christmas cheer."

"I beg your pardon?"

He smiled. "There's a pine grove just beyond the cottonwoods."

Ah, now she understood, and since Captain Clark was to be the obvious escort... "I know it well," she said. "It is not far."

Claire followed his gaze toward her mother. Despite their limited language skills, Captain Lewis and Evening Sky were still managing a cheerful conversation.

"We could be back before she even knew we were gone," Mr. Lafayette said. "We could surprise her."

Claire liked the idea of a surprise, and since her mother was being looked after and Captain Clark was willing to provide escort, she agreed to the plan. Moving nonchalantly toward the fort's gate, she waited for it to open.

Beyond its walls lay a vast, motionless, moonless landscape. Claire was thankful for the lantern, for the only light visible was the faint glow of cooking fires on the far side of the Missouri. Sadly, her people were passing this long winter night like any other.

The trio started off. Claire soon found that broadcloth was not nearly so useful in the snow as buckskin. Normally fast on her feet, she now struggled to keep pace with the men. The hem of her skirt grew wetter and heavier with each step. Nevertheless, she continued on. They passed the stumps of the cottonwood trees the soldiers had felled to build their fort, moved past the remaining timbers until they came to the grove of pine.

While Captain Clark kept his ear and musket cocked for any sounds of approaching danger, Claire held the lantern. Mr. Lafayette hacked away at the boughs. For a polished, city-bred gentleman, he worked with speed and skill. He knew how to handle himself in the wilderness. She supposed that was one of the reasons the captains had asked him to continue westward.

Soon a bundle of greenery lay at her feet.

"Do you know where we might find berries?" he asked.

She shook her head. "My people would have picked all that are edible by now, and the birds will have taken the rest."

"I suppose we will have to do without them," he said.

Instinctively she bent to pick up the bundle. "No," he said. "It's heavy. Allow me."

Such kindness, she thought. A man of her tribe would have not only expected her to carry the boughs but also commanded it. Mr. Lafayette handled her the hatchet instead. Claire shivered slightly as his fingers brushed hers. All of a sudden, she couldn't help but wonder what it would be like to have this man caress her face, her hair.

Shock jolted her senses now far more than his fleeting touch. Why was she thinking such absurd thoughts? Was she so starved for affection and security that she had taken to imagining things? She quickly turned her attention to Captain Clark. The man's eyes were scanning the dark horizon.

"I think we have all we need now, sir," Mr. Lafayette said. "Besides, Miss Manette is getting cold."

Claire felt the blood drain from her face. He had seen her shiver. Thankfully he had not recognized it for what foolishness it actually was.

"Then we'd best be on our way," Clark replied.

The merrymaking was still going on when the trio returned to the fort. Captain Clark barred the door behind them.

"Meet me at the blacksmith's hut," Mr. Lafayette whispered to her.

"Very well."

He took the direct way, she the more roundabout. Her mother and Captain Lewis were still sitting by the fire. Evening Sky offered her a curious smile as Claire passed by.

She knows I have been scheming, she thought. Giving her what she hoped was an innocent-looking smile in return, Claire continued on.

Mr. Lafayette was already sorting through the greens when she arrived. "In what way would your mother prefer these to be displayed?" he asked.

There was no mantel, but there was the writing desk. "We could arrange them around that," she said.

He had separated the greens into small and large piles. The small ones Claire twisted together as garland. The larger ones he formed into the shape of a wreath. Her excitement grew.

"There may be a bit of scarlet fabric left from my dress," she said. "We could fashion a bow from that."

He nodded, smiled. "That's a capital idea, and we may have enough here for a second wreath."

"Then let's give it to the men," she said.

"I think they would enjoy that."

When they had finished, Mr. Lafayette poked his head out the door of the hut. "We'll have to do some skulking to get these back without being seen."

She couldn't help but giggle.

"Are you opposed to skulking?" he asked with a grin.

"There is little point. My mother already knows we are plotting something."

"Well, still, there is no need to announce our scheme. Let us try to make a surprise present." He gathered the wreaths on his right arm and draped the garland around it also. "If we walk tighter perhaps they'll be less noticeable."

She was not all that eager to do so, especially given what she had been thinking in the pine grove. "Would our walking tightly together not arouse suspicion enough?"

He conceded her point with a smile. "You are correct. Take the garland and hide it beneath your cloak. I'll follow along with the wreaths in a moment or two."

She did as he suggested, making her way back to her hut as casually as she could. Stepping inside, Claire fumbled for a candle and lit it. One stick of tallow wasn't going to produce much of a warm glow, but Claire was determined to make the best of what she had.

She laid the garland upon the desk, but before she could see to it properly, a fist pounded upon the door. Captain Clark was standing on her threshold, holding a box of candles. Mr. Lafayette was not five steps behind him. Knowing the parade would attract all the more attention, Claire beckoned them both inside.

The captain grinned, apparently somewhat amused by her distress. He then handed her the box of candles. "We can spare these for tonight," he said. "After all, it is a holy celebration."

"*Merci*, Captain." After a curtsy, she hurried to place the candles about the room. The music outside had stopped. She knew the party was ending. With little time to spare, Claire hurriedly searched through her mother's sewing supplies, found a few scraps of scarlet cloth. She tied a bow on each wreath, and then asked Captain Clark if he would be so kind as to present one of them to the men.

Clark cast a quick glance at Mr. Lafayette for translation, then smiled. "*Oui,*" he said, "and I'll see to it that your mother is detained for a moment or two longer." He stepped outside.

Mr. Lafayette lit the extra candles while she finished arranging the garlands. "It's a pity we don't have a crèche," he said, "but I'm afraid I'm not very good at carving—especially not in five minutes' time."

"Carving!" Claire gasped. She'd almost forgotten her mother's Christmas gift. From beneath her bedding, she retrieved a wooden cross necklace with a leather cord.

"Did you make that?" he asked.

"Yes."

"It's beautiful."

She could feel a blush of pride darkening her cheeks. She had fashioned the necklace from cottonwood, smoothed it with river sand and then notched a Mandan-style border. She had done most of the work while her mother was sleeping.

"It isn't a crèche," she said.

"But it will do quite nicely."

Grinning, she placed the necklace in the garland.

"Shall I hang this wreath here?" he asked, pointing to the wall beside her mother's bed.

"Yes, please."

When he had finished, Claire surveyed their surroundings. It wasn't Illinois. It wasn't her father's doing, but the little hut now looked cozy and cheerful, and she knew her mother would dearly appreciate this gift. Claire appreciated the one who had thought of it. Greatly.

The forceful knock again sounded. As Claire brushed pine needles from her dress, Mr. Lafayette opened the door. Evening Sky stood at the threshold on the arm of Captain Clark. "Madame, I believe these two young people have crafted a surprise for you," he said. He transferred her arm to Mr. Lafayette and then, with a smile, turned back for the parade ground.

Claire held back her tears as the Frenchman escorted her mother inside. Evening Sky's eyes were wide with wonder and delight.

"For you, Mother," Claire said. "In memory of father."

With tears in her own eyes, Evening Sky kissed her daughter. She then turned and placed a kiss on Mr. Lafayette's smooth cheek, as well. *"Merci,"* she said. *"Merci."*

Claire's heart was completely full. As her mother then went about the hut, fingering each bough, Claire looked back at Mr. Lafayette. "Thank you," she said, although the words seemed wholly inadequate.

"It was my pleasure," he said. He studied her for a moment, then said, "I should go."

Yes, she supposed he should. The surprise had been presented and it was late, but she wasn't all that eager for him to leave. She had enjoyed this evening immensely. "I suppose I shall see you tomorrow morning."

"Actually, no. I'll be on the hunt."

"Oh?" She could feel disappointment rising inside her.

"There will be no work tomorrow. Captains' orders. Tomorrow is to be a day of freedom, of frivolity and feasting...at least, as much feasting as our food supply will allow."

He flashed her an adventurous, slightly roguish smile. She took no offense in it, however, for she knew any trickery he had up his sleeve would be directed at the animals he hoped to capture tomorrow. "Then I wish you a good hunt," she said. "Thank you again, Mr. Lafayette, for everything."

"Pierre," he gently corrected her. "And *Joyeux Noël*, Mademoiselle Manette."

She hesitated, but only for the briefest of seconds. "Claire," she said, "and a Merry Christmas to you as well."

He took her hand, bowed gallantly over it and kissed it gently. "Claire," he repeated with a smile. Then he turned and closed the door behind him.

Chapter Seven

Although the boom of a cannon and a volley of musket fire jolted Claire from her dreamy sleep, she was not alarmed by the sounds. She knew their significance. The firing of the guns was the soldiers' way of marking celebration. Christmas morning had come.

Claire drew in a deep, satisfied breath, filling her lungs with the scent of wood and pine. Across the hut her mother still lay sleeping, her face toward the wall. *Good*, Claire thought. Evening Sky needed the rest after the previous evening. The two of them had talked until the wee hours of the morning, till the candles waned and their eyelids grew heavy. Her mother had loved the cross necklace Claire had made for her and repeatedly told her how much she had enjoyed the gift of a celebration, particularly the decoration.

"Young Lafayette is a kind and considerate man," she said.

"Indeed, he is."

Long after her mother had drifted off to sleep, Claire lay beneath her own pile of blankets and buffalo skins, recounting every detail of the moments shared with

him. The Scripture reading and singing had strengthened her soul. The hanging of the greens had delighted
her senses. The feel of Mr. Lafayette, of *Pierre*, taking
her hand in his and pressing it to his lips had stirred
her heart.

It stirs it still. She didn't know whether to blush or
giggle, to feel ashamed or happy. Pierre Lafayette was
on the verge of stealing her heart, a feat no man had
yet to accomplish, and she knew she could not allow
that to happen.

Last night, for one quick moment, she had the audacity to wonder if he just might be the answer to her
prayers. *But that cannot be!* He was handsome, yes,
and he had come to her aid. He'd shown respect to her
and her mother. He'd become a friend, but that didn't
make him a potential husband.

Mr. Lafayette was an honorable man. He was not,
however, interested in courtship. *The chill of winter
will eventually surrender to the warmth of spring. The
Missouri will thaw and he will be on his way. He has
his duties. I have mine. I cannot allow myself to become distracted from my true purpose here, to bring
the good news to my family, my tribe.*

Yet as much as she wanted to discount the thoughts
that had passed through her mind last night, to claim
they were the simple product of a lonely woman reaching out to a kind soul, she couldn't.

She tried to force Pierre from her thoughts but found
her curiosity only growing. Claire couldn't help but
wonder where he was at that moment and what exactly
he was doing. Had he been successful in his hunt? Was
he now in the process of dressing a prize elk or buffalo?

She remembered how skillfully he had worked with

his hatchet last night, how deft his hands had been fashioning the boughs into wreaths. He was quick and strong, but he'd been most gentle when he had touched her.

She indulged for a moment in that vein until a forceful knock on the door jolted her back to reality. Hastily donning her buffalo robe, Claire answered the summons. Captain Clark stood waiting outside. He cast her what she thought was a curious look, one that made her cheeks warm with embarrassment. Could he tell what she had just been thinking?

"My apologies for disturbing you, Miss Manette," he said.

Claire blushed even further. It was a holiday, yes, but this man was dressed in his full uniform, and his boots were already muddy. Clearly he had been up and about for hours. Here she was with her hair still loose about her shoulders.

"Captain Lewis wishes to see you," he said.

"Oh?"

"Yes."

Limited language skills aside, she could tell he did not wish to elaborate. A chill shivered through her. Something was wrong. Her thoughts immediately flew to Pierre. Had he been injured on his hunt?

Or was it something even worse? Had she mistaken the cause behind the discharge of weaponry? Was there some impeding danger? The Sioux had come marauding only weeks ago, as they often did, thieving and bent on bloodshed. As Pierre had once so ruefully remarked, war was a way of life here on the frontier. *Have the Sioux returned? Have they captured Pierre?*

Her knees felt weak, her throat dry. Unable to formulate further words, she nodded to Captain Clark. He quickly turned on his heel. Closing the door behind him, Claire hurriedly pulled on her leggings and moccasins. Rather than take the time to plait her hair, she twisted it into a bun. Her hands were trembling, but she managed to secure the locks with her twigs. During all this, Evening Sky stirred slightly beneath her bedding, but Claire was able to slip outside the door without waking her.

Low, heavy clouds shrouded the fort, speaking the promise of more snow. The air seemed colder than it had last night. The chill went all the way through her bones. There were few soldiers on the parade ground this morning. Claire wanted to think them still sleeping or off on the hunt, but fear told her they were preparing for battle. If so, what would be the outcome for them? What would be the outcome for her and her people?

She reached the officers' quarters. Captain Lewis met her at the door. His features were grave and taut. "Thank you for coming, Miss Manette."

"Are men danger?" she asked in stunted English. "Hunt? Sioux?"

Lewis blinked, and then realized her concern. "No. No. I've had no word of anything amiss with the hunt, nor with the neighboring Sioux."

She heaved a sigh of relief but realized she had just betrayed herself. If this man was as observant and intelligent as he appeared to be, he'd have little trouble knowing why, or rather, *for whom* exactly she had first been concerned.

How foolish am I? I've left no secret as to where my heart is becoming inclined.

Lewis ushered her inside his quarters. Claire

stepped in to find Toussaint Charbonneau leaning casually against the wall. Sacagawea was seated on a stool in the corner. She smiled at Claire. Claire returned the expression, but not without difficulty. She knew what the couple's presence here, clearly on good terms again with the captain, would now mean for her.

Captain Lewis cleared his throat. "As you can see, Miss Manette, Mr. Charbonneau and his wife have returned. Therefore, your services will no longer be needed."

Her disappointment was palpable. The only emotion stronger was guilt. *Foolish girl! Why do you mourn? You knew this work was only temporary. You should have been more careful. You have allowed Pierre Lafayette to become a distraction from your real purpose here!*

Captain Lewis walked to his desk. His chair creaked as he sat down. After studying her pensively for a moment, he said, "Miss Manette, I must confess, I am hesitant to see you return to your village. If you wish, I could find other work for you. You could remain here, but you and your mother would have to share the living space with Charbonneau and his wife."

He signaled for the Frenchman to translate, but Claire held up her hand. She understood the message. *If you wish, I could find other work for you...* A part of her did wish just that. For all her prayers, for all her talk of faith, she *feared* returning to her uncle's lodge.

But what good is postponing the inevitable? She was going to have to go back one day. The longer she remained in Pierre Lafayette's company, the harder it would be when the time came for him to leave.

And there was a bigger issue at stake here, bigger than the matter of her personal safety. *My people need the Lord. And if that means sacrificing my life, my health and happiness, what price is that to pay in the light of eternity?*

Her mind was made up. Rather than try to stumble through an explanation in English, she asked Charbonneau to translate. "Thank you, Captain, for your concern. I do appreciate all of the kindness you have shown me and my mother. It has been a great honor to be of assistance to you, but I must return to my people. My family has need of me, and I must not delay any longer."

Lewis leaned back in his chair, studied her again for a moment. She prayed he would not ask her to reconsider her decision. If he tried to persuade her to stay, she would likely do just that. His kindness served only to make the choice harder to accept. How different her thoughts were of this place than when she first arrived. Here she was protected. Here she was treated with respect.

But I cannot stay! I have to go back to the village!

Captain Lewis sighed. Evidently he recognized her decision as final. "I'll have one of my men ready a horse. He will escort you and your mother back to the village."

It would be better if I simply went, she thought, *for what soldier might he choose?* What if Pierre arrived back at the fort in time to become the commanded escort? Would she be able to say goodbye to him without revealing her growing feelings? "Thank you, Captain, but do no not trouble your soldiers, especially on this day of celebration. I've no need for an escort, but if I may beg your indulgence, I'll take the horse. After I deliver my mother safely to her lodge, I'll return it to you, along with the first animal you loaned to my uncle."

If, that is, Running Wolf is willing to return it without incident. Uncertainty washed over her in waves. *Oh, God, am I doing the right thing?*

But the Almighty did not answer. Captain Lewis shook his head no. "I'll come for my horses tomorrow," he said.

Tomorrow. Just what would tomorrow bring? Her uncle had said that her year of mourning had come to an end. Would she be given to the first warrior in sight upon her return to the village? Would Pierre Lafayette sympathize with her plight? Seek to rescue her? Would he even think of her at all?

She was very close to panic, and she knew she could not allow herself to go there. *Lord, please give me the courage to follow Your path. Reclaim my heart and please, forgive me for allowing myself to become distracted by earthly pursuits of happiness. Help me remember that no man is my hope. You are my hope.*

Her breathing slowed somewhat. "By your leave, Captain," she said, and with a final curtsy, she turned to go.

Returning to the hut, Claire found her mother up and dressed.

"There is sadness in your eyes," Evening Sky observed at once.

Claire tried to explain without explaining too much. "Sacagawea's husband has returned. They have no need for me here now."

"And we are to return to our village?"

Yes, she should have said, but again she wavered. She told Evening Sky of the captain's offer.

"And you said no to him."

Claire nodded. "I did not think it was proper to take work from Sacagawea."

Her mother smiled knowingly. "That is not all of it."

"No, it isn't," Claire admitted. She could feel the heat building in her cheeks but couldn't bring herself to admit what exactly was causing it. There *were* other reasons to leave, very important ones. "We are no longer needed here," she said. "We *are* needed there. Besides, these walls are too thin. This cold is not good for you. A warm lodge will be better."

"You wish to honor me, I know," her mother said. "But do not try to humor me." She kissed her daughter's head. "I am not the only one who occupies your heart."

"That will soon pass," Claire said, more for her own benefit than that of her mother. Then she began gathering her belongings. There weren't that many to sort, just her Bible, comb and brush. The scarlet dress was hanging on a peg in the corner of the room. Conscious of the tremble in her hands, provoked by what it represented, Claire took it down, folded it carefully and placed it inside her deerskin pouch.

With her mother's meager belongings now packed as well, Claire took one last glance about the hut, gave one last thought to the lists she had compiled here and to the man she'd worked alongside. Swallowing a lump in her throat, she picked up her and her mother's sacks and stepped outside.

Private Cruzette had readied a horse. He was standing at the gate, waiting for them. Claire helped her mother mount the animal. After securing their bags, she took the reins from the soldier.

"Merci," she said.

He doffed his cap, then moved to open the door. The wide, white prairie stretched out before her. Resisting the urge to scan the horizon for any sign of the hunting party, Claire started forward. She kept her eyes solely on her destination, the village across the river. There was her future.

Steeling her resolve, she determined to put all thoughts of Pierre Lafayette out of her mind, but as the gate closed behind her, the thoughts came once more. Why did she feel as though she were somehow leaving her life behind?

"Well done, Lafayette," Private Howard cheered as the buffalo fell to the snow with a thud. "With this and Coulter's elk, there will be good eating for the next few days."

"Indeed," Pierre said. "A feast." *Just like I promised.*

His chest swelled with pride until Jessaume said, "Maybe your squaw can make us some *poudingue blanc.*"

Pierre's jaw immediately tightened. It wasn't that he disliked white pudding, or any other buffalo delicacy. It was who Jessaume thought should prepare the meal—and the way he'd characterized her. "She *isn't* my squaw," he insisted.

Jessaume laughed. "It certainly appeared as though she was last night."

"Indeed," added Coulter, "you practically pushed poor Howard out of the way when he tried to sit next to her."

Now all the men were laughing, except, of course, Pierre. Handing Jessaume his smoking musket, he

moved toward his kill. He knew if he were to respond
any further to the ribbing he would be in danger of telling a lie—or worse. He'd own up to what he was really
thinking about Claire Manette, and that was something
he wasn't about to admit to anyone, especially himself.

Claire.

Words could not adequately describe the feeling that
came over him when she had given him permission to
address her by her Christian name, nor the near rap-
ture he'd experienced as he pressed his lips to her hand.

She was an adventure in her own right, a mixture
of mystery and frankness, softness and steel. *A woman
like that could snuff the flame of wanderlust in a man.
And if I'm not careful, that is exactly what will happen to me. I'll find my roaming cut short, leaving me
bound, just like this poor beast here.*

Pushing his thoughts of her aside, he began to field
dress the animal. As long as he kept focused on his
task, he was fine. The second he thought about returning to the fort, he knew he was in trouble. Why was
she so prominent in his thoughts? He had seen pretty
faces, shared friendships with intelligent women before, but they had never affected him like this.

The men loaded the buffalo on to the sleigh, secured
it for transport. Pierre wanted to trek farther, see what
else they could find, but Jessaume, Coulter and Howard were against it.

"It's well after noon now," Coulter said. "We had
better start back if we want to reach the fort before
dark."

"It is supposed to be a holiday," Pierre grumbled
under his breath, but he knew Coulter was right.
They had stayed on the plains overnight before and in

weather much colder than this, but previously they'd had their captains' permission to do so. *Today we do not*.

"Cheer up, man," Howard teased. "Your mademoiselle will be waiting."

That was exactly what Pierre feared. He had seen the look in her eyes when he'd bid her good-night. Was she enjoying his company as much as he was hers? If so, that would put a serious strain on his resolve to avoid romance.

It would be a romance that could lead nowhere, have no point. I'm leaving this place and she will remain here.

He sighed to himself. *I've no one to blame for this but myself*. Why had he asked her to dance? Why had he gone to all that trouble, trekking through the snow, gathering greens? It wasn't completely a wish to bring Christmas cheer to her mother.

Tomorrow will be back to business as usual, he told himself. *The frivolity of Christmas will be only a memory. There will be tasks to complete, drills and inspections*. They were a military expedition, after all. Eventually the snow would melt and they would march westward.

Today spring seemed like an eternity away and the fabled Pacific Ocean even farther. The snow was deep, and the fresh flakes falling made the going even harder. By the time they reached the south bank of the Missouri, Pierre was chilled to the bone. He was tired, and he was miserable. Christmas or not, he was in no mood for socializing tonight. *If Mademoiselle Manette is waiting at the gate, I won't be captivated by her eyes this time. I won't linger. I'll give her a nod, tell her the hunt was good and inform her when she can expect to claim a piece of meat. After that I'll collect a mug of something warm, change my clothing and climb into bed.*

And yet as soon as he stepped into the fort, his eyes betrayed him. While Captain Lewis came to inquire of their success, Pierre found himself scanning the grounds, searching for her. She was nowhere to be found. Toussaint Charbonneau, however, was.

"Mademoiselle Manette was relieved of her duties and returned to her village this afternoon," Lewis said, as if reading his thoughts.

Pierre's heart quickened, and all desire to distance himself from her vanished like ice under a warm spring sun. "Returned to her village?"

"Yes."

"You mean, to her uncle?"

"Yes." Evidently the captain considered the matter finished, for he turned his attention to Jessaume, Coulter and Howard, giving them directions concerning the distribution of the meat.

Pierre's mind was reeling. "You sent her back to him? *How could you* after what he did?"

Captain Lewis's eyes narrowed. "You forget yourself, Mr. Lafayette. Do not take such an accusatory and insubordinate tone with me."

Insubordinate? I'm not one of your enlisted soldiers. As a French voyager, I am free to come and go as I please. And accusatory? Did he *not* send her back to Running Wolf? Surely accusation was warranted! *Any officer stupid enough to send her back to such a man doesn't deserve my allegiance or respect.*

He turned on his heel, started for the gate. There

was only one thing on his mind right now, one mission. He had to be sure Claire was alright.

Private Howard caught his arm. "Don't do it, man. You'll suffer the lash—or worse. Remember Newman?"

John Newman, an original member of the expedition, had been court-martialed for insubordination. He was the man who would be returning to Saint Louis on the keelboat in the spring, the man Pierre was replacing.

Lewis called out, "Stand fast, Mr. Lafayette!"

Only then did Pierre realize his foolishness. He froze. What was wrong with him? Had he been touched by fever? Had he really intended to defy his captain's orders, set out alone to find Claire? Then what? Spirit her away from her uncle, her tribe? And go where? And at what cost?

One step more and I'll be on the keelboat with Newman. Or was he already? Pierre turned back to face his angry captain. Lewis's face was seething. Pierre didn't know if an apology would help or hurt, but he took a chance and spoke first.

"Forgive me, Captain. You are right. I forget myself."

Lewis's hard expression remained. He stared at Pierre, clearly trying to decide what course of action best to undertake. Pierre held his breath.

"You walk on thin ice, Lafayette," Lewis said finally, his teeth clenched. "I advise you *never* to place yourself in such a position again."

"Yes, sir."

The captain turned on his heel, strode away, but Pierre felt little relief. He had maintained his position with the expedition, at least for now, but what about Claire? Sacagawea, who had watched the entire scene from the left of the gate, came to him. She made several signs, obviously trying to tell him something important, but just what, Pierre had no idea.

Her husband came to translate. "My wife is trying to tell you that your squaw left the fort of her own accord," Charbonneau said.

"Of her own accord?"

Charbonneau nodded. So did Sacagawea. "I was there when Lewis summoned her. He offered her the opportunity to stay, promised to find her other work, but she said no."

With that, the Frenchman and his wife walked back to their hut, the one Pierre had once worked in with Claire.

Pierre stood there on the parade ground. The snow continued to fall and the temperature had dropped considerably. He was shivering, but he paid his physical condition little mind. Charbonneau's words echoed in his ears.

Of her own accord? Why would Claire go back to her uncle if the captain had granted her leave to remain here? Pierre had seen the tears in her eyes, felt the tremble in her hands the night Running Wolf had attempted to trade her. Why would she willingly go back to such a man? Why would she knowingly put herself in harm's way?

And what, if anything, was he to do about it?

Chapter Eight

The three-mile distance to the village seemed more like thirty today. Snow seeped inside Claire's moccasins, making her toes ache. The horse upon which her mother sat snorted and resisted her lead.

Ahead were her people, her own flesh and blood. Was it not her privilege to live among them? Her opportunity to introduce them to Christ? Yet the closer she came to the village, the more her feelings of inadequacy and fear grew.

Her uncle wanted nothing to do with white man's religion, and he'd made it perfectly clear he'd part with her without her approval or consent if the price was right. She felt she should return despite the danger, but was she doing so because God had told her to, or was she simply trying to escape another danger? The danger of falling for a man who would never marry her, who could be no permanent help to her in her circumstances?

He would never be content to remain here, nor would I wish him to be. He must move on. It is part of his nature. He must have his adventure. He must gain his land.

She would not begrudge him that. She was not jealous of him for it, even though she and her mother had lost her father's land. The night she had spoken with Pierre on the subject, the night he had promised to pray for her, she had finally been able to put the past to rest. She'd been able to forgive Mr. Granger at last. But as for bravely facing her uncertain future, she wasn't quite there yet.

"Fear not, for I have redeemed thee, I have called thee by thy name. Thou art mine. When you passeth through the waters, I will be with thee. And through the rivers, they shall not overflow thee..."

Claire recited the verse from book of Isaiah over and over again in her mind. *It comes down to a matter of trust,* she thought. *Either God is with me or He isn't. Either He loves me in spite of my weaknesses or He does not. He placed me in this village because this is where He truly wishes me to be.*

She drew in a breath. The air was cold but refreshing. *I choose to believe He does. I choose to believe.*

So she walked on.

As she and her mother reached the village, the women were scurrying about with their daily work. Some paused long enough to offer Claire a disapproving glare. Others whispered. *I have been talked about,* she thought, and she wondered exactly in what way.

Was the rumor circulating that she was improperly consorting with white men, or did they think her audacious for not going along with her uncle's plan to sell her to one?

"They stare at me," Evening Sky said, having no-

ticed them, as well. "They whisper because surely my
brother has told them how boldly I spoke to him at the
fort." Evening Sky gave a slight laugh. "They act as
though they are shocked, but deep down they probably
wish they had my courage."

Claire offered her mother a smile. "We all wish we
had your courage."

"You have, child," she said.

She wasn't so sure about that, but she nodded respectfully and tugged on the horse.

The men of the village were gathered in their usual
place. Beneath the tree of the Lone Man they sat, visiting and discussing their ideas. Running Wolf was
among them.

Claire's stomach knotted at the sight of him, but, repeating the verse again in her mind, she continued toward her family's lodge. Little Flower poked her head
outside the door just as Claire was assisting Evening
Sky to the ground. With a squeal, her cousin came
running.

"Oh, Bright Star! Such a surprise! We did not expect your return so soon!"

Claire took comfort in Little Flower's enthusiasm
and embrace. So did her mother. They were pleased to
see her, as well. They had missed her.

"And how are all the children?" Claire asked.

"Very well. Spotted Eagle claimed his first elk, and
River Song has another tooth."

"I am most pleased for you and for them, cousin."

Little Flower's smile faded. Claire felt her uncle's
ominous presence fall over her. Cautiously she turned.
"I have returned, uncle," she said.

His frown was unmistakable, as was the harshness

of his tone. "What displeasure did you bring? Why did the white chiefs send you back so quickly?"

Claire swallowed hard, searching for the words. Her mother found them first.

"She caused no displeasure, brother. She has completed her work. The white chiefs no longer have need of her. They send her back with their greetings."

The frown remained. "Then you will return the horses."

Claire wasn't certain if the previous sentence was a command or a statement of disappointment. Nevertheless, she nodded humbly to show she was willing to do his bidding. "Captain Lewis insists he himself will come tomorrow for the horses," she explained.

To that, Running Wolf nodded contemplatively. "Chief Black Cat says that no Mandan must visit fort today. Today is a day of powerful medicine for white men."

"Not the day itself, brother," Evening Sky gently corrected him. "The day is but a celebration for the one who came to earth this day, the Creator's son. The one born to save."

The significance of Christmas held no meaning for Running Wolf. He simply crossed his arms over his broad chest and sniffed at his sister's explanation.

"The Son is a gift to us," Evening Sky said, "and I bring you a gift to mark this occasion." She withdrew the beaded moccasins from her pouch and handed them to her brother.

Whether the footwear served as appeasement for the impending loss of the horses or he truly appreciated his sister's gesture, Claire could not say. Her uncle's expression did not change, but, gesturing toward the lodge, he indicated that they should go inside.

We are welcome, Claire thought, *at least for now.*

Evening Sky started toward the door with Little Flower, but Claire remained where she was. There was something she needed to do. She wasn't certain how her uncle would receive it, but she felt compelled to speak all the same.

She nodded humbly once more. "I thank you for your welcome, uncle. I know I have not been as grateful for it as I should..."

His eyebrow arched.

"I have held bitterness in my heart. I have pined for my father's land. Forgive me. It was wrong of me to do so."

Running Wolf looked as if he did not know what to say to that. Once more he motioned for her to go inside the lodge. Claire did so.

After hugging her little cousins, then fetching the herbs so Little Flower could steep her father's favorite tea, Claire settled in next to her mother on her pallet.

"You have done well," Evening Sky whispered to her, "both here and at the fort. You speak peace, and God is pleased by that."

Claire drew in a breath. She appreciated her mother's words. She hoped God was indeed pleased with her. She hoped Running Wolf would be, as well.

Christmas and the days that followed passed as any other winter days on the plains. There was corn to grind, meat to roast. There were cakes to bake and children to feed. Claire immersed herself in the daily activities of tribal life but found her thoughts drifting repeatedly back to the fort.

Aside from thinking of Pierre, whom she indeed

missed but was determined to forget, Claire couldn't help but second-guess her decision to refuse Captain Lewis's offer of continued work. One reason she had returned to the lodge was that it was warmer for her mother, but the cozy earthiness had not helped Evening Sky's health, and neither had the cheerfulness of Little Flower's children.

Evening Sky's face grew thinner, in spite of the availability of food. She showed no interest in eating. Something was wrong.

Would it have been better to be under Captain Lewis's medical supervision? Claire wondered. But even if they had stayed at the fort, there was no way to know if her mother would have accepted the captain's help. She repeatedly told Claire not to fret over her, but of course the daughter could not refrain from doing so.

"Mother, please…take more nourishment."

"It does not suit me, child. But if you insist, I'll take a little tea."

Despite her lack of appetite, Evening Sky's spirit remained strong. Claire heard her singing hymns each morning as she washed River Song's face. The one-and-a-half-year-old girl giggled at her great aunt's touch and tried her best to emulate her songs. The words, however, were still babble.

Evening Sky repeated them patiently. "Love… heart… Great Spirit… Jesus…"

Claire wondered what Running Wolf would say to that last word. The man had said little to her and her mother since their return, which was worrying. And yet that also meant that he had said nothing further about the marriage agreement. Claire did not bring the matter up for discussion.

* * *

Pierre had plenty of time to think about what he had done and what could happen in the future as he tanned the hides his group had brought back from the hunt. The skins had been stretched upon the palisade wall to dry, and now Pierre painstakingly scraped away the animal hair.

He wanted to do his best because that was his character, but he also wished to do so because of what had happened between him and Captain Lewis.

"It is your choice, Mr. Lafayette, whether you choose to continue with this expedition or not," Lewis said that morning as Pierre was beginning his work. "You alone will bear the responsibility for your future."

Pierre humbly conceded the captain's point. He knew he had gravely jeopardized his standing in this man's eyes. He'd made himself a fool, and to make matters worse, he had done so *unnecessarily.*

"Of her own accord..." The words repeated again and again in his mind, yet for the life of him, he still couldn't reconcile her decision to leave. He had seen the tears in her eyes, felt the tremble in her hands the night her uncle had attempted to trade her. He knew she was committed to sharing her faith with her tribe, but she herself had told him her uncle's heart was hardened to the message.

Captain Lewis won't be around to rescue her from the next trapper or warrior who has something of value to barter, and neither will I. What could village life offer her except further restriction and fear?

Then another possibility hit him square between the eyes. Was there a particular warrior, one who showed at least some interest in the gospel? Did she hope *he* would claim her? He paused in his work long enough to consider that.

If that is the case, then I should be happy for her.

He returned to his scraping. He wasn't happy. He did not like the thought of any man, Indian or white, saved or not, making her his wife.

And yet, *he* wasn't willing to claim her. Doing so would mean the end of his adventure for certain. *She knows her own mind*, he told himself. *Whatever her reasons, she has chosen to return to her village. What happens to her from here on out is not my concern.*

But he couldn't quite convince himself of that. His stomach continued to churn. He tried to pray for her safety and for the success of her mission, but that didn't make him feel any better. He then tried imagining the height and color of the mountain ranges he would be crossing come spring, the size of the bears he hoped to take down. He thought of the Pacific. Was it as peaceful and as blue as the Spaniards claimed, gray like the great Atlantic or muddy like the raging Mississippi river after a heavy rainstorm?

He didn't know. The only thing he could fully envision was Claire Manette's enchanting green eyes. How quickly his heart beat whenever she leveled her gaze upon him.

See to the tasks at hand, he ordered himself.

Dutifully he scraped the last of the hair from the hide, then began treating it with a mixture of fat and oil. He rubbed. He smoothed. He laid the skin over a smoking frame positioned carefully above a smoldering fire. The last step would keep the leather supple even when wet.

And wet we will be. By the information they had

been gathering from the natives, there were places ahead where more than likely they'd be ferrying the canoes through the river instead of the canoes ferrying them.

Pierre repeated the tanning process all that week. The final days of December passed interminably slowly. By the time January arrived, he was no closer to putting Claire Manette from his mind than when he'd first had the audacity to argue with Captain Lewis.

The first morning of 1805 dawned cloudy but relatively warm, at least by measurements on the plains. Captain Clark and a party of musicians planned to visit the lower Mandan village that afternoon at the chief's request for a New Year's celebration. Pierre had no interest in frivolity that day, or in joining the second group that Captain Lewis would lead to the upper village, *Claire's village*, the following afternoon. He continued tanning hides, and when finished with that task, he chopped wood. Still he thought of Claire.

Upon the second party's return, Private Cruzette mentioned having seen her carrying a heavy pot into her lodge. Sergeant Ordway stated that he had passed her later in the village plaza.

"She did not look happy," he said.

The hair on the back of Pierre's neck stood on end. Was she ill? Was she *married*? "What exactly do you mean?"

Ordway shrugged. "Worried, I suppose… I'm not certain. Just…unhappy."

"Did you speak to her?" Pierre asked. "Did you see her uncle?"

"I did not speak to her," Ordway said. "I didn't dare.

That uncle of hers looks as though he'd scalp any man who did."

"He watches her like a hawk," Cruzette added, "and so does the medicine man. I saw him talking with her uncle. I couldn't hear what they were saying, of course, let alone understand it, but the medicine man was definitely eyeing her."

Pierre had yet to meet this medicine man formally, although he knew him to be somewhat older, with gray streaks in his long, dark hair. Whether that made him beyond marital interest, he did not know. Either way, he didn't like the thought of any man *eyeing* her.

When an invitation was made by Chief Black Cat to visit again the following day, both captains declined the request. Pierre, however, and one of the privates asked to represent the fort. The request was granted, although Lewis seemed hesitant about saying yes where Pierre was concerned.

"I expect your immediate return when the festivities are concluded," the captain said.

"Yes, sir," Pierre replied. He did not actually intend to stay in the village for very long, only long enough to see her, speak with her if the opportunity presented itself. He just wanted to be certain she was alright.

"What are they celebrating tonight?" Pierre asked his comrade as they started off through the snow.

"Not sure exactly. Apparently this gathering is different, some sort of medicine dance."

Pierre inwardly groaned. *Dancing.* He had no interest in that. The last time he had done so only caused him trouble.

"It could be amusing," the private suggested.

"I think I'll just wander about," Pierre said.

"Suit yourself."

They parted at the main lodge. As his fellow expedition member disappeared inside, Pierre tried to remember exactly which dwelling was Claire's. The gathering darkness made the task more difficult, and he could not seek help because the village was deserted. Apparently most inhabitants were gathering for the medicine dance.

The sound of drum beats echoed in his ears. He wondered if he should return to the main lodge. Would he find her there? He didn't think so, unless of course she had been forced to go. It was a medicine dance, after all, which as far as he understood would mean customs and practices contrary to the Christian faith.

A chanting cry was rising from the location. It was not quite a cheer, not quite a wail, but the eerie sound prickled his skin. Pressing on, he at last he found the lodge, or at least, the one he thought was hers. *Now what?* he thought. When he had come to the village before, he had either waited outside or been escorted in by a member of the tribe. *But Claire doesn't know I am here, so she isn't going to come out to greet me*, and he didn't think entering on his own would be proper.

He couldn't call for her, either. She'd never have been able to hear him over the drums. They were growing louder by the moment. As he stood there trying to decide what to do next, a child popped out of the entryway. His dark eyes widened at the sight of a white man, but then he grinned. Evidently he recognized Pierre, for Pierre had recognized him. It was Spotted Eagle.

"Is Bright Star here?" he asked in halting Mandan.

The boy grinned once more and waved, wanting him to follow. Pierre stepped inside the lodge to find

Claire tending a comfortable fire. She was once again dressed in buffalo skin, and her long, dark hair was parted down the middle and plaited. Evening Sky was seated by the fire, surrounded by children. On her lap looked to be a small Bible.

Startled, everyone paused to look at him. When Claire discovered him, she gasped. Pierre wasn't certain if it was a sound of surprise or fright.

"What are you doing here?" she asked.

"I came to inquire of your safety," he said.

The look that came over her face then told him she was pleased to see him, although apprehension lingered. "I thank you for that," she said as she slowly came toward him. That guarded expression was in her eyes. Still they were captivating. "But you need not worry. I am well. You should go."

"Go?"

Spotted Eagle came up beside her. "Does he not, either?" Pierre thought he understood him to say.

Claire looked at the boy. Her face softened as it always did whenever she spoke to a child. "No, he does not," she said.

"I don't what?" Pierre asked curiously.

"Dance in an attempt to call the buffalo. The ceremony tonight is an effort to bring them near and to impart hunting powers to the warriors."

"I see."

"Spotted Eagle and the others wanted to know why my mother and I did not dance for the warriors," Claire said. "I told him it was because we pray to the Creator, that we trust him to provide food and other necessities for the tribe." The drumming suddenly stopped. Her look of apprehension grew. "You should go before my uncle sees you. He may think there is something improper."

Pierre wondered how he could think that, especially when her mother and the handful of children were with them, but he wouldn't argue with her reasoning. Still, he had to be sure of her safety before he left the village. "Are you certain you are alright?" he asked. "You're uncle hasn't forced you into marriage?"

"Not yet."

It was not a very comforting reply. However, before he could inquire further, a sudden gust of cold wind swept through the lodge. The fire sputtered. Pierre turned to find Running Wolf standing in the entry-way, his arms crossed over his chest. He was most definitely angry.

Claire drew in a shallow, shaky breath at her uncle's arrival. She had not expected him to arrive so soon. Neither had Spotted Eagle. He hurried to greet him.

"Grandfather, Bright Star says our dance does not call the buffalo, that they are instead under command of the Great Spirit's son, Jesus, and that we must ask Him to send them to our village."

The comment was made innocently enough. Spotted Eagle was a young, inquisitive boy. Presented with two paths, he was trying to decipher which of them was the true one to travel. Running Wolf's face, however, flashed with anger.

"He asked why I did not dance, uncle," Claire hurriedly tried to explain. "I simply told him."

Ignoring his grandson, Running Wolf advanced toward her. Like an honorable gentleman, Pierre immediately stepped in front of her, attempting to shield her from the tirade her uncle was surely about to display.

He had no idea what he was doing. Though she appreciated his gallantry, his actions were only making them look guiltier, as if she had invited him here to preach with her to her family. He planted his feet. Part of her rejoiced at his willingness to come to her aid. The other feared just what his actions would provoke.

She touched his arm. "Please," she said, "it would be better for you if you do not interfere."

"I am not concerned for myself," he said.

Contrary to what she thought, Running Wolf had no desire to speak with either of them. He pushed past them both and snatched the Bible from Evening Sky. Having captured it, he then turned and kicked over the cooking pot at the edge of the fire ring. Boiling corn spilled everywhere. The children, wide-eyed with incredulity, scooted back from his path.

"You," he said, glaring at Evening Sky. "You condemn our ancestors' rituals, and yet you encourage your daughter to engage in her own?"

"No, brother, I do not! The children simply asked a question."

He turned to Claire. "You think yourself better than your people. You will not help them bring the buffalo."

She desperately wanted to help her people, but the dance tonight would not bring good hunting, would not put food in their bellies.

"And now you both poison the children with your lies. You seek to make them white, like this dog here—he and his chiefs seek to make the Mandan weak. They say no more war with our enemies!"

He tossed the Bible into the still smoldering fire.

The flames ignited at once. The precious pages blackened and curled.

"No!" Claire cried. Immediately she lurched for it, only to be caught by Pierre's strong arms.

"Let it go," he said.

"But it belonged to my father!"

"I know…but it's too late."

Mustering her strength, Evening Sky pushed to her feet. "You speak of what you do not know, brother. Claire has only spoken truth. Both she and this man seek only a better life for our people, our children."

At that, Running Wolf cursed his sister.

Claire wanted to take her mother's place, take the words upon herself. She moved at once to stand beside her mother, but Pierre's forceful hand pulled her back. Instead, he moved forward.

"How dare you speak to a lady in such a fashion," he said.

Running Wolf did not understand his words, but he clearly recognized the tone of the rebuke. He turned the full force of his anger on Pierre and the God he represented. Out of his mouth flew a venomous stream of words, ones Claire dared not translate.

Running Wolf started toward the Frenchman. Pierre advanced, as well. Both stood with hands ready to draw their weapons, Running Wolf his tomahawk, Pierre his knife. *God, no!* Claire breathed. *Please!*

Running Wolf drew his weapon first.

Claire screamed.

"Brother, no!" Evening Sky rushed toward him.

It was an accident, of that Claire was certain, but as Running Wolf turned to fling his sister aside, his weapon slashed her stomach.

"No!" Claire screamed.

Pierre immediately surged forward, wrestled Running Wolf's arms behind his back, but he was too late.

Scarlet bloomed on Evening Sky's tunic.

"Mother!"

Dazed, Evening Sky sank to her knees. Claire raced to catch her. Laying her as gently as she could on the hard-packed ground, Claire pressed her hands to the wound. The bleeding aside, there was something else that gave her great alarm. Evening Sky's stomach was swollen, as if she were with child.

But that was impossible. Her mother had told her once she was now beyond childbearing age. Claire's mind quickly offered her another explanation. *The weakness in her legs these past months, the intermittent pain...* The wound from the tomahawk was not life-threatening, but if her mother truly did have cancer... *Oh God...please...*

Claire called to Little Flower's youngest sister, not yet thirteen, She Who Walks Tall. "Fetch me hot water!"

As the girl moved to do so, Claire heard the tomahawk drop to the ground. "The wound was not meant for you, sister," Running Wolf said.

The man for whom the wound was surely meant then spoke. "What would you have me do?" he asked Claire.

Evening Sky's eyes pierced her daughter's. Claire knew the answer without her mother even saying the words. "Let him go," she said, although her heart was not as willing as her voice.

"Are you insane?" Pierre asked.

Evening Sky waved her hand, uttered the command

in Mandan. Pierre reluctantly obeyed, but keeping his own knife ready, he moved to shadow Claire.

Running Wolf crept toward his sister and laid a hand upon her forehead. It was the closest thing to an apology a man like him would offer, but Evening Sky accepted it with a nod. The warrior then gestured for one of the children to fetch Claire's needles.

Yes, the wound would need to be stitched, but Claire wasn't certain she could do it. Her hands were trembling so, and as for the other matter... *God...please... do not let it be so...*

Pierre saw how shaken she was. "Shall I send for Captain Lewis?"

"Please."

He motioned for Spotted Eagle, choosing him because he was known at the fort. Claire was glad Pierre hadn't offered to fetch the captain himself. She needed his presence right now. She needed him to think for her. Finding a piece of tanned hide and paint, Pierre scribbled a short message to the commanding officer, then sent Spotted Eagle on his way.

Meanwhile, Claire kept her hands pressed to her mother's wound and prayed. She prayed like she never had before, frantically, and desperately. She longed for the captain's quick arrival, yet at the same time dreaded just that. Surely he would inform her of what she already knew.

Chapter Nine

Unbeknownst to Pierre, Spotted Eagle had gone to fetch not only Captain Lewis but also Chief Black Cat. Upon their arrival at the lodge, the captain did not ask what had precipitated this circumstance, although he surely had an idea. He had witnessed Running Wolf's temperament before. Just what he thought of Pierre's in this moment was unknown. Lewis simply went straight to work doctoring. Chief Black Cat did inquire, first of Running Wolf. Pierre listened hard but sadly understood little of the warrior's explanation.

Claire was too busy helping tend her mother to translate, but when Black Cat turned to Pierre to ask of the situation, she came to his aid.

"He wants to know why you are at the lodge," she said.

Why? That had a clear-cut answer. "Tell him I wanted to be certain you were well. Tell him that Running Wolf displayed much anger toward you and your mother at the fort, and I was therefore concerned for your welfare."

Black Cat gave no indication at first what he thought

of Pierre's answer. Then, after a pause, he said something that made Claire redden. When she hesitated to relay the question, the man gestured forcefully for her to do so.

"What did he say?" Pierre asked.

The blush further darkened. Clearly she did not wish to tell him. He remembered what she had said about Running Wolf accusing them of impropriety. The only impropriety the man could cite could be in terms of his own religion, that according to him, Pierre and Claire were undermining it. Still, Pierre felt terrible. If he had somehow tarnished Claire's honor, besmirched her reputation, he would never forgive himself.

"What did he say?" he asked once more.

Claire lowered her eyes to the ground. "He wants to know if *you* wish to claim me."

"Claim you?"

"As a wife."

Pierre felt the blood drain from his face. Had he gotten himself dangerously close to an arranged marriage yet again? Yes, he wanted to help Claire, but no, he did not wish to *claim* her. He detested the thought of anyone claiming anybody. Love was supposed to be a choice. A mutual choice, made of one's own free will.

When Pierre's tongue failed him, Black Cat spoke again. Claire explained, "The chief says he does not understand why you would interfere in this matter if you did not have such intentions."

He didn't? Well, that Pierre could *easily* explain. "Tell him that as a gentleman, *as a Christian*, it is my duty to look out for others."

She repeated his response. Black Cat stared at Pierre, his lined face marked by a most puzzled expression. He turned then to Spotted Eagle, asked him what he had witnessed.

The child chattered quickly, gesturing and pointing to each of the adults while they looked on in silence. At one point, Running Wolf interjected. Claire waited until both he and the boy had finished before translating.

"Running Wolf accused you of trying to turn his children from Mandan ways, but Spotted Eagle says that you did not tell him he should not dance or that he should seek to become like the white man. He says that my mother and I did not tell him or the others to do so, either."

So the boy had confirmed the truth. Whether it was to be believed or not was yet to be seen. Pierre cast a glance at his captain, thinking it odd that the man had not plied him with questions. Pierre's superior officer appeared to be totally preoccupied with his stitching, but he knew from experience the man was listening intently and evaluating everything that was happening. How *he* would respond to the situation was yet to be seen, as well.

Chief Black Cat then raised his hand, a signal that he had come to a decision. Was Pierre about to be banished from this village? Would Running Wolf be punished for what he had done to his sister? And the question that had plagued him for two weeks now remained forefront. What would happen to Claire?

The chief looked Pierre square in the eye. "Do you wish to live in peace with the Mandans?" he asked, according to Claire.

"Yes," Pierre answered adamantly.

The chief then turned to Running Wolf, asked if he

wished to live in peace with the men of the fort. The warrior answered affirmatively, as well, although with far less enthusiasm than Pierre had shown.

"We will then speak no more of this," Black Cat decreed. "Running Wolf will put away his tomahawk and the white man will put away his knife."

Pierre was surprised at the leniency of the chief's words, and the lack of consequences for both him and Running Wolf. After all, it had been a dangerous confrontation, and someone had already gotten hurt. Then he realized Claire had not translated everything Black Cat had said. He knew that because when the chief again looked directly at her, she hesitated. Running Wolf was practically grinning.

Pierre watched as Claire bowed to her chief and spoke again in Mandan. He struggled to gather the general meaning of the words, for they were spoken much too quickly. Running Wolf's grin faded. Black Cat said something else. This time Claire remained silent. The chief gave a short nod and then, with apparently nothing more to say, exited the lodge.

"What just happened?" Pierre asked her.

"Nothing." She returned to her mother's side. Running Wolf remained near his sister's pallet, with a look on his face that Pierre could not quite read. Pierre stood where he was, trying to interpret the situation. Clearly more than *nothing* had happened, and whatever it was, Claire did not wish to tell him.

He found himself rather annoyed by that fact, yet told himself he had no right to be taken into her confidence. He had just told her and everyone else in this lodge that he had no intention of claiming her. The memory of what Sergeant Ordway had said earlier con-

cerning the medicine man flashed through his mind.
Had Claire just agreed to marry him instead? His stomach rolled at the thought.

*But if she had, wouldn't that have pleased Running
Wolf greatly?* He didn't look all that pleased. *What is
going on?* He *had* to know. "Claire…"

She glanced over her shoulder. Pierre held her gaze
firmly until she turned fully toward him.

"What did you promise the chief?"

She blinked.

"Are you to marry the medicine man?"

"Certainly not!" She came to him once again, and
this time she finally explained.

Evidently Chief Black Cat's solution for maintaining peace between her uncle and the Frenchman was
for Claire to stop speaking of Christ to her family. His
heart sank to the pit of his stomach.

"And what did you say?"

"I told him, respectfully, that I must obey God rather
than men, but that I would promise not to speak unless
I was spoken to, not to teach unless asked."

"And what did your uncle say to that?"

"He quickly promised that he would make certain
no one, at least in this lodge, ever asked."

With that she returned to her mother. The stitching
now finished, Captain Lewis rose to his feet and came
to Pierre. "You handled that well, Lafayette."

Did he? The conflict within him intensified. He had
promised peace, but at what cost? He said as much to
the man.

"We are here to appreciate the culture, study it, if
you will. Not interfere. Need I remind you that the re-
sults of doing so could be disastrous?"

"But sir, what about decency? Faith? Are we not bound by a higher duty to advance such things?"

"We are indeed, but I believe one must cultivate peaceful relations *before* doing so." Lewis lowered his voice, looked him square in the eye. "Unless you plan to marry this girl, remain here as a member of this tribe and change the culture from within, which I highly discourage, by the way, you must respect her uncle's authority over her. If you do not, you will find not only yourself in danger but also your fellow expedition members. We are sixteen hundred miles up the Missouri, Lafayette. No one will come to our aid if we find ourselves in conflict with the tribe."

Sadly, Pierre knew he was right. He had seen what his interference had accomplished tonight. He could not risk war. *But are we already not engaged in conflict? Is there not a war between light and darkness, life and death?* What was he to do?

For now he focused on the most immediate concern. "What about her mother?" he asked.

The captain drew in a breath, just as Claire moved from her mother's side and came to stand with them. Running Wolf kept vigil at his sister's pallet.

"Lafayette," Lewis said, "I know the mademoiselle understands English fairly well, but will you be good enough to translate so that there is no mistaking what I say?"

"Of course, sir."

She, however, spoke first. "It's the cancer, isn't it?"

"I'm afraid so."

There were tears in her eyes, but she set her jaw most bravely. Pierre wanted nothing more than to pull her into his arms, give her permission to cry, comfort

and shelter her, but that was something he knew he had
no right to do. He stood where he was, arms at his sides.

"We have herbs and poultices that sometimes treat
such things," she said, "but never at such an advanced
stage. Have you medicine, Captain? Have you something that will help her?"

Pierre could tell she knew the answer for herself
already. He could see it in her eyes, but she was desperate for hope.

"Only for the pain, my dear," Lewis said. "I'm sorry."

Giving in to feelings, Pierre laid his hand softly
upon her shoulder. Claire's lower lip quivered slightly.
How much time her mother had, they did not know,
but Pierre suspected by the look on Lewis's face that
it was not long.

God in Heaven…help her…

The captain cast a glance then in Running Wolf's
direction. He sat guard over his sister, eyeing the white
men with an obvious look of suspicion. "If you would
like, we could move your mother back to the fort,"
Lewis said. "If you think she would wish it."

To move an injured woman—already weakened by
illness—was a risk all of its own, perhaps bringing de-
mise by way of the wound. *But that is his point*, Pierre
thought. *She is going to die anyway. Is it more merciful for it to happen more quickly, and in a place where
she and her daughter will not be tormented?*

Pierre didn't want to bring more harm to Evening
Sky, but he also didn't want to see more harm come to
her daughter. Running Wolf had promised peace for
now, but what would happen to Claire if she was left
on her own?

Claire drew in a shallow breath as if she herself was

thinking of such possibilities. "*Merci*, Captain. I shall inquire of my mother's wishes."

"Very well," Lewis said. He looked at Pierre. "In the meantime, I believe I shall see what has become of your comrade." He bowed to the mademoiselle, then turned on his heel.

Pierre's hand was still on Claire's shoulder. As Lewis left the lodge, she slipped from his reach and returned to her mother. She spoke to her in Mandan. Pierre couldn't catch even half of the words, but he could guess their context.

Why did you not tell me? Why did you keep this hidden for so long?

Evening Sky patted her daughter's hand, said something in return. Claire went on to explain the captain's offer, for Pierre clearly heard Lewis's name amid the Mandan. At that, Running Wolf's jaw tightened slightly. He cast Pierre another suspicious glance.

The Frenchman's hand inadvertently touched the handle of his knife, but he did not draw it out. He wanted the man to know that despite his own promise of peace, he was not foolish enough to let down his guard. He would protect these women if he had to.

The warrior held his look for a moment then turned back to his family. There was more talk. There were more tears from Claire. Pierre moved closer to her but kept his attention focused on her uncle. Running Wolf's expression shifted from anger to pleasure and then to questioning. At the last, he again patted his sister's head, like a man who knew not what to do or expect next.

Claire covered her mother with a second buffalo

skin, then stood. The worry in her eyes was still there, but she was trying hard to appear calm.

"What did she say?" Pierre asked.

"She wishes to remain here."

Somehow he knew that was going to be the answer, but he did not like it. How could he look after her properly if she remained here? "Claire..."

"She is confident that God will bring healing."

Pierre didn't doubt the Almighty's ability to do so. The question was, would He? While Pierre believed with all his heart that the Lord worked all things for good in the end, God's plans could seem unfathomable at times. "And your uncle?"

"My mother believes God will bring healing to him, as well."

Which, despite his own personal faith, Pierre had to admit seemed a more difficult task than the first. But whatever healing Running Wolf required concerned him less than the pain Claire was feeling. He knew how hard she had struggled with Phillip Granger's betrayal. How would she deal with the fact that her uncle had injured her mother? "And you?" he asked.

He could see the tension building in her face. She was trying hard to keep her emotions hidden, but her green eyes flickered with determination and a hundred other emotions.

"I must remain here, even if my prayers are not answered," she said. "It is not, however, safe here for you. I fear there will be trouble. You should return to the fort."

He knew what kind of trouble she meant. Running Wolf was watching them intently. He had made a promise to his chief to put away his tomahawk and his anger, but "accidents" could happen. In fact, one already had. *And if one were to happen again, how would the men at the fort respond, and likewise the tribe?* Captain Lewis's words repeated through his mind: *"We are sixteen hundred miles up the Missouri. No one will come to our aid..."*

He hated this feeling of being caught between two nations. "I fear it is not safe for you," Pierre said. "Come with...us.*" With me*, he almost said.

She shook her head. "They are my people, and this is my mother's decision. I must remain."

My people. Your people. Why must the world be divided in such a way? But her mind and that of her mother's were firmly decided, and when Captain Lewis returned a moment later, she told him so.

"Very well, mademoiselle," he said, though the tone of his voice expressed his reluctance, as well. "Should you have need of anything, send word immediately."

"*Merci*, Captain. I will do so."

Lewis then looked at him. "Mr. Lafayette..." It was an unspoken order but one he knew he must obey. His captain had bid him leave. So had she. As much as Pierre wanted to remain, he knew he couldn't. After one last look at her, he turned away and walked out of the lodge.

The midnight sky was clear and cold, a black velvet canopy studded with a billion diamond-like stars. Usually it was a sight to take his breath away, make him stand in awe of the majesty and timelessness of the Lord. Tonight, however, it boded uncertainty. Evening Sky believed God would intervene. If Providence was to bring healing to this place, of both body and soul, Pierre prayed He would do it quickly.

* * *

Claire had never spent a more lonely or desperate night. When Little Flower had returned from the medicine dance, she had shown concern for Evening Sky and an eagerness to be of assistance. At once she took to brewing tea and pounding yarrow in preparation for poultices to stave off infection in Evening Sky's outer wound. Claire was careful to keep the details of the accident to a minimum. How could she tell her cousin that the damage to her aunt was of her own father's making?

But word in the village traveled fast. When the rest of the family arrived, they all knew what had happened, and they all knew why. Claire and Evening Sky would not worship in the ways of their ancestors, and according to whispers among the other cousins, the spirits were angry.

She was angry herself. It was bad enough when Running Wolf had been threatening Claire. But drawing his tomahawk on Pierre? Injuring his own sister in the process? Claire knew he acted in ignorance and superstition, and she knew she must forgive him for doing so, but oh, the difficulty!

It all seems so futile! Phillip Granger, her uncle's marital arrangements for her... Every time she committed herself to forgiving, to trusting God with her future, things seemed only to get worse! And now her mother insisted on remaining here in this lodge, so confident that God would intervene in her condition. Would He? Or would He disappoint her just as Pierre had done tonight?

She told herself she should not be thinking such things of the Almighty *or* the Frenchman. Even if

Pierre Lafayette had wanted her—which he didn't—
there could never be anything between them. Running
Wolf had marked him as an enemy. She had tried to put
such foolish thoughts of him rescuing her, of him wanting her as a wife, far from her mind, but every time
she saw him, she found herself drawn closer to him.

He had come tonight to inquire of her safety. He had
sought to defend her honor, and the comfort he gave
when he had touched her made Claire want to seek the
shelter of his arms and never leave them. But he had
sworn to her chief right in front of her that he had no
desire to marry her. He would be her friend, her assistant in dealing with the captains and their medical
help, but nothing more.

God help me...fill me with Your strength...Your
love...Your forgiveness. I cannot live without it.

Running Wolf watched her all night with a stoic expression. He showed little enthusiasm when his son-
in-law Two Bulls announced the triumph of the dance
and boasted that there would be many buffalo to hunt
come spring. Running Wolf simply claimed his honored place by the center fire and sat in brooding silence. What he was thinking, Claire could not tell.

Pallets were soon placed. Children were put to bed.
The men finished their stories, and after making the
necessary preparations for morning food, the women
settled in for the night, as well.

Claire alone remained awake. Beside her Evening
Sky now slept, although her grimaces when she moved
told Claire her rest was anything but peaceful. Claire's
own breath hitched every time she observed the pain-
filled expression.

Father God, my mother believes You will bring healing. Please do so... Please...

Outside the lodge, the wind howled viciously. Claire's eyes burned from exhaustion, yet no matter how hard she tried, she could not settle. Her thoughts drifted endlessly from her mother to her uncle, to God and to Pierre.

Sunrise came and with it the duties of the day. There was snow to be gathered for water, corn to be mashed. There were hides to tan and children to feed. Running Wolf spent the day sipping ceremonial tea at the fire and conversing with the other warriors of the village. While he and the rest of the family were out, and Claire was changing the dressing on Evening Sky's wound, Captain Lewis paid a call.

This time he had brought Toussaint Charbonneau as his translator. Claire understood the wisdom of such a decision, but she couldn't help but feel disappointed that it was Sacagawea's husband who now stood in Pierre's place.

It is better this way, she told herself, *for everyone.*

As the captain examined Evening Sky's wound, Claire asked Charbonneau about his wife. "Her time is soon, yes?"

He nodded and then grinned broadly. "A few more weeks, then I shall have a son."

He boasted of what every man on the plains wished for, a child to continue his name, further his legacy. Claire wondered if he would be as proud if the baby turned out to be a girl.

"I pray that all goes well with Sacagawea and that she is delivered of the child quickly."

Charbonneau nodded.

As for Claire's mother, the yarrow seemed to be helping her injury. The internal illness, however, was making its presence known now by more than just the swollen abdomen. Her mother's color was an odd shade. Captain Lewis asked how she had slept.

"Fitfully," Claire said.

From his kit the captain retrieved several small packets of powder. "If the willow bark isn't enough for the pain then give her these." He handed them to Claire, then added, "I have something for you, as well."

He handed her a letter. It was sealed, but Claire recognized the outer handwriting. She knew immediately who it was from. Her heart swelled even though she told herself it shouldn't.

"*M-merci*, Captain," she said, her voice trembling slightly.

Knowing Running Wolf could return any moment, Claire slid the letter inside her moccasin. The men took their leave.

Not a moment after they had gone, her uncle returned. Walks with the Sun, the medicine man, was with him, so was his son, Golden Hawk. Both men were dressed in their finest array, with their highly decorated spirit sticks in hand.

Claire recognized their intentions even before her uncle announced them. Running Wolf had brought Walks with the Sun to say an incantation over his sister. The incantations had no power, but if God did choose to heal Evening Sky, Running Wolf and the others would be convinced their own rituals had caused the change.

Lord, what do I do? What do I say? She had promised Black Cat that she would not speak of spiritual matters unless spoken to. If she protested, Running Wolf could turn both her and her mother out of the village for good. They could seek shelter at the fort, yes, but even that would be only temporary. Besides, it would break her mother's heart to leave her family. It would break Claire's, also.

Despite her pain, Evening Sky was alert, and she pushed to her elbows. "Brother, you honor me with your presence," she said most respectfully.

He nodded to her, then gestured toward his guests. "They are my honored gift to you, sister."

"I know, and I am most grateful." She paused for the space of a heartbeat. "However, I *cannot* accept."

Running Wolf looked confused.

"To do so would be an affront to my God," she explained.

His look moved to a scowl. "Yet you would accept the white man's spells?" He pointed to the packets in Claire's hands. "You accept the chants of the white chief in the three-cornered hat?"

Claire would curse herself if she thought it would help the situation. Why had she not hidden the captain's powders along with Pierre's letter? Once again she had allowed herself to become distracted. What would be the cost this time?

"They are not chants, brother," Evening Sky insisted. "And the powder is little more than our willow bark."

He turned to Walks with the Sun. "You see?"

The medicine man nodded. His disapproval and his son's were most evident.

"If you are so against them, brother, I will not take the powders."

What? Claire thought.

This seemed to please Running Wolf, and it certainly pleased the medicine men. They nodded affirmatively. Claire, however, was anything but pleased. "Mother...the pain..."

"God will sustain me, daughter," Evening Sky said, and then she looked her brother fully in the face. "You shall see."

Chapter Ten

It was well after midnight and the lodge was full of snoring. Evening Sky now slept, as did the rest of her family. With that relative privacy, Claire took the opportunity to open Pierre's letter.

"Dear Claire…"

It was little more than a greeting of cordiality, of friendship, but the phrase warmed her heart all the same. Pierre's handwriting was bold and precise, yet fluid, the mark of a highly educated gentleman. *A man who does not belong here. A man who has vast dreams, as endless as the western sky.*

She studied his script in the flickering firelight.

It is with great regret that I pen these words. Perhaps I should not risk writing them at all, let alone having them delivered, but I was compelled to offer my sincerest apologies for what has occurred…

He went on to say how sorry he was for all that had happened to her and her mother.

Had I, a white man, not come into your lodge the
night of the medicine dance, then perhaps Running Wolf would not have become so enraged
and your mother would not have become injured.

He was probably correct in assuming that, but Claire
did not begrudge his intrusion. Had he not come, she
would not have learned of her mother's true physical
condition, and he would not have been there to steady
her when she did.

Oh, how she had needed his encouragement in that
moment. When Captain Lewis declared nothing could
be done except treat her mother's pain, Claire thought
her own life would drain out of her. Were it not for the
steady look in Pierre's eyes, she was certain her knees
would have buckled. He might be bound by the expedition's code not to interfere in tribal matters, but he
had transmitted his compassion nevertheless.

Pain raked her heart afresh, but Claire forced herself
to keep reading. He informed her that Captain Lewis had
insisted he stay away from the village, at least for a few
days, in order to be certain Running Wolf's anger toward
him had abated. Pierre promised that he was with her in
spirit. "I am praying for you…" and in hopes of offering
her encouragement, he had enclosed several pages that
he had removed from his own Bible. He'd sent her the
book of Philippians and had marked a particular verse.

"But my God shall supply all your need according to his riches in glory by Christ Jesus…"

Claire clutched the paper to her chest. *Supply all
my needs…* It had been difficult to believe such things

when marriage and complete assimilation into the tribe were her only concerns. Those matters paled in comparison to what burdened her now. She knew God was not one to broker deals, but she'd pay any price for the return of her mother's health.

Evening Sky stirred in her sleep. She grimaced as the pain of both her external wound and internal ones intensified. Claire pulled the buffalo robe to her mother's chin, then lightly stroked her hair.

"'My God shall supply all your need…'" She repeated the verse softly, forcing herself to believe. Whether her mother heard or not she did not know.

Sunrise came and the lodge stirred to life. Although normally chatty and pleasant, Little Flower seemed distant this morning. She was not the only one. Spotted Eagle and River Song offered no hugs or accounts of their previous evening's dreams. They spoke not a word to her or to Evening Sky as they breakfasted around the fire. In fact, Spotted Eagle would not even look at them.

What has happened? Has Running Wolf told our family not to speak to us?

Claire supposed she should have suspected such a thing, especially after she had declared she would still speak the name of Jesus if asked. *And now that Mother has refused the medicine man's chants…what difficulties lie ahead?*

Swallowing her fears, Claire whispered a prayer and continued with her tasks as she always did. Her family might not be speaking to her, but she would still continue to speak to them.

"Come, River Song," she said cheerfully, "let me

wipe your face. Your great aunt is in need of rest this morning."

The child obeyed. She even giggled when Claire touched the warm cloth to her skin. Spotted Eagle, however, came and stole her away.

"We stay on this side of the lodge, sister," he told the girl.

Claire swallowed back her hurt, then took a bowl of corn to her mother. Evening Sky was now awake but managed only a spoonful of food.

"That's all, Bright Star. Thank you."

"Some tea?" Claire asked hopefully.

"No. Just let me rest."

Reluctantly Claire returned to the center fire. As soon as she did, Little Flower gathered up her children and took them outside. Evening Sky returned to sleep. Claire did her best to go about her usual routine, but the stillness of the lodge was heartbreaking. She was sitting by the fire, grinding dried corn, when Three Horses, a respected warrior of about Running Wolf's age, stepped into the lodge. Silencing her mortar and pestle, Claire immediately nodded to the man.

"My uncle is not here, honored one. He has gone to the lodge of our chief."

"I come not for him," Three Horses said. "I come to speak with you."

Claire couldn't hide the surprise in her voice. "With me?" What would he want with her?

Laying aside her tools, she stood and invited Three Horses to claim a seat beside the fire. He declined.

"Come," he motioned. "See my son."

Claire hesitated slightly, but knowing a warrior's command could not be easily dismissed, she laid another blanket over her mother and followed Three Horses to his home. His teenage son, Black Raven, had recently suffered a severe case of frostbite to his toes while staying overnight to hunt on the prairie. Three Horses had gone to the fort for assistance. Claire wondered if the captains' treatment of the boy had failed.

And if it has, why is he calling upon me? Had word gotten around the village already that she and her mother had turned away the medicine man? Did Three Horses believe Claire's God more powerful?

She stepped into the warrior's lodge. Three Horses's wife, Cries Like a Dove, sat beside her son's pallet. A worried expression filled her face.

"Show her," her husband said.

As Cries Like a Dove lifted the buffalo skin from her son's feet, Claire sucked in a breath. The toes of one had turned completely black.

"The white Chief with the beaver skin hat said this could happen," Three Horses said. "That if it does then the toes must come off."

Claire winced.

"Do you believe this to be true?" he asked.

She did not wish for it to be so, but even she could tell something must be done, and Captain Clark had much more expertise in this area than she. "If that is what he said, then yes, I believe it to be so. He is an honorable man. He would not wish to inflict pain upon your son."

"But there will be pain," Cries Like a Dove said.

Claire hated to be the bearer of such bad news, for this family had suffered through more hard times than most in this village. Cries Like a Dove had once been called by a different name—She Who Smiles, but smiles had turned to tears after the loss of not one but four children, all before they had seen the light of day. She was pregnant once again, and Claire prayed the circumstances would be different this time.

"But you believe there will be worse pain if nothing is done," Three Horses said to her. She nodded her agreement.

While husband and wife discussed the matter further, Claire knelt before Black Raven's pallet. "You are a strong young warrior," she said.

The boy tried to smile, but she could see the fear in his eyes.

"Will you pray to your God that He will grant favor, that I will soon be hunting again?"

Her heart was touched with encouragement. She tried to offer Black Raven the same. "Yes. I will gladly pray to my God. It will be my privilege to speak to Him on your behalf."

This time the boy offered more of a smile. Three Horses then came and scooped him up into his arms.

"I will take him to the white chief," he said.

Claire nodded respectfully, and then looked at Cries Like a Dove. Her face was beset with tears, but she, too, nodded.

"Go with them," she pleaded, "for you speak the white man's tongue."

Claire wanted to be of assistance, of course, but beyond moral support for the family, she wasn't really needed at the fort. Sacagawea's husband would be there. He could speak the languages necessary for communication. She did not wish to leave her mother, especially now that the rest of her family was slighting her.

Cries Like a Dove must have guessed as much, although what details she actually knew, Claire could not say. "I shall tend to Evening Sky in your absence," she offered.

This was a tender woman, and Claire knew she would care for her mother most gently. Though appreciative, Claire still hesitated. If she went to the fort, she might see Pierre.

But this is an opportunity to show this family the love of God. "Very well," she told Three Horses's wife. "I shall accompany your family to the fort."

Pierre recognized Claire even before she had finished crossing the ice. A warrior was traveling with her. In his arms he carried a bundle. Pierre's heart thumped at the sight of her, half in excitement, half in fear. Why was she coming to the fort? Had something dreadful happened to her? To her mother? Was Running Wolf putting her out of the village? Had Pierre precipitated such by his letter?

Worried for her welfare, he had labored over the correspondence for hours by the flicker of candlelight. He would much rather have spoken to her face-to-face, seen for himself how she and her mother were faring, but Captain Lewis had insisted he remain at the fort. He could not go against the man again. If he did, Pierre doubted Lewis would even wait for the ice to thaw before sending him back to Saint Louis. He was liable to send him packing now—and that wouldn't do Pierre or Claire any good.

He had been especially grieved that her father's Bible had been destroyed. He knew how much it had meant to her and her mother. Desperate times called for desperate measures, and thinking a few pages of thin paper could be hidden easier than an entire book, Pierre had torn out his favorite Bible passage and enclosed it in his letter.

"But my God shall supply all your need according to his riches in glory by Christ Jesus."

The verse from Philippians was the one that had given him courage to finally step out on his own. Now he wondered if his good intentions had caused further trouble. Had Running Wolf found the Scripture pages? Although the warrior could not read French, he was smart enough to know what they were if he found them—especially since he had probably seen the pages of his brother-in-law's Bible many times.

Captain Lewis's warning echoed in his ears. *"You are here to observe, not interfere..."*

The sun glare upon the snow was wreaking havoc on his eyes, but as she came closer, Pierre realized the Indian accompanying her was not her uncle, and the bundle he carried was not a collection of blankets and goods but an injured boy.

Leaving the hunting party that was about to depart, Pierre hurried to meet Claire. As she recognized him, a momentary look of happiness filled her face, one that warmed his heart. The look, however, was quickly replaced by an expression of seriousness as she explained why she had come.

"Captain Clark told Three Horses that if this should happen, he was to come to the fort."

Pierre felt sorry for the child and even sorrier for the father who carried him. The man was obviously struggling with his decision to bring him here. Surely he knew what was about to happen. "Captain Clark is presently tending a soldier down with pleurisy," Pierre said, "but Captain Lewis is available."

Claire explained this to the warrior. Apparently convinced that one captain was as good as the other, he nodded his approval.

"Would you kindly escort us to Captain Lewis?" she asked Pierre.

"At once." He almost added that it would be his pleasure, but of course, given the circumstances surrounding her presence, it was anything but. He wanted to ask her how she and her mother were faring, and if she had read his letter, but he didn't.

He marched them straight to the captain's quarters. Lewis was once again at his desk, this time surrounded by the preserved animals and pressed plants he had collected thus far along the route. He left them at once to see to the boy.

"Tell his father that, regrettably, the toes must be removed."

Claire did so. Three Horses' strong jaw twitched, but he nodded his consent.

"Mr. Lafayette," the captain then said, "I could use your assistance."

"Yes sir." Pierre would do whatever necessary to help, of course, but surgery was a skill he had not yet acquired. Thankfully the only real assistance asked of him was fetching bandages and blocking the child's view of the procedure.

The Indian boy bore the gruesome trial bravely. The few times he wavered, Pierre had laid his hand to his shoulder, patted him encouragingly or showed him his knife. The boy took a special interest in that. According to Claire, he wanted to know if Pierre had killed many buffalo with it.

He couldn't help but chuckle at that. He was brave with a musket, but not so brave as to sneak up on such a monstrous beast and prick it with a pin. If Black Raven had felled an animal this way, then he was a warrior indeed.

Captain Lewis removed all of the toes from the boy's left foot, then carefully wrapped a bandage around it. "Your son will need to remain here for a few days so that I may observe his progress," he said.

Claire translated the words with grace and reassurance. Her voice was like music to a restless, stormed-tossed soul. The Indian father again nodded his consent.

The captain then offered the man the opportunity to stay with his son. The invitation did not extend to Claire, though he did ask her if she would be kind enough to help settle father and son in a hut.

"Of course, captain," she said with that quick and proper curtsy. Watching her, Pierre couldn't help but wonder what her life would have been like if her father had lived. Would she have remained in Illinois or would she have embarked on other adventures?

How different would my life be if I had met her in New Orleans? Pierre had never been interested in courtship or marriage, *but perhaps that was because I had yet to find the right woman.*

The thought jolted him so that he nearly dropped the bandage roll he was now holding. A smile, a dance, a touch of the hand to convey compassion was one thing, but this was not New Orleans, and he was not in love.

This is an Indian Village, a temporary stop en route to the Pacific.

Besides, she wasn't interested in him like that, anyway. She had turned blood red in embarrassment at the chief's suggestion that Pierre might make her his wife.

Awkwardness aside, he couldn't let her go back to her village without making certain she was alright. After she had settled the guests, he asked her, "May I speak with you for a moment?"

She nodded.

Pierre drew her gently toward the forge. She did not resist his lead. Evidently the blacksmith had gone to gather supplies, but his unattended fire lay smoldering. Pierre gave it a poke. As he did, an odd feeling came over him. This was the place where they had once conspired to bring Christmas cheer. "Are you well?" he asked.

"Yes." Her eyes told him otherwise. No doubt she was worried about what the future would bring. He couldn't blame her for that.

"And your mother?"

"She is keeping faith." Her jaw twitched slightly. "I am trying my best to do the same."

Pierre swallowed hard. There was so much he wanted to say to her, but he couldn't coherently phrase his thoughts.

"Thank you for your letter," she said. "It was a great comfort, especially the Bible passage."

"I hope it did not cause you further trouble."

"No. I hid it safely beneath my pallet and read it only when others are sleeping. I must be especially careful now that—"

He waited for her to finish. When she didn't, he prompted her, "Now that what?"

She looked away.

"Claire?"

Reluctantly she told him about what had happened when the medicine men had come to visit, and how her family had treated her this morning in the aftermath. Listening, Pierre drew in a breath. The chief and Running Wolf were tolerating her faith for now, probably because of what had happened to Evening Sky, but if God did not intervene, the mother was going to die. What was to become of Claire? Forbidden to interfere with tribal customs or not, Pierre had to do something.

"Captain Lewis offered to find you work once before..."

"No," she said immediately. "That is not the way."

She turned quickly for the parade ground. He admired her commitment to her family, to her faith, but it scared him to think what she might be asked to give up for the sake of them. He followed her as far as the front gate. The western sky was awash in various shades of gold, red and orange.

She paused to take in the view. "Such beauty," she said.

He could hear the longing in her voice, the desire for freedom, for peace. "Indeed," he said. "Sacagawea says that west of here, the great mountains look purple in the fading light." He paused, then mused, "I wonder how the ocean will look."

"I should like to see such things..."

"Perhaps one day," he said.

She turned her eyes to him. "Man is to the road. Woman is to the hearth."

Wind tugged at her buffalo robe. The fur about her face skimmed her cheeks. Pierre had the sudden desire to reach out and brush it away, but he refrained from doing so.

He looked at her. She looked at him.

"I must go," she said abruptly. "Cries Like a Dove will be concerned for her family…" She took a step, then stopped, turned back. "And I think that, given the circumstances with my family, it would be better if you did not visit our lodge again."

Not visit? He could understand if she, like Captain Lewis, thought it best for him to stay away for a few days to allow her uncle's anger to cool, but the way she'd thrown the sentence to him told him she wanted a more permanent separation. Had he offended her? He asked.

"No," she said, "of course not." But she would no longer look him in the eye. "It would just be better if…"

"I promised I would protect you." He waited. "Claire, look at me…"

When she finally lifted her eyes, her look was hard, stubborn. For the life of him, he couldn't figure out why. "I don't need your protection," she said. "Now, if you'll excuse me…my mother has need of me."

With that, she hurried off. Pierre stood dumbstruck, watching her disappear in the fading winter light.

Claire hurried from the fort as fast as she could manage. She knew coming here had been a mistake. She was thankful that Black Raven had been tended. Thankful that Captain Lewis was confident his foot could be saved. She was thankful Three Horses had been permitted to stay with his son during his recovery. But when she thought of Pierre, gratefulness battled with a hundred other emotions.

She had stood beside a noble and kind man, clad in buckskin, his beard and hair once again as ragged as any ruffian trader. He, like her, was caught somewhere between two civilizations, not fully at home in either. Today, though, in the middle of the dark, ramshackle hut, they had helped a suffering Mandan boy and comforted a worrying father. Between them, they had exchanged glances and assured each other that things would be alright. She had never felt more at home. With him at her side, Claire felt as though she could face any challenge, meet any danger that came her way.

And then, the way he looked at me when I told him about my family...when I told him how Spotted Eagle pulled his sister away and how my own cousin fled my presence as if I carried the plague...

He'd felt her pain, and in sharing it added an entirely new level to her own. She could claim that all she felt for him was friendship, the fellowship of a Christian brother or the longing for her father's culture, but she knew the truth. She was falling in love with a man who did not share her feelings.

And he will be gone by spring.

Claire felt the air rush from her lungs. If it hurt this badly to think of him leaving, what would she suffer when he actually did? He had spoken of purple mountains, of vast oceans, all things she would never see, although when he had spoken of them, she'd wanted nothing more than for him to gather her in his arms, kiss her and then carry her off to that place.

How can I even be thinking of such things, let alone desiring them, when my family, my tribe is in such

*desperate need? How can I long for escape when my
mother needs me so?*

She quickened her pace. Despite Claire's prayers,
Evening Sky was gravely ill, and Cries Like a Dove
would be most anxious to learn of her son's fate. Captain Lewis had assigned Pierre to tend the boy. Claire
knew both Black Raven and his father would be well
looked after.

*I was right in asking him not to visit the lodge again.
He has his duties. I have mine. And with Running Wolf
suspicious of him, it will be better if he remains at the
fort. It will certainly be better for me.*

She told herself that repeatedly, but her heaviness
of heart stayed with her all the way back to the village.

Chapter Eleven

January drifted into February, and the knee-deep snow and the cold winds of winter brought further hardship to the prairie. Despite tribal efforts to call the buffalo, not a single animal had made an appearance for weeks. Food stores were running low.

Evening Sky grew weaker, although her spirit remained strong. She insisted God would bring healing. Claire did her best to believe, but the dire predictions Captain Lewis made on his visits did little to encourage her faith. Nevertheless, Evening Sky had a sense of peace about her, one that resonated in her eyes. The calmness fostered a sense of curiosity in Cries Like a Dove.

The young woman had come often to see Claire's mother during the time her husband and son stayed at the fort. Although Running Wolf and the rest of the lodge continued to shun them, he did not forbid the woman's visits. When curiosity turned to questions, Claire and Evening Sky told her stories of Jesus. Although at this point Cries Like a Dove accepted only that Christ was a wise and kind teacher, Claire held on to hope.

The day then came when the woman wished to say a prayer to Jesus. "I wish to ask Him that my son and husband would return well from the fort."

Three Horses and Black Raven returned to the village by the time of the hunger moon, the name given in these parts to the full moon of the month. The boy, although walking now with a slight limp, was no worse for wear. Three Horses was most grateful for the kindnesses the white men had shown him, particularly Pierre. Claire felt the double emotions of joy and pain at the mention of his name.

Three Horses was also pleased by the friendship his wife was forming with Claire and Evening Sky. Apparently Cries Like a Dove had shared the women's stories with her husband, and told him of her prayer.

Claire wondered how Three Horses would take such news. Would he, like Running Wolf, believe his wife was forsaking the path of her ancestors?

Evidently he did not. "Your stories dry my wife's tears," he said to Claire. "You help my son. You help my squaw. Both good for my child."

Meaning, the baby who would soon join the tribe. Meanwhile at the fort, Sacagawea had given birth to a healthy baby boy. Charbonneau came boasting of the news just before sunset on the eleventh of February. He had given the child a French name—Jean Baptiste. But already the Mandans as well as Captain Clark had taken to calling the boy Pompey—*Little Chief.*

Although food was scarce, there were music and rejoicing in the village to celebrate the baby's birth. Evening Sky had done her best to craft a tiny set of moccasins for the child but was unable to complete them. Claire was seeing to the task, her mother looking on, one evening when the call went out through the village to assemble at the tree of the Lone Man. Chief Black Cat was to address the tribe.

Evening Sky tried to rouse herself but was far too weak to do so.

"Stay, Mother," Claire insisted gently. "I shall make your excuses to our chief if he asks for you."

When Claire stepped from the lodge, the western sky was the color of fire. Beautiful and captivating, it reminded her of the night she had parted with Pierre. Absence did truly make the heart grow fonder, because Claire was no closer to forgetting him than the day she had promised herself that she would.

She missed him terribly. She missed his curly black hair, his handsome smile, the stately way he carried himself. Every time she caught a distant glimpse of a man carrying a musket, clad in a buckskin coat, her pulse quickened, only to slow in disappointment when she discovered it was not him.

It did so now as she recognized Captain Clark. He and Charbonneau were standing in the plaza with Chief Black Cat. The taut look on her chief's face told Claire that something was terribly wrong. Whispers circulated around her. When Chief Black Cat raised his hands to speak, a hush fell over the crowd.

"The white chiefs say our great enemy has attacked."

No one needed to be told who the *great enemy* was. There was no one the Mandan tribe feared more than the Sioux. Claire's stomach knotted as the story unfolded. According to Black Cat, by way of Charbonneau and Clark, a party of men from the fort had been out hunting several miles below the river. Upon their return, a band of Sioux, an estimated one hundred warriors, had rushed on them.

Claire's heart went to her throat. Instantly she thought of Pierre.

"Our great enemy has stolen the white men's horses, weapons and game."

According to the report, the small hunting party had been completely outnumbered and were forced to surrender their goods. Thankfully no one was killed, but since thieving could not be tolerated, especially when a sleigh of meat could mean the difference between eating and going hungry, the American captains had decided to pursue the Sioux and reclaim what was rightfully theirs.

Chief Black Cat agreed with their course of action. "White Chief Lewis will lead the hunt at sunrise," he announced. "Any Mandan who goes with him will share his game."

Running Wolf instantly volunteered. So did Golden Hawk, the medicine man's son, and several others. While provisions were a motivating factor, Claire was certain it was not the only one.

"Mandan and Sioux will never live in peace," she heard Running Wolf say to Golden Hawk, "no matter how much the white chiefs wish it."

Claire's stomach knotted. Was Running Wolf expressing his opinion or proposing a course of action? Was he joining Captain Lewis's party to add strength of force or to attempt to provoke further trouble? Claire again thought of Pierre. If he had not been part of the first hunting group, then he would most certainly be part of the second. Would her uncle's aggression put Pierre in danger?

As her fellow villagers dispersed, Claire lifted a silent prayer. *Oh, God, grant wisdom, restraint and protection for all those involved...especially Pierre.*

In the pale gray light just before daybreak, the men had assembled at the fort. Apprehension snaked its way up Pierre's neck at the sight of Running Wolf among the Mandan men who would accompany them. Beside him stood a younger man about Pierre's age whom he soon learned by way of Captain Lewis was Golden Hawk, the medicine man's son. Neither of them was painted for war, but the expressions on their faces told Pierre they would welcome it if it came.

Peace through strength, Pierre thought.

It was the maxim Captain Lewis preached, believing the tribes could prosperously coexist if they would cease hostilities and promote peaceful relations and trade. Pierre couldn't help but wonder, though, despite the Captain's sincerity, if the philosophy was doomed to fail. Human nature went against it. In each tribe they had encountered, the old men liked the idea of peace, but not so the braves. The Mandans were no different. In this culture, young men earned respect and advancement by triumphing over their enemies.

Although no longer a young brave, Running Wolf still seemed itching to prove himself and just as bent on teaching the Sioux a lesson as the younger men of the party. Golden Hawk appeared to be cut from the same cloth. Pierre recognized that like Claire's uncle, he had completed the Okipa ceremony twice. Both of his little fingers were missing.

The sun had breached the eastern horizon, casting the barren landscape in a fiery orange glow. Pierre couldn't escape the thought that it wasn't just the Sioux whom these men marked as an enemy. Though he'd had no dealing with Golden Hawk specifically, Pierre was fairly certain the son of a medicine man would not be open to a Christian message, either.

A dreadful thought crossed his mind then as he remembered once more what Sergeant Ordway had said. The medicine man, Golden Hawk's father, had been seen watching Claire while speaking to Running Wolf. *Perhaps the father wasn't eyeing her for himself but for his son.*

He was sickened by the thought. Pierre hadn't seen her since that day at the fort, but as usual, he had thought of her constantly. For some reason, they were like oil and water, and why that frustrated him so he did not know. He could choose to stay away from her, but he did not wish to. One moment he despised her stubbornness. The next moment he foolishly wanted to kiss her.

He wondered if that had been evident at their last encounter. Was that why she had become offended? Did she think he was like some of the other men here, eager to steal affection with no thought of a lasting commitment?

He wasn't certain what she thought. He was not even sure what *he* was really thinking. All he knew was that being near her seemed to fill something inside him, something that hunting and exploration had yet to satisfy, and that troubled him more than she herself did.

The party began to march, each man carrying his musket, bow or spear. Pierre marched a respectful distance from the warriors, mindful of their movements. He did not trust them, at least not the two that he'd been watching so closely.

Southward the men trekked. Each man kept his eyes on the horizon for any sign of the Sioux.

About midday, they spied at a distance the primitive shelters Captain Clark had erected on the previous hunt. Here they expected to find a cache of meat. The yield had been so great, they had not been able to transport all of it previously. That had been a good thing, for if they had, the Sioux would have stolen the extra, as well, when they'd attacked the hunting party. Nearing the spot, however, Pierre and the rest of the men's hopes fell. The huts had been burned, and among the charred remains of wood was the load of burned carcasses. The Sioux hadn't even claimed the meat for themselves.

Pierre's anger flared. *What a waste.* It was one thing to steal when starving. It was quite another to induce starvation in others. The food stores at the fort were extremely low, and word was in the village the situation was even more desperate. Thinking more of Claire and her mother than his own growling stomach, Pierre was first in line behind Captain Lewis when the officer gave the order to continue marching. Doggedly the party moved forward, but no further trace of the Sioux remained.

The sun was now high in the sky, reflecting blindingly on the prairie. One of the Mandan men claimed a painful condition of his eyes. Two others insisted the trail was cold and the cause hopeless. Although displeased by their complaints, even Running Wolf moved to abandon the search.

"The Sioux are far away. No meat. Better hunting north of the river."

Captain Lewis was just as disgusted as anyone else by the lack of progress, and although bent on continuing, he agreed to send the native men back. Private Howard would travel with them. His feet were frosted and in need of medical attention.

"If you do not tarry, you should reach the fort by dusk," Lewis said. As for the rest of the men, he ordered them to continue.

Pierre tugged at his cap and did his best to shield his eyes as he moved forward. He understood the captain's tenacity. If what belonged to them was not recovered, it would only further emboldened the Sioux. What if they were to attack again? What if this time they came to the village? Would Running Wolf defend his niece, his sister?

God watch over them.

He reckoned they had marched about thirty miles when they came upon two abandoned tepees with Sioux markings. Daylight was fading fast and the winds were building. Conditions would not allow them to travel farther tonight. Besides that, the party was thoroughly exhausted.

Settling into the abandoned site, Captain Lewis ordered the men to sleep. Pierre volunteered to keep the first watch.

"Alert me at once if there is any movement," Lewis said.

"Yes, sir."

Taking his place, Pierre wondered if Running Wolf had yet returned to the village. Would he accept today's disappointment quietly, or would he take his anger out on Claire and her mother? The thought kept Pierre's muscles taut and his senses alert all through his watch.

Running Wolf returned to the lodge that evening with a frown. Claire knew at once that the efforts to recover the horses, weapons and meat had failed. But how so? Had the Sioux attacked, or had the men simply been unable to locate them?

And what of Pierre? She longed most of all to ask about him but did not dare.

Evening Sky lifted her head from her pallet. "How was your hunt, brother?" she asked.

Running Wolf huffed as he sat down by the fire. Claire dutifully placed his tea at his side. There was no more corn. Her uncle crossed, then uncrossed his legs restlessly. "There is no meat," he replied. "The White chief with the three-cornered hat still walks, but he will not find what he seeks. The enemy has fled."

Claire drew in a breath. It was greatly discouraging that the food had not been recovered, but at least there had been no bloodshed. *At least, not yet.* How long would Captain Lewis and his men march before they admitted defeat and returned to the fort? The memory of Black Raven's frozen feet skittered though her mind. Shivering, she whispered a silent prayer on Pierre and the other men's behalf.

"I am sorry for you, brother," Evening Sky said, "but I trust you will find meat soon."

Claire moved to refill her uncle's cup. He caught her arm before she could do so. His grip was so tight it threatened to bring tears to her eyes. "The spirits are angry with us," he said. "That is why our enemies provoke us. That is why there are no buffalo."

His hold and intimating glare told Claire exactly who Running Wolf thought was the target of their anger.

"If you would marry and give up these white men's ways, things would be different."

Claire lowered her eyes, not out of humility but in an effort to hold her tongue. If anyone had a right to be angry, it was her! How could her uncle treat her this way? He was her own flesh and blood! How could he seek to barter her off to strangers all those months ago? And now, with her mother sick, how could he *still* insist she wed?

"A strong warrior is what is needed to keep you on the path of our ancestors."

He did not name a specific warrior, but it mattered very little. She was desperate just the same.

God help me. I know he acts in ignorance. I know that walking Your path of forgiveness is the only way to shine Your light...but Lord, it is so hard! Help me! Defend me!

"You say nothing to this?" Running Wolf said.

Claire had no words. No voice at all. With sudden great strength, however, Evening Sky raised herself to a sitting position. Her voice was clear, her eyes as bright as fire. "She tries to show you respect, brother! You do not wish for her to speak the name of Jesus, but I tell you once again that He is the true Great Spirit. He is more powerful than all the others. He will provide."

Running Wolf practically tossed Claire aside as he rose to his feet. "He has not provided for you! You scorn the power of our medicine man. You place your life in the hands of a dead man."

"He is not dead," Evening Sky said. "He lives."

Running Wolf turned his eyes again on Claire. She nodded in agreement with her mother, a quiet confidence infusing her. Whatever doubts she might have, whatever fears and emotions with which she struggled, Claire was certain of this. Deep in her bones she knew it to be true. Come life or her death, she knew it was true. Christ was alive.

Running Wolf turned for the door. "Foolish women! I will suffer no more of this talk!" Snatching his buffalo robe, he stormed out of the lodge.

Cries Like a Dove had watched the entire exchange in wide-eyed silence. When Running Wolf had gone, she asked, "Do you not fear displeasing him? Do you not fear what he may do? What if he calls his spirits against you? Do you truly believe your God is more powerful than Running Wolf's spirits?"

"Yes," Evening Sky and Claire both said at once.

"We do not wish to displease Running Wolf," Claire said softly, "but as my mother said, our God is the true God. If angered, my uncle can only hurt my body," *or offer it to another*, she thought. "He cannot touch my spirit. The true God holds power over both body and spirit."

"And He does not wish to punish," Evening Sky said. "He wishes to forgive all those who turn to Him. He offers love. He brings peace to the heart." She paused. "Peace despite pain."

Cries Like a Dove's eyes began to water. "I should like peace of heart," she said. "I should like to know forgiveness. My husband never says that I have failed him, but I know that I have. The old women tell me that is why I cannot give birth." She wrapped her arms around her unborn child. "I fear I shall fail again."

Claire slowly stepped forward, embraced the woman. She knew that fear of failure. Although not a mother, she knew what it was like to feel responsible for the lives before her. The weight of the burden at times was almost unbearable. No wonder she had wished to escape with Pierre that night. *But if I rode off toward the sunset, I would not have the privilege of witnessing moments like this*, she thought. *God is indeed moving.*

"The old women say that I have done wrong," Cries Like a Dove said. "They say that I must seek the medicine man's provision, but I have done so before, and he was no help."

"We have all done wrong," Evening Sky said, "but no medicine can help. Our wrong must be atoned, and there is only one who has the power to do so."

"Your Jesus?"

"Yes," Claire answered, feeling hope surging inside her as she could see Cries Like a Dove's heart opening to the truth. "He loves us even in our weakness, even in our shame. Only He can lift us from such and fill the emptiness inside our hearts."

He was doing it right now inside Claire. The fear she felt, the restlessness were melting away. Assurance filled her now. *This* was where she was meant to be. *This* was her family. No matter what happened in the future, no matter what her uncle tried to do to her, this was where she was supposed to be. Phillip Granger, for all of his scheming, had actually done her a favor. His actions had led her here.

Cries Like a Dove clung to her, her tears falling upon Claire's shoulder. "Then I want your Jesus to do so for me. I want him to take my wrong and give me peace."

"All you need to do is ask Him," Claire said.

And so she did, and as Cries Like a Dove cried out to the Savior, Claire's heart leaped with joy. Evening Sky smiled with equal gladness. This woman was the first of the tribe to come to the light. "Thank You, God," Claire whispered. "Thank You. May there be more… May there be many, many more…"

Almost a week after his party had first set out, Pierre spied the palisade on the horizon. The primitive fort had never looked so good. His feet were sore and cold, but thankfully ten toes remained. His muscles ached, but the two sleighs full of meat that he and his compatriots pulled behind them were worth the strain.

They had never found the Sioux, but trekking still further south, they had located a second cache of meat that the enemy had not discovered. In it were two sleighs and a few small deer. With provisions enough to last them for a couple of days, the party set to hunting.

By the time they had finished, they had procured thirty-six deer and fourteen elk. In their full-bellied exuberance, the men had taken to guessing the weight of the collection all the way back to the fort. Sergeant Ordway estimated twenty-four hundred pounds. Pierre reasoned it was more like twenty-eight. Captain Lewis believed it to be three thousand.

Despite the loss to the Sioux and whatever the newly gathered meat's true weight, God had indeed blessed them. There had been no battle, and there was food to spare. In the interest of maintaining friendship, the captain decided to share the bounty with the Mandan.

Upon reaching the river, Lewis directed that a portion of the meat be taken to the village. Pierre was the first to volunteer for the task of delivery. He wanted to see Claire. Since there had been no quarrel between Running Wolf and him on the hunt, Lewis agreed.

A party of villagers, mostly Chief Black Cat and his family, was now coming toward them. "You found what was taken?" the chief asked.

Charbonneau explained this was not the meat that the Sioux had stolen. "It is a fresh kill," he said, "and it is the white chief's desire to share it with our friends."

Black Cat smiled his approval. "It is good you have come," he said. "Our hunters have not yet returned. Our women and children are hungry."

Pierre glanced around for two particular women. With the Mandans now clustering about them, they hauled the sleigh into the heart of the village.

Upon their arrival, the celebratory drums began to beat. Chants of thankfulness echoed. Among the throng, Pierre spied Claire. She was standing just outside her family lodge, a little thinner in the face than the last time he had seen her but still just as lovely.

Noticing him, she smiled. He hadn't known exactly what her response toward him would be, given how they had last parted. In fact, he still wasn't certain. Was she glad to see him or simply grateful for the meat he had brought?

He didn't care. He was glad to see her, and that was enough. Only as he approached her did he think of his appearance. He had once again let his hair and beard grow. His buckskin clothing was ragged and unkempt. He was hardly presentable to meet a lady.

Even so, she offered him another smile. "I thank God that you are well," she said.

"It is because of your prayers."

She lowered her eyes, blushed, as if embarrassed by the fact that he knew she had been praying for him. Perhaps he presumed wrong, but he didn't think so. He knew someone had been praying. He had felt the strength unleashed by the petitions.

"How is your mother?" he asked.

Her eyes returned to his. They were vibrant and penetrating, more so than he believed he had ever seen before. A new light seemed to shine in them. Pierre self-consciously rubbed his scraggly chin. "Her health is much the same," she said, "but her heart is happy… as is mine. I have much to tell you."

"Oh? Good news?"

"Indeed!"

Her face practically glowed as she told him then of Cries Like a Dove's decision to follow Christ. Pierre rejoiced at the news, but a small part of him couldn't help but wonder what the woman's husband thought of her newfound faith. Three Horses was a likeable man, and Pierre had formed something of a friendship with him during his time at the fort. Still, Christianity was a divisive issue. He asked Claire.

"Oh, that is the best part. Her husband said if Christ could dry her tears then he would not object to her worshipping him. He even gave his wife a new name."

"What does he call her now?"

"One Who Smiles."

Hearing that, Pierre smiled himself. He couldn't help but think then of Claire's own Mandan name,

Bright Star. She was indeed just that, a light that shone in the darkness. "That is wonderful news," he said.

At the tree of the Lone Man, Chief Black Cat raised his hands, preparing to speak. His villagers drew near to pay the hunters honor. Just before they did so, a cry came from the main entrance. Startled, Pierre turned quickly in the direction of the sound, alert for danger. It was not, however, a cry of war or distress but apparently celebration. The Mandan hunters had returned. Their people rejoiced at their entrance.

Running Wolf, his face painted, his jaw set proudly, was leading the party. Behind him were four other braves, including Golden Hawk. Each hunter carried a deer on his shoulders.

"They bring food, as well," Claire said.

"Indeed."

But when the animals were laid beside the sleigh load of meat, it was obvious which hunting party had been most successful—particularly since the hunters from the fort had brought only a portion of all that they had captured. Chief Black Cat nevertheless proclaimed welcome to his men and bestowed the same honor as he had upon the whites. It was obvious to Pierre and anyone else with eyes that Running Wolf did not wish to share such honor. The warrior's disapproving glare burned through Pierre as Running Wolf located him among the crowd.

Instinctively Pierre stepped in front of Claire, blocking her uncle's view of her. He did not wish trouble with the man, but Pierre would make it clear that he would not tolerate even so much as a shadow of discomfort directed toward Claire or her mother.

Claire, stubborn as usual, would not be shielded.

When Black Cat gave the command, she stepped forward with the other women and began to carve the meat, leaving Pierre and Running Wolf to glare at one another.

Claire walked a fine line between excitement and caution when Pierre arrived in her village. He was safe. He had been successful. She was glad to see him, and she wanted to share with him all of the news of what had happened in his absence. Yet she knew she must separate from him, if not for her sake, then for his. Running Wolf was clearly jealous of him.

When the women were called to skin the meat, she moved to the deer her uncle had brought. One Who Smiles, formerly Cries Like a Dove, moved up beside her.

"Your uncle's eyes are upon you," she warned.

"I know."

As One Who Smiles reached for her knife, she staggered just a little. Claire immediately steadied her. "You are weak, sister. Allow me."

Unbeknownst to Claire, Chief Black Cat was circling the group. Noting the pregnant woman's difficulty, he paused. Although it was customary for all of the meat to be dressed and distributed first to the hunters before any other person ate, Chief Black Cat made an exception.

"Give a small portion to her now," he said to Claire, speaking of One Who Smiles. "Let her rest inside her lodge."

Highly surprised but extremely grateful, Claire nodded to her chief.

"You are most generous, great chief," One Who

Smiles said. "Might I prepare this in the lodge of Evening Sky?"

Claire smiled at her friend's thoughtfulness. Her mother needed nourishment as well.

The old chief nodded his approval. Claire moved to slice the meat, but Black Cat stopped her. "Take from the white man's portion," he said. "It is better quality."

Claire nodded obediently, then moved toward the sleigh that Pierre and the others had brought. She was thankful for Black Cat's kindness yet was left uneasy by it at the same time. She could feel Running Wolf's eyes upon her. She dared not look toward Pierre.

In an unprecedented move, the chief then suddenly announced, "Cut the meat for the sick and old first."

The village went silent in shock. On the plains, where the old were often told, "You have lived long enough, and it is now time for you to die," twice in a matter of minutes her chief had shown deference to the weakest members of the tribe. Were the teachings of Jesus penetrating even further than Claire had realized? Was this the true reason for Running Wolf's frown?

Pierre moved up beside her. "Let us unload the sleigh for you," he said. "Suggest to your chief that representatives for those most in need wait in queues while the meat is prepared."

It was a wonderful idea, and Claire turned at once to Black Cat. "If it is the chief's pleasure..." she said before explaining Pierre's idea.

Black Cat nodded approval. With his permission, Pierre then organized the people into lines. There was disbelief but relief at the same time for those who suffered.

Claire relished the concern Pierre showed for her people. She admired his willingness to take leadership and the gentle way he did it—so different from the autocratic ways practiced by most of the men in her tribe. Claire watched as he escorted a particularly feeble grandmother to the head of one of the queues. She in turn offered him a toothless grin.

Claire's heart swelled so much that she thought it would burst. Pierre Lafayette was a man of strength and gentleness, of ferocity and faith. This was the kind of man with whom she wanted to live out her days. This was the husband whose name she wished to carry.

Admitting to herself what her heart had already known for some time, Claire felt a bubble of laughter rise inside her, one, however, that quickly burst. Without a doubt she had fallen in love, but she had fallen in love with a man who would not, *could not* be her husband. Spring was just a few weeks away. Even if the expedition was not continuing westward, even if Pierre did have some interest in her that went beyond Christian concern, it would still be impossible.

She cast a glance toward her uncle. Running Wolf had taken post beneath the Lone Man's tree, his arms crossed upon his massive chest. He and his hunters had been deprived of the honor of eating first not only by the white man but also by their chief. Claire saw the piercing look her uncle gave Pierre. If looks could kill, Pierre would have been lying in the trampled snow.

Black Cat's kindness could easily vanish if another confrontation flares between Pierre and my uncle, she thought. *And if the American captains become angered...* She shoved away the thought.

"You should go," she said to Pierre.

"But there is still more meat to—"

She touched his sleeve. The action stilled him. "My uncle is angry with your handling of the meat. He thinks what we have done today is an insult to the spirits."

"You mean an insult to himself."

"Pierre, please…" She heard the tone of her own voice. It revealed more concern for him than she wished to admit.

"If you are worried for my safety, I assure you I can take care of myself."

"I know you can." She didn't say anything else. She feared if she did, he would come to understand what she truly felt. Even now it seemed as though those dark charcoal eyes were burning a hole through her soul, exposing everything she had ever thought about him. He cast a glance then in her uncle's direction.

"I know you told me you did not want my protection, but that won't keep me from rendering it when it is warranted."

Her heart swelled once more. She wanted him to stay with her always but dared not say it. "I do not despise your offer of such," she said. "I only think of the consequences of the last time you faced my uncle when his ire was raised."

She could tell by the change in his expression, the uncertainty in his eyes, that he followed her thoughts.

He opened his mouth to say something else, but an approaching soldier kept him from doing so. Despite the ragged clothing and unkempt hair, Claire recognized him. It was Private Cruzette, the fiddle player.

He nodded to her, then said to Pierre, "The captain

is looking for you. He wants a report on conditions here in the village."

Pierre hesitated. To an officer it would have been infuriating. To her it was endearing. He was torn between his duty to his captain and his promise to her.

But she refused to be the cause of trouble to him. "Go," she encouraged him. "All will be well here. Black Cat has shown me great favor today." She didn't give him a chance to respond but instead quickly turned back to carve the remaining meat.

Chapter Twelve

Pierre hadn't liked leaving the village, but he did so reluctantly. Given what had happened the last time he had tarried, coupled with his previous hesitancy to obey Captain Lewis, he thought it prudent to do so. Claire had insisted all would be well, but just in case, he asked Charbonneau to keep an eye on her.

The Frenchman returned to the fort just before dark. "All is quiet," he announced. "Full bellies produce sound sleep."

"Did you see her uncle?" Pierre asked.

"Yes. I saw him sitting at the chief's special fire before I left. Evidently Black Cat had smoothed over his ruffled feathers by inviting him and his hunters to dine with him."

Charbonneau told him not to worry, but of course that was easier said than done. Pierre tossed and turned in his bunk for hours. The bugle sounded all too soon. He slid from his bedding only to greet another cold morning. A skin of ice coated the water in the wash basin, causing most of his fellow adventurers to forgo that morning ritual. Grumbling and yawning, they each layered up their clothing, tugged on their hats and gloves. Grabbing their muskets, they headed for the parade ground.

Captain Clark was already afield. Pierre and the others assembled in front of him, but before the officer could issue the daily assignments, a call came from the catwalk. Private George Shannon, the sentinel on duty, announced that an Indian rider was approaching.

"He's comin' in awfully fast, sir. Looks to be some sort of trouble."

At that, Pierre's muscles tightened and every man, including Captain Clark, stood a little straighter. Were the Sioux once again on the prowl?

"Is it a single rider?" Clark asked.

"Yes, sir."

"Can you yet tell who it appears to be?"

"Appears to be the boy who stayed here. The one who lost his toes."

Pierre blinked. Why was Black Raven coming to the fort? Then he remembered the story Claire had shared about the boy's mother having decided to follow Christ. His pulse quickened. Has there been some sort of trouble because of that decision? Was Claire in danger?

Captain Clark gave the order to open the gate for the boy. With Charbonneau already dispatched on other business, Clark called Pierre forward to assist with translation. Pierre did the best he could, but the boy was talking so fast that even if he'd had a better grasp of the Mandan language, the task would have been difficult. He heard Captain Lewis's name mentioned. Then he thought he heard the word for baby.

"Has your mother's time come?" he asked. "Is she in distress?"

The boy made signs to indicate the child was on its way but something was wrong. "Medicine," he said.

Pierre looked at Captain Clark. The officer nodded. "Fetch Captain Lewis."

Pierre hurried to do so. He was relieved to know Claire was not in danger, but it distressed him greatly that her friend was.

Having heard the commotion on the parade ground, Captain Lewis stepped from his hut. "What is amiss?" he asked.

Pierre quickly explained. Fetching his doctoring kit, Captain Lewis ran for the gate. One of the soldiers had already saddled his horse, and apparently under Captain Clark's direction, a mount had been prepared for Pierre, as well.

"Sir, I'm not certain how much help I can be," he said. "I speak very little Mandan."

"But you speak French," Clark said. "And so does Miss Manette."

So he and Captain Lewis, along with Black Raven, galloped toward the river. Navigating the ice carefully, they burst again into speed once they had climbed the far bank. The snow impeded their pace somewhat, but they still managed to make it to the village in record time.

Women there were going about their daily chores, while the men were visiting in their usual spot beneath the great tree. Though a few cast a glance at the white men, no one seemed all that alarmed. Pierre noted Running Wolf was suspiciously absent from the group, but having no time to ponder the potential reasons, he continued on with the captain.

Reaching the lodge, Pierre and Lewis left the horses

in the care of Black Raven, then stepped inside. It took
a moment for Pierre's eyes to adjust to the semidark-
ness. When they did, he was surprised by the emptiness
of the lodge. Upon entering he had expected to find
a gaggle of women, busy tending to or at least whispering about the pregnant mother. Instead only Claire
was at One Who Smiles's pallet. Standing over them
both was Three Horses, the worried-looking husband.

I didn't know she was a midwife, Pierre thought. Was
there nothing this woman could not do?

Claire looked as though she'd never been more
relieved to see them. She came to them at once, explaining the circumstances, alternating her attention
between Pierre and Captain Lewis.

"The pains began last night," she said, "just after
you left the village. The midwives all gathered. One
Who Smiles sent for me. She wanted me to come and
pray for her. She did not wish for the women to recite
incantations over her."

"Where are they now?" Lewis asked.

Pierre wondered the same. "Did the women get
angry about the prayer? Did they leave?"

"Not at first, but when it became clear that the baby
wasn't progressing, the midwives blamed One Who
Smiles. They said she had angered the spirits by refusing their assistance, and they would not stay."

So they abandoned her? Pierre looked at the woman
on the pallet. She was in obvious travail.

"How long has she been like this?" Lewis asked.

"Hours. Captain, I am not skilled in bringing forth
children. I begged Three Horses to send for you, but
at first he refused, saying he did not wish to anger the
spirits."

So he believed the women, Pierre thought. *God, help his wife...help the child...*

"I wanted to come to the fort myself, but One Who Smiles forbade me to leave her side. She insisted God would be with her, and she wanted me beside her to help her pray. I reminded Three Horses of Black Raven's trouble with his feet, of how God had helped him recover."

Pierre noted to whom she gave credit—not the American captains but to the Great Physician.

"Three Horses now asks for your help."

The warrior nodded to the men, then pointed to his ailing wife. Captain Lewis went to her at once. The woman said something to him, but neither Pierre nor the captain could understand.

"She asks for rattlesnake powder," Claire said. "She asked me for it earlier, but I was afraid to give it to her. She says you gave it to Sacagawea and then her child came."

He felt her abdomen, then shook his head. "You did right in not administering the powder. It would only have heightened the danger. The child has not yet turned."

Pierre was hardly an expert in such areas, but even he knew the woman's condition was grave. "Have you a remedy?" he asked.

Lewis looked doubtful. "I can try."

"What would you have us do?" Claire asked.

Us, Pierre noted. Oil and water aside, they were a committed team.

"Fetch clean cloths and some sinew," Lewis ordered.

By now Black Raven was standing in the entryway, his dark eyes wide with fearful curiosity. Spying him,

Claire asked him to gather the necessary items. He did so at once, while his nervous father looked on.

Pierre laid his hand upon the man's shoulder. They were of different blood and culture, but they could each understand what they would suffer if they lost someone for whom they cared.

If that were Claire lying there...

Language could not convey the communication, but the look the man gave him told Pierre he appreciated the gesture of friendship.

"I'll need you to keep her still," Lewis said to Claire, and then he looked at Pierre. "Perhaps it would be best if you took the boy and his father outside."

"Of course." Pierre looked again to Three Horses, motioned to the door. Claire translated his request, adding a smile of reassurance at the end. It was a token of comfort Pierre was certain even she herself did not feel. Not only was a woman's life and that of her child in the balance but also the potential faith of a husband and son.

Three Horses might have given pause over the old wives' claims that the spirits had been angered, but the fact remained that he'd entrusted his wife's care to the judgment of her friend who worshipped the white man's God.

Pierre didn't know who needed prayer more in this moment—the woman in labor, the child, Three Horses, Claire or the captain. *Or perhaps us all...the entire expedition...for what will happen if the woman dies? Will the spirit-worshiping midwives blame Claire and Captain Lewis?* Would they convince Black Cat and the others to revoke the friendship they had thus far given?

Running Wolf is already inclined against us. If hostilities ensued, what would be the outcome? The river was still covered in ice. There could be no easy retreat.

"We are sixteen hundred miles up the Missouri. No one will come to our aid..."

Pushing aside the disconcerting thoughts, Pierre chose instead to lift a silent prayer while he followed Three Horses and his son outside. Life in the village continued around them as it had previously, although now he heard the district sound of drums. Three Horses immediately frowned and said something that Pierre did not understand.

What did the drums mean? Was trouble brewing? Did the sound come from outside the village or within it?

He thought of informing the captain, but just then a cry came from inside the lodge. He'd once heard Indian women were taught to make no sound when giving birth. If that was true and One Who Smiles was breaking that rule, then she must have a very good reason for doing so. The captain could not be disturbed.

Three Horses turned a worried eye toward the lodge. Pierre tried to distract him. Using signs and his limited Mandan vocabulary, he inquired of the drums. The man offered a disgusted look and answered in a tone much the same. Black Raven translated his father's remark. He had apparently learned a little French.

"Drums for death," the boy said.

The hair on the back of Pierre's neck stood up. "Whose death?"

"My mother. Tribe expect no live."

That's the work of the midwives, Pierre supposed. So they *had* truly given up on the poor woman. Well, he would not, and apparently Three Horses wasn't about to do so, either. He shook his head adamantly.

"Tell your father that Christ is more powerful than the spirits," Pierre said. "That He alone holds the keys to life and death."

Black Raven repeated the words. At first Pierre wasn't certain if the man understood, but then Three Horses pointed to Pierre, and he pointed to the sky. Next the warrior raised his arms heavenward and lifted his voice in a native cry. It was plaintive but not unnerving. Pierre recognized it for what it was, a man in anguish pouring out his soul to the Creator.

"He pray to this Christ," Black Raven explained. "Asks you to do same."

"It would be my honor," Pierre said.

And there in the midst of the earthen huts and cooking fires, one man danced and called out, the other bowed his head in reverent silence, but Pierre was certain the Savior heard them both just the same.

Claire cried tears of joy when a writhing, dark-haired baby boy was laid at last upon his mother's breast. His face was a bit bruised by his prolonged and rather traumatic entry into the world, and his cry was somewhat kitten-like for the moment, but Claire was confident he would gain strength. Overall he appeared healthy.

Though exhausted, One Who Smiles exerted what little of her strength remained to count her infant's fingers and toes and then whisper her thanks to the captain, to Claire and to God Almighty.

Lewis smiled as he wiped his hands on a piece of

cloth. He then looked at Claire. "She'll need nourishment."

Claire nodded. "I prepared a broth."

"Good. Fetch it while I better examine the child."

Claire moved at once to the fire, gathered a bowl of warm liquid and then returned to her friend.

"Our God is good," One Who Smiles said.

"Indeed," Claire replied. "Here, drink this and then I shall tell Three Horses the momentous news…that he now has *two* sons."

Tears trickled down One Who Smiles's face, but Claire knew they were tears of joy. When the broth had been sufficiently drained from the bowl, Claire walked to the door. Bright afternoon sunlight stung her eyes, but the cold air was invigorating. She drew in a deep breath. Never before had she been so scared, or prayed so fervently for assistance, and never before had she felt such joy when God answered her prayer.

A new life has entered this village. Despite the midwives' dire predictions, my Christian sister has survived. Thank You, God! Thank You!

She was certain she hadn't been the only one praying. Pierre was doing so, as well.

She found him along the side of the lodge with Three Horses and Black Raven. The men were sitting cross-legged on the snow-packed ground, speaking to one another with signs and limited vocabulary. Her heart leaped at the sight of such obvious friendship and respect.

Black Raven saw her first. He excitedly tapped his father's knee. Surely he could tell by her expression that all was well. Pierre stood immediately and brushed the snow from his trousers. Three Horses remained seated, but as soon as Claire delivered the news, he jumped to his feet with a shout. What followed then surprised her beyond words.

Three Horses lifted a prayer of thanks, not to his ancestors but to the Creator and sustainer of life. Claire's jaw dropped when she heard the name of Jesus on the warrior's lips.

Pierre simply grinned.

Having finished his song of thanks, Three Horses came to her and laid his hands upon her shoulders, just like an elder would do when bestowing a blessing on a younger member of the tribe. "The other women went away," he said. "but you did not leave my wife. Your God will be my God."

Tears filled Claire's eyes, blurring her vision. She had done nothing to convince this man of the truth. She had simply cared for her friend in her time of need, and to think that God had somehow used her to assist the birth of one soul into the world and one soul into His kingdom…it was overwhelming indeed.

"You give me great honor," she said.

With the smile only a proud father could offer, Three Horses then moved toward the lodge. His oldest son scampered happily beside him.

"Don't look so surprised," Pierre said as he came up beside her. "Are we not taught to believe that God answers prayer?"

"Indeed." She laughed joyfully, heartily. She couldn't help herself. He did, too.

"Thank you," she said. "Thank you for everything you did."

"I didn't do anything."

"But you did. You kept company with Three Horses and Black Raven and you prayed."

He flushed slightly as if embarrassed by her praise. "It was my privilege."

Only then did she realize that he had once again shaved his beard and trimmed his curls. He was so handsome. Claire had the sudden desire to let her fingers trace his strong jaw, linger over the cleft of his chin. She didn't dare do so. Such behavior was unseemly for any maiden, French *or* Indian.

"What will they name the child?" he asked.

"I do not know. In our culture, children are not given their names until ten days after birth. It is part of an official naming ceremony."

"I see." He paused, rubbed his clean-shaven chin.

"You must be cold," she said.

He chuckled slightly. "I am."

"Come with me," she said. "I know where there is a warm fire." Fearing that the invitation had sounded utterly improper, she quickly explained, "I need to look in on my mother for a moment before I return to assist One Who Smiles further. Will you come with me? She would enjoy your company." Then she added, "Running Wolf is not here. He has gone hunting and will not be back until the morrow."

"Well, in that case," he said. Then, as if he were to escort her across a ballroom floor, he offered his arm. "Shall we?"

Claire stifled a giggle as she laid hold of his sleeve. She was so happy. She couldn't resist replying in the same manner. "You are most kind, dear sir."

With a shared laugh, they tramped through the snow.

* * *

Pierre's mood changed the moment he entered Claire's lodge. It wasn't because he was stepping into the domain without Running Wolf's permission to do so. He had been invited, and the presence of Little Flower and her children assured propriety. What troubled him was the sight of Evening Sky. Pierre had not seen her for several weeks, and the change in her constitution was deeply disconcerting.

She was lying on her pallet. Her face, arms and legs had withered away, but her abdomen was abnormally large for someone so thin. Her coloring was a sickly shade of pale, enough to tell Pierre that despite persistent prayers, the woman's time was drawing nigh.

Did Claire not see it? Had the change been so slight each day that she simply failed to notice the signs? Or did she not wish to see them?

Evening Sky welcomed him with a tired but contented smile, like the look of a weary traveler who had at last reached his final destination. Pierre took her frail hand in his, kissed it gently.

Kneeling beside him, Claire excitedly told her mother all that had transpired with One Who Smiles and Three Horses.

"You have done well, Bright Star. God has answered our prayers," she said. A pale bluish tinge colored her lips. She looked back at Pierre, indicated she wished to take his hand once more. Pierre noted that her fingertips held the same bluish tint.

Her hands were ice-cold, but it wasn't for lack of heat. Claire had laid another buffalo skin over her mother when she had arrived, and in the center of the lodge, Little Flower stoked a roaring fire. It was so warm that Pierre was perspiring.

"God *has* brought healing," Evening Sky said to him.

Pierre's throat constricted, for he understood the message she was delivering. Bodily healing for her was not to be. She knew that. But she also saw that God *was* working in matters of the heart. Three Horses and One Who Smiles were the evidence.

"We must remember that," she said as she gave his hand a feeble squeeze. He recognized the second message. Claire would have trouble accepting that. Her mother wanted him to help her.

Pierre's throat further tightened, but he managed a dutiful nod. In few words, Evening Sky had said much. She had honored him by giving Pierre this charge. There was much he wanted to say to her, but he kept it back. Claire still apparently failed to grasp what was happening. He sensed Evening Sky wanted it that way. Perhaps it was a tribal custom when approaching death to speak of it as little as possible.

If it was, he must disobey, but he would do so delicately.

Evening Sky told her daughter she should return to Three Horses's lodge to look after the mother and newborn child. "You are needed there," she said. "There you can do much good."

Claire hesitated, but after Evening's Sky's gentle insistence, she bent to kiss her mother's cheek and then stood. Pierre pushed to his feet, as well.

"I think you should stay," he whispered to Claire in English.

She blinked, looked at her mother, and then looked

back at him. He saw the questions in her eyes. Pain pierced his heart, for he knew what was coming for her.

"But mother said...the baby—"

He stopped her with an upturned hand. He knew the newborn and recently delivered mother needed continued care, but despite Evening Sky's charge, Pierre did not believe Claire was the one to provide it. *At least, not right now.*

He turned to her cousin. "Will you go to One Who Smiles?" he asked Little Flower in Mandan. "Help mother and child?"

Little Flower looked somewhat surprised, then fearful, but it was no match for the expression that now filled Claire's face. Her lovely bronzed skin drained white. She knew full well Pierre would not ask her cousin to assist a woman the midwives had shunned were it not absolutely necessary.

"Please," Pierre said to Little Flower.

The woman looked back at Evening Sky, then Claire. She nodded.

"Thank you," he said, "and please...tell Captain Lewis where I am."

She nodded once more. Then, grabbing her buffalo robe, she threw it over her shoulders and hurried outside.

When she had gone, Pierre turned back to Claire. She was standing stone still. The joy of new life was no longer in her eyes. Tears now filled them. One soul had come into the world. Another was about to depart. Such was life out on the frontier.

Chapter Thirteen

Pierre moved to take her hand, draw her close, but Claire resisted. She could not accept his comfort. If she did, she knew she would give in fully to her tears. *And I cannot do so. The time is short. I have to remain strong.*

He must have recognized her need to maintain her composure, for when she pulled away, he offered neither apologies nor words of condolence. He simply followed her back to her mother's pallet and took up post a few paces behind her. Evidently he wanted to give her privacy, but he also wanted her to know he was near if she needed him. Claire appreciated that more than he could possibly know, and once again she fought the urge to seek the shelter of his embrace.

Kneeling, she took her mother's hand. Evening Sky's eyes reflected a measure of joy and sorrow.

"You should have gone to One Who Smiles," she whispered, but her expression told Claire she was glad she had not.

"My duty is to you," she said.

The older woman shook her head. "No. Your duty is to God. Follow His path, always. Although sometimes the way will seem very dark, you will eventually come again into the light."

At that, Claire broke down. There was so much darkness. Her father's passing, her mother's struggle, her uncle's superstitious fear. Why couldn't God simply bring that light now? He could. She knew He could. Why couldn't He simply banish darkness, despair, pain and death now? Why must they wait?

But she did not ask because she knew the answer. With the exception of Three Horses and his family, her entire village still needed Christ. There was still love to be shared. Her mother's work was done, but Claire still had tasks to complete. And they overwhelmed her.

God, I cannot do this alone. Help me.

Evening Sky squeezed her daughter's hand. A loving mother knows her child's thoughts and fears, no matter how old that child has become. "God will provide for all of your needs," she whispered.

Needs, Claire thought. *There are so many.* Not just spiritual matters, but regular earthly chores, as well. There were so many ordinary tasks to undertake even now, tonight, at the lodge. With Little Flower absent from the dwelling, there was snow water to be gathered. There were children to feed.

It was then she realized she smelled the aroma of stew. Claire turned to find Spotted Eagle busy stirring a pot at the fire and Pierre seating River Song and the rest of the children near him. Claire watched as Pierre then doled out a bowl full of liquid to each of them.

The two were doing women's work, but neither seemed to think it beneath his dignity. How Pierre had managed Spotted Eagle's cooperation, especially given his attitude of late, she did not know, but she was thankful for it.

When Pierre looked up, caught her eye, she offered him a smile. He nodded, then said to Spotted Eagle, "Watch the others and I'll gather more snow."

Spotted Eagle nodded as if he had been given an honored charge.

"The children are in good hands," Evening Sky whispered.

"Indeed," Claire replied.

"You are in good hands, as well."

Captain Lewis arrived sometime later along with Chief Black Cat. It would have been unseemly for the chief to be waited on by a man, and when Claire whispered such to Pierre, he quickly took his place at the fire with the other men. Claire served the broth, then gathered the children around her.

"You have acted most bravely, taking on a role that is not your own," she whispered to Spotted Eagle.

"The white man said my hands could honor Great Aunt by doing so," the boy said, "and I wished to pay such honor because I have acted *dishonorably* toward her."

Claire knew Pierre would not have condemned the child for his earlier rudeness to Evening Sky. After all, the boy had only been following his grandfather's command, but clearly Spotted Eagle's conscience had been pricked.

"Your great aunt holds no anger toward you," Claire assured him. "She forgives you. She did so even before you realized you had done wrong."

He looked at Claire with dark, inquisitive eyes. "Do you forgive me?" he asked.

"Of course," she replied, giving him a squeeze. "If the Great Spirit forgives me of my wrongs, how can I not do the same for others?"

Spotted Eagle smiled, then turned his attention back toward the guests. "Our chief thinks highly of Great Aunt."

"Indeed."

It was a high honor for a chief to visit Evening Sky on her deathbed, an honor usually only bestowed upon warriors and medicine men.

Perhaps Black Cat had come only because the captain had done so, but given what Claire had witnessed, with his willingness to distribute meat to those in need first, she wondered again if it was possible that he was being drawn toward the teaching of Christ. He had never actually been hostile to such. His utmost goal seemed to be preserving peace and safety for his people.

Black Cat offered no spirit blessing as he would have done for a warrior, but he did lay his hand upon Evening Sky's forehead and wish her peace on her journey before leaving the lodge.

Captain Lewis remained a little longer. Claire left her place with the children and returned to her mother's side.

Lewis asked if there was anything he might do for her. "Perhaps alleviate the pain?" he offered.

"I am beyond pain now," Evening Sky told him. She then asked of Three Horses's son.

"He is well," the captain said, "and so is his mother."

Evening Sky smiled. Although it was weak, Claire could tell she was content. Once again she took her mother's hand. It was much colder now. Claire swallowed back her emotions as Captain Lewis took his leave. To Claire's surprise, he had granted Pierre permission to stay. She was glad he did. She needed his quiet presence, even if she could not fully explain to him why. As if sensing so, he laid his hand upon her shoulder for a moment, then returned to the children.

Twilight gave way to darkness. Darkness to the coming of a new day. Claire could tell the changes by the smoke hole in the center of the roof. The pale pink streaks of dawn now colored the sky.

The children slept soundly and Evening Sky held on. "You remember the hymn your father used to sing to us?" she asked in a voice barely above a whisper.

"Yes," Claire replied, her own voice cracking. It was not of French origin but German. "A Mighty Fortress Is Our God."

"Sing it for me."

Heart in her throat, Claire did her best to sing her mother's favorite hymn but found she could only hum it at first. Recognizing the tune, Pierre came to join them, adding his own comforting baritone to the small choir. Claire's faith and voice strengthened as they plunged further into the verses.

"'Let goods and kindred go, this mortal life also, the body they may kill, God's truth abideth still, His kingdom is forever…'"

Listening, Evening Sky closed her eyes. The faintest of smiles graced her lips. When the song was finished, she looked at her daughter.

"Your father would be so proud of the woman you have become," she whispered.

"Give him my love," Claire said. She held her mother's hand to the last, and only after her mother's

eyes closed for the final time did Claire allow herself
to give in to tears.

This time she let Pierre console her.

The children were beginning to stir, but Pierre did
not move from his post. Instead he cradled Claire's
head against his chest. Her sobs were almost voiceless,
but they shook her entire frame. As a man, he wanted
nothing more than to dry her tears and promise her everything would be alright. He couldn't. Evening Sky
might have passed into her eternal rest, but the trials
for her daughter were only heightening.

Running Wolf chose that exact moment to return, breaking them abruptly apart. Apparently Chief
Black Cat had informed him of the news of his sister's
passing, so he did not look surprised, nor did he ask
questions. Neither did he voice objection at Pierre's
presence. He was, however, far from willing to let his
niece grieve in peace.

Running Wolf had returned with Little Flower,
whom he had apparently snatched from Three Horses's
lodge. In a forceful tongue, he instructed his daughter to prepare Evening Sky's body for a Mandan funeral, and for Spotted Eagle to remove the children
from the lodge.

The words were no sooner out of his mouth when
the medicine man, Walks with the Sun, arrived. He'd
brought with him his son, Golden Hawk. Pierre knew
exactly what was about to happen. Claire did, as well.
The moment Golden Hawk lifted his hands to recite
an incantation, she objected.

"Uncle, please...my mother would not wish for this."

Pierre stood beside her, guarding her. He didn't like

the way Golden Hawk was looking at her. It was not so much a look of desire, although Pierre would not have liked that, either. It was more one of determination. The kind one showed a wild horse he intended to break.

Pierre was just about to step in front of her, deny the man his view, when Running Wolf shouted something at her in Mandan.

Pierre couldn't recognize the words, but whatever he had said drained the color from Claire's face. Everything within Pierre wanted to attack the Indian, but Claire's knees were buckling. He quickly steadied her instead.

The older medicine man said something. Golden Hawk and Running Wolf seemed to agree. Without the aid of translation, Pierre had no idea what was happening until Golden Hawk and Running Wolf moved to the pallet and lifted Evening Sky's lifeless body from it.

They are going to carry her away. "Stop!" Pierre shouted, but it was Claire who stopped him.

"Let them go," she said. "It is better if you do."

"What?"

"Pierre, please…"

Her words were more than a polite entreaty. She was practically begging him not to interfere, yet she offered no explanation. As the Indians carried Evening Sky to the door, Pierre looked to Little Flower. She offered no explanation, either. At her father's command, she gathered up items for her children and hurried to the door.

He and Claire were now completely alone, and Pierre was thoroughly confused. Why had Claire allowed her uncle to take her mother's body away? It was obvious some tribal medicine rite was to be performed, and he knew she did not wish for it.

"Why didn't you let me stop them?"

"There was nothing you could do."

"I'd like to think there was. What did Running Wolf say to you?"

Her breath hitched. Her chin quivered. "He forbade me to attend my mother's funeral."

Anger surged within him. She might be bound by some tribal custom of respect that kept her from disobeying her uncle, but he was not. "I'll go to Black Cat. I'll go to the captains. I'll make this right."

She caught his arm as he turned for the door. "My uncle said he would make war on the men of the fort if I disobeyed his commands."

A chill raced up his spine. Now he understood why she'd done it, but still. "One man could hardly—"

"It would not be just one man. He says there are others. Many others."

Many? No. Pierre didn't believe that. The Mandans had shown them extreme generosity. "He's bluffing."

"Would you take that chance?"

Captain Lewis's words echoed through his mind. *"We are sixteen hundred miles up the Missouri."* There was more at stake here than a family funeral. He didn't like it, but he knew she was right. *How can she do that?* he wondered. *How can she separate her personal emotions from facts of the matter?* He admired her coolheaded demeanor, yet it irritated him at the same time. He realized he wanted her to need him more than she did.

"Let my uncle claim what he wishes," Claire said, "but my people will know the truth. He will confer it with his own lips."

"He will tell them *why* he has not allowed you to

attend the ceremony," Pierre reasoned. "He will tell them that you worship Christ."

She nodded slowly. "I know where my mother is. I know Whom she served…"

He marveled at her strength, but she was a human being with limitations, and her strength waned. Her chin began to quiver again, her eyes to cloud, but before he could take her hand or offer any physical comfort, she moved away from him.

Outside the drums were beating. They had begun sometime late last night. Their pounding matched the rhythm of his heart. *She does not belong here, any more than I do.*

She was wiping her eyes, trying to regain her composure.

Ask me to take you from this place and I will, he thought. *Ask me…*

"You should return to the fort."

"Come with me."

Her eyes flickered with surprise and something else, something he couldn't quite identify. Offense? Fear? She shook her head. "No. I cannot come to the fort."

"Why not?"

"My presence there will only cause trouble, as your continued presence here may well do."

She might be right about that, but he didn't like the fact that she seemed determined to handle this on her own. "I promised you once that I would look after you."

"And you have. But there are others whom you must protect, as well. You should tell your captains what Running Wolf said. It may well be just an idle threat, but—"

"—they should be aware."

She nodded.

"What will you do?" He wasn't going anywhere until he got a satisfactory answer on that point.

She drew in a breath. "I shall ask Three Horses for permission to shelter in his lodge for a few days. One Who Smiles will be in need of help."

So far Three Horses had proven to be an honorable man, but would the new believer have the strength to defend Claire or her faith if Running Wolf mounted an attack? *It is there or the fort*, he thought, and she had already told him she wouldn't come to the latter. *Why must you be so obstinate?*

He let out a sigh. "Then allow me to escort you to Three Horses's lodge."

"I would appreciate that."

Pierre watched her quietly while she gathered what few belongings she possessed. A couple of deerskin pouches, one that looked to contain the dress she had worn the night they danced. He also thought he caught a glimpse of his letter and the pages of Scripture he had sent her before she hid them away. Last she claimed her mother's cross necklace, and her bag of beads.

He took the bundles from her. She then glanced about the lodge. Tears glistened in her eyes. This had been her home for nearly a year. No matter what difficulties had transpired here, she was having trouble leaving it.

She might not allow him to do much for her, but he would see to this. "Before we go…" He took her hands in his. Pierre couldn't help but notice how perfectly they fit in his. "Let's pray."

She offered no objections, but bowed her head.

"Father God, I ask You to comfort Claire in this

time of loss. I ask for Your protection on her, on this village and on the occupants of the fort. Grant her people knowledge and understanding of You, and may this particular lodge come to know Your peace and salvation."

When she lifted her head, there were tears in her eyes, but Pierre thought she had never looked more beautiful. There was a light in her face, one of hope, of strength and renewal. It quickened his heart.

"Thank you," she whispered.

"It is my honor and privilege, mademoiselle." He led her to the door.

To Claire's great relief, Three Horses welcomed her with open arms. He invited her at once to lay her pallet beside One Who Smiles. By signs and gestures, he offered Pierre a seat at the center fire.

"It is not right that your uncle forbid you to attend your mother's ceremony. I will go," he said. "I will tell Running Wolf you will remain here in my lodge until my wife recovers. Perhaps longer."

Claire bowed graciously. One Who Smiles's time of confinement would last at least a month. If Claire was permitted to stay, she could mourn her mother's passing in safety and in the comfort of those who shared her faith. *"Perhaps longer..."* If Running Wolf allowed her to remain here, if Three Horses would claim her as an adopted sister, then she could be freed from her uncle's marriage demand. Her Christian brother would surely understand her refusal to marry a nonbeliever.

She explained all of this to Pierre when Three Horses left to speak with her uncle. Upon hearing the last part, he looked as though a great weight had been lifted from his shoulders.

He can stop worrying about me now, she thought. She knew he had been or he would not have offered to take her back to the fort. Deep down, however, she wanted to believe there was more to his offer than that. She wanted to believe he was willing to claim her.

Nothing would make her happier than to know the comfort and shelter of his arms—not for a moment but forever—but such a thing could never be. The captains would never allow him to take her westward with the expedition. There were already enough mouths to feed. Likewise, Pierre could not remain in this village. It was far too dangerous for him to do so. *We'd be forced to travel elsewhere.* He would lose his promised land grant, and she would lose what remained of her family.

He would become a displaced adventurer saddled with a half-breed wife. He couldn't return to his wealthy family in New Orleans. White society would not accept her. Mr. Granger back in Illinois had proven that.

Pierre might care for her as a friend, as a Christian brother, but without love, the pure passionate bond between a husband and wife, how long could it last? What if he encountered a woman he truly did love? Surely the sacrifice would be too great. *He would come to despise me.*

But all of this was foolish thought, a waste of time and energy. He had not indicated any interest in marriage to her and he never would. Her mind was simply searching for happiness no matter how fanciful. She was exhausted, worn out from fear and grief.

"I am pleased to know he will look after you," Pierre

said. "He is a good man. You will be safe with him and his family."

"Yes, and now you can return to your true duties. The captains have been most gracious concerning your attention to me, but I would not wish to trespass upon their favor any longer. I would not wish for them to hold it against you."

"You need not worry about me," he said.

"I cannot help but do so." The words were out of her mouth before she could stop them. Claire felt herself flush, hoping he hadn't read more into the comment.

"Any more than I can stop worrying about you," he said. He offered her a sad although still handsome smile. "Are you certain I can't convince you to come to the fort?"

"Yes," she said. *Go*, she silently willed him. *Please go before I tell you that I want to go with you. That I want to be with you no matter where you are.*

"Do not hesitate to send for me if there is the slightest need," he said.

"I won't," she promised.

With visible reluctance, he turned for the door. The ache in her heart swelled. *I am not alone*, she told herself as he left the lodge. *God has provided refuge. He will fill my needs.*

She prayed He would fill her heart, as well.

Chapter Fourteen

Pierre trudged back through the snow toward the fort. He could hear the chants rising from the village. Captain Lewis's order again came to mind.

"Do not interfere with tribal customs. Respect the culture..."

There were many things he dearly admired about the Mandan people—their hard work, their knowledge and ability to live off the land, their hospitality... Chief Black Cat had been the epitome of graciousness when it came to welcoming strangers into his territory. Running Wolf, however, had not shown graciousness, even when it came to his own flesh and blood. He was a controlling, wrathful, manipulative man. How was Pierre to respect someone who did not respect the rights of others?

Claire isn't even permitted to attend her mother's funeral, let alone have any say in how it should be conducted.

He told himself that she was safe, at least for now. Three Horses would look after her while Claire helped tend to his wife and newborn son. *But then what?* One

Who Smiles's time of confinement would last until the end of the month. It was early March now, and Lewis and Clark hoped to resume their westward journey by the first week of April.

He remembered that he once couldn't wait to be on his way. Now the idea of a lengthy winter did not frustrate him so. The thought of leaving this place did.

What will happen to Claire?

It was obvious Captain Lewis was itching to move. Last week he had ordered the keelboat hauled ashore so that repairs could be made to it. It was some feat breaking her from the ice, but the men accomplished it and were presently getting her ready for sail. The boat was to return to Saint Louis with the mail, the scientific specimens, the French oarsmen and disgraced Private Newman. The two pirogues, along with others they planned to build, would convey Pierre and the rest of the party on to the Pacific. Pausing for a moment, he studied the canoes. Was there room in them for one more passenger?

He continued on to the fort. Captain Lewis had asked him to report to his quarters immediately upon arrival. Pierre wondered if the man had been expecting trouble with Running Wolf. He knocked upon the man's door.

"Enter."

Pierre stomped the snow from his feet before stepping inside the hut. Lewis, as usual, was at his desk.

"Ah, Lafayette. How is Miss Manette?"

Pierre noted he didn't ask about Madame Manette. Apparently the wind carried so today that he too could hear the sounds of the funeral procession. Pierre told him of the older woman's final hours. "In the end she passed peacefully, and her daughter was beside her."

Pierre's heart quickened then with the memory of holding Claire in his arms. He pushed the thought aside as Lewis asked, "And her uncle?"

"There lies the issue, sir."

"In what way, pray tell?"

Pierre informed him of Running Wolf's declaration that Claire was unwelcome at her mother's funeral. Then he told him what the warrior had threatened if she disobeyed his command.

The captain's eyes widened with alarm. "Did he speak to you directly? Did he make any signs or gestures?"

"No sir," Pierre replied, "and I can assure you that Claire—" He caught himself. "That is, *Miss Manette* has no intention of disobeying her uncle's command."

Lewis nodded gravely. "Did you observe any changes of behavior or attitude toward you or our other men by the villagers? Did Chief Black Cat offer any cause for alarm?"

"No, sir. In fact, it was quite the opposite." Pierre told him what Three Horses had done, how he had welcomed Claire into his lodge and had given Pierre a seat of honor at his fire.

The captain visibly exhaled. "Then in all likelihood, Running Wolf is simply blustering. He is, after all, experiencing his own grief."

"Yes, sir, but with all due respect, I believe it is more than that. With the exception of our efforts to locate the Sioux, this man has offered little cooperation toward us, and from what I have observed, he even has issues with his own chief."

Lewis again nodded. "He has proven himself in a land of war. Now that he sees that way changing, be it by tribal alliances, trade or the spread of Christianity, he fears he will have no place in the future."

"Frankly, sir, I'm rather concerned for the future."

"You need not be. We'll post extra sentries. Scrutinize our visitors a little more carefully before allowing them admittance into the fort, and keep the men from the village for a few days."

Pierre appreciated Lewis's efforts, and while he was concerned for the captain's well-being and the safety of his comrades here at the fort, that was not his only thought. If he was to remain here, how could he look after Claire? *Her mother has just died. She needs a friend now more than ever.* "If I may ask, sir, how long do you think that will be necessary?"

"Not long, I hope. Black Cat and some of his secondary chiefs were to visit in a few days to discuss the possibility of traveling to Washington to meet with President Jefferson. By then, we shall know better the lay of the land, so to speak. For now, however, it's best to keep to ourselves."

Pierre knew that was the prudent course of action. If there was no interaction then there could be no chance of offending any of the natives, particularly Running Wolf. Still, no matter how much he respected Three Horses, Pierre did not like the idea of leaving Claire solely to his care.

He decided to tell his captain plainly, "I am greatly concerned for Miss Manette's welfare, sir."

"I know you are," Lewis said simply, "but as I advised you once before, it would be better for us all if you refrain from further interference. Life here is different, Lafayette. Though it is harsh and at times, I grant you, unfair, we cannot risk angering our hosts. If the Mandan people turn against us, then so will the other tribes. The safety of the expedition will be the least of concerns. There will be no hope for expanded trade or peaceful relations. The purchase of Louisiana will be for naught if we cannot coexist."

Trade and relations with the neighboring tribes were indeed important, but what about the life of one single woman? *Where does she fit into this plan? Where do I?*

Lewis sensed his inner turmoil. "Is there something else, Lafayette?"

Yes, Pierre wanted to say. "No, sir. Nothing further." And with the captain's permission, he took his leave.

The task of caring for a recovering mother and an infant left Claire little time to brood over her own losses. The still unnamed dark-haired son of One Who Smiles grew stronger each day. For the most part, Claire was ignorant in the ways of tending infants. To a degree, so was her friend. Many of the prescribed rituals One Who Smiles had performed after the birth of Black Raven so many years ago were rooted in superstitions she no longer wished to practice. As a Christian, she now considered the burning of purification incense and ceremonial washings taboo.

So between the two of them, they did what they thought necessary. Claire wrapped the newborn baby in cloths, then changed them when needed. Often she showed One Who Smiles the Bible pages Pierre had given her, and although her friend could not read or understand the words written in French, Claire translated them into Mandan. They also prayed. Claire prayed that this child would grow up in a loving household and eventually a village of faith. One Who Smiles thanked God for a Christian friend to stand beside her. Though the issue had yet to be firmly laid to rest, they did not speak much of Running Wolf's anger, nor of his insistence that Claire marry by the spring. One Who Smiles, like Evening Sky previously, insisted that all would sort itself out in time.

Claire lay awake at night, praying for a happy resolution. She also prayed that God would ease the pain of her heart, that of her mother's departure and Pierre's absence. She had not seen him in days. He had sent a note by way of Black Raven, informing her of Captain Lewis's decision to keep the men on alert and occupied at the fort.

"When Chief Black Cat makes his scheduled visit, we will have a better grasp of the situation," he had written.

From her perspective, the situation was that she was hopelessly in love with a white man, and now, even if one of the Mandan warriors came to Christ, Claire knew she would not be able to marry. *I'd never be able to give any other man my whole heart, be the marriage partner he deserves.*

She sighed heavily, for her situation had not improved in the least. To remain unmarried was a burden on the tribe, unless Three Horses was wholly willing to adopt her as his sister. Claire hoped for that, for it was sisters that One Who Smiles and Claire were fast becoming.

As the woman's strength slowly returned, she began to make clothes for her infant and instructed Claire on how to bend willow branches to frame a cradleboard.

"Now we will cover it with buckskin."

Together they worked to shape the oblong bag that the baby would be placed into eventually. One Who Smiles nodded approval at the result. "You work well, Bright Star. You are quick to learn."

"You are a patient teacher." As the words fell from Claire's lips, the memory of working with Pierre on vocabulary lists drifted though her mind. He had given her the same compliment.

"When I have more strength, I shall decorate the brace with strings of beads so that they may sway and tinkle and amuse my child when we walk," One Who Smiles said.

It reminded Claire of what her own mother had done. Though Claire had long outgrown the need for a cradleboard, Evening Sky had kept hers hanging on a peg on the wall in their cabin back in Illinois. In her younger years, Claire had been constantly strapped to her mother's back and traveled everywhere, just as One Who Smiles's son would soon be.

Tears collected in Claire's eyes. She missed her mother terribly, but she did her best to remind herself that Evening Sky was now at peace and reunited with Claire's father.

"Who are you thinking of, Bright Star? Your mother? Or the handsome Frenchman?"

Claire flushed. So her feelings for Pierre were obvious to her friend. Had they been obvious to him, as well? Was that the true reason he was staying away?

"I was thinking of my mother," she said, but there was no point hiding what this woman already knew. Pierre was always in the back of her thoughts. One Who Smiles had suffered her own great disappointments in her life. Claire might learn something from her. "I do, however, think of him, as well."

The woman smiled. "You are right to do so. He would make a considerate husband."

"Yes, he would, but such things cannot be."

"Because of your uncle?"

"Because of many things."

A week later, Running Wolf appeared at the lodge. Thankfully Three Horses was in attendance. He had just sat down to eat the meal Claire had been preparing. She couldn't help but jolt at the sudden appearance of her uncle, so much so that she nearly dropped the bowl of stew she had been about to serve Three Horses.

Surprisingly, Running Wolf appeared not to have come in anger. He entered with a placid look on his face. Taking the man's arrival at face value, Three Horses offered him a seat at the fire. Claire delivered venison stew and tea to each of them, then returned to the cooking pot to fill a bowl for One Who Smiles. Her hands were shaking badly, but she managed to serve the remaining food, then take a seat beside her friend. Stealthily they both eyed the men.

Running Wolf presented Three Horses with a handsome knife. "A gift to you on the birth of your son," he said.

Proudly accepting it, Three Horses then presented Running Wolf with a colorful woven blanket. "A gift to you for allowing your niece to care for my family."

Running Wolf nodded and accepted his gift. Claire watched silently, unsure exactly of what was taking place. Were the two men making a contract? Would Running Wolf allow her to remain here? Was he freeing her from her marital obligation to the tribe? One

Who Smiles didn't seem certain, either. Claire could see the questions in her eyes. Still, she patted Claire's hand hopefully.

"Bright Star will stay until your squaw's confinement has ended," Running Wolf said. "Then I wish for her to return to my lodge."

Three Horses said nothing to that. Claire held her breath. One Who Smiles continued to hold her hand.

"I have been given two horses with sleek black manes," Running Wolf said proudly. "It is a very good price for one such as her."

Claire's heart slammed into her ribs. So her uncle had gone ahead and brokered a marriage deal after all! To whom was she to be given?

Three Horses asked just that.

"Golden Hawk wishes to make her his squaw," Running Wolf announced. "This will please the spirits. The medicine man's son will return Bright Star to the path of our ancestors."

One Who Smiles's grip tightened on Claire's hand. By now she was trembling all over. Was this really to be her lot in life? Was she to be wed to a man who was not simply unaware of God's saving grace but flatly opposed to it? She had seen how this man treated his animals. Golden Hawk would try to force her to submit to his ways, and beat her if she did not.

Three Horses knew this, as well. "Bright Star is now a guest in my lodge." He turned to her and, in a manner highly uncustomary in these parts, asked, "Do you wish to wed the medicine man's son?"

"No!" she cried.

He turned back to Running Wolf. "She has given her answer."

Running Wolf was unfazed. Apparently he had expected such and was prepared. "I have allowed her to remain here because of the birth of your son, but as her uncle, I retain authority over her. She may reside in your lodge until the new moon, and then she will return to mine."

Claire knew full well what would happen then. She would not see the April moon's first quarter before being wed. Three Horses knew it, as well. He lifted his chin. "She will not return to you. I will welcome her here, always."

"You cannot," Running Wolf insisted. "She is not of your clan. I must give permission to you, and I will not, because you also have forsaken our ancestors' ways."

"Then I will pay your bride price."

Running Wolf looked momentarily shocked, and Claire felt the air rush from her lungs. She realized what her friend was proposing. Running Wolf did, as well. "You would take a second wife? White men take no second wives."

Claire's head was spinning. Although she appreciated Three Horses's attempts to rescue her from Golden Hawk, becoming his lesser wife was not the solution. It wasn't fair to One Who Smiles, let alone the fact that it went against the principles of Scripture.

Oh God...please...

"I will not accept your bride price," Running Wolf said. "No matter what you offer."

"Then I shall go to Black Cat."

Running Wolf gave back the blanket. Three Horses returned the knife. Rising, Claire's uncle stomped from the lodge. One Who Smiles's husband promptly exited, as well, presumably on his way to see the chief.

The baby was crying, but neither Claire nor One Who Smiles moved to settle him. Both women were far too overcome with shock. After a few moments, One Who Smiles spoke. Her voice was soft but forced. It was the sound of a woman resigned to make the best of a terrible situation.

"If this is what must be, Bright Star, then I welcome you."

"No," Claire said. "This is not the way."

With a sudden burst of energy, she got to her feet, dashed from the lodge. She ran toward the village entrance. The icy crust that had previously covered the snow was now giving way to slush. Still at full speed, she pressed on.

I will leave this place! I will not agree to Three Horses's solution, and I will certainly not marry Golden Hawk! Lifting her skirts higher, she ran toward the river.

On its bank, she froze. Where was she to go? She couldn't go to the fort, although that was exactly what she wanted to do. She wanted to run to Pierre and beg him to take her from this place. *But I cannot do that. Running Wolf will lose the horses that Golden Hawk has given him, and that could anger him enough to drive him to start war on the members of the expedition.*

She looked back toward the village. She couldn't return there, either. Surely Chief Black Cat was growing tired of the trouble she was causing him. If he didn't force her to marry Golden Hawk, he was liable to wed her to Three Horses on the spot just to end this matter.

She turned then toward the west. The endless prairie stretched out before her. From the horizon, a man

was approaching. He was clad in buckskin and shoul-
dered a musket. Claire recognized him at once by the
way her heart leaped at the sight of him.

Recognizing her, Pierre broke into a full run.
"What's wrong?" he asked as he came charging toward her.

She could see the concern in his eyes, hear it in his
voice. Unable to control her emotions, she flung herself into his arms and spilled the entire sordid tale. "I
don't know what to do! I don't know where to go!"

"Shh…" He cradled her head against his chest.
"Shh. I'll take care this… It will be alright." He smelled
of black powder and wood smoke. In his arms she felt
safe. She truly believed that he *would* make everything right. She didn't know how or what he would do
to accomplish that, and she was too tired, too weak to
consider any of the potential consequences of his actions or hers.

"Come," he said, taking her by the hand. She followed him to the fort.

They entered the palisade. The gate shut securely
behind them. Pierre led her to her old hut, the one
she had shared with her mother. Depositing her in Sacagawea's care, he then headed off to request an audience with his captains.

"What is it now, Lafayette?"

Pierre detected a hint of irritability in Captain
Lewis's voice. Knowing that hesitancy would only
further annoy the man, he cleared his throat and
plunged in.

"Sir, it is about Miss Manette…"

As he told the man all that she had revealed to him

on the riverbank, Lewis listened quietly. His face was unreadable.

"Sir, surely you are as disturbed by this as I am," Pierre said. "Would it be possible to take on one more member for the expedition?"

Lewis eyed now him with a look of incredulity, but he didn't say no, so Pierre pressed further. "The mademoiselle is strong and quite skilled in tanning, doctoring, foraging for food—"

"We are not taking a woman along with us."

"But Sacagawea—"

"—Sacagawea speaks Shoshoni, the language of the western tribes, and she has a *husband*."

Pierre understood the meaning. Lewis wasn't going to be responsible for an unmarried woman in a dangerous unknown land, not when he was charged with the responsibility of looking after his men. Pierre then said something that surprised even him.

"What if *I* were to claim her as my wife? What if *I* alone took responsibility?"

At that the captain's chair scraped across the rough-hewn floor. He pushed to his feet. His face was disciplined and controlled, but his words had bite. "Have you lost your senses, man? Has infatuation so blinded you that you are no longer capable of reason?"

"With all due respect, sir, I am not infatuated."

"Then you claim you are in love?"

Pierre swallowed hard. Was that it? No…it couldn't be. "No, sir. I merely wish to do my duty, as any Christian gentleman would."

Pierre saw the flicker of offense in his captain's eyes. He hadn't meant to imply that his officer wasn't such a man. He simply—

"At what cost?" Lewis asked. "What if *your wife* becomes ill along the journey? What if some hostile Pacific tribe holds us hostage and seeks to make her a slave? Would you be able to do your duty then? Would you think clearly, rationally, for the benefit of your expedition brothers *and her*, or would you forge a war on your own?"

He saw the man's point. Pierre didn't want to believe he would fall to pieces or do anything to jeopardize his fellow comrades, but he realized he had already come very close to doing so several times when he feared for Claire's safety. *And if someone were to seek to harm Claire physically in my presence, I would come unhinged.*

"I know you believe it your duty to protect her," Lewis said, his tone softening slightly. "That is an admirable quality, but believe me when I tell you, she is safer here among her own people than out there in the wild."

Pierre knew Lewis truly believed that. He was not a man to say one thing and think another, but Pierre wholeheartedly disagreed with him. The captain had not seen the way Running Wolf looked at her, spoke to her. *He hated her.* And as for Golden Hawk, Pierre had yet to forget the lascivious glare he'd given Claire when he entered her lodge. Pierre knew exactly what the medicine man's son had been thinking, and it sickened him.

A decision had to be made. Pierre had always wanted to believe that his quest for adventure, his reason for signing on to this expedition, was more than just pursuit of vainglory. He believed God had a plan for him, a plan that could not be fulfilled in New Orleans.

Perhaps this was it. This woman needed to be rescued. It would mean sacrificing his dream of seeing the Pacific Ocean, of bringing down that grizzly brown bear. He'd have to forgo his land grant and the fame that would otherwise be forever attached to his name by being a member of the Lewis and Clark expedition. In all likelihood he'd be forced to return to New Orleans, at least for a while, once again come under his father's authority in terms of his shipping business.

And that presented another problem. Would his parents accept an Indian woman for a daughter-in-law? True, she was half French, but would that be enough? And could Claire be happy there?

He did not know. But at least she would not have to choose between polygamy and being forced to marry a man who scorned her faith and who would treat her as a slave, make her old before her time. *I will not allow that.*

His mind was made up. He would make whatever sacrifice needed. It was the right thing to do. "What about the keelboat, sir?"

Lewis's eyes narrowed. "What are you saying, Lafayette?"

Pierre drew in a breath. There was no going back now. "I'm saying that with your permission, I would like to return to Saint Louis with the keelboat—that is, myself and Miss Manette."

"As your wife."

"Yes, sir. Please do not misunderstand me. I am greatly honored to be a member of your expedition, and if I could, I would continue westward."

"But you won't."

"No, sir, not now. I believe I have been given a higher duty."

Lewis drew in a calculated breath, then conceded Pierre's point with a slight nod. "Will the lady accept you?" he asked.

In all honesty, Pierre hadn't even thought of that. "I don't know," he said.

"Then you had better go and find out."

Chapter Fifteen

Claire did her best to rein in her emotions as Sacagawea handed her a cup of tea. Her hands were still shaking. "Thank you," she whispered.

Sacagawea nodded gracefully. "Drink," she said, "and then there is more."

Claire could barely swallow what she had, but she was determined to honor her hostess by partaking of the young mother's kindness. Sacagawea smiled at her sweetly. How much of Claire's story she knew, she did not let on, but Claire realized she could indeed relate. Sacagawea had been taken from her family, a captive, a prisoner of war, when she was but a child. She and Otter Woman had been claimed by a man old enough to be their father, almost their grandfather.

Claire, however, had never once heard Sacagawea complain about Charbonneau or his second wife, but she could not help but wonder if the young woman had ever wished for something more. Had she wished for a dashing young man who would make her heart thump? Had she wished for love?

Or did she simply accept her fate and try to make the

best of it? Part of Claire wanted to ask, but the girl was two years younger than she, and Claire wasn't about to burden her with her troubles. Sacagawea had enough of her own. She was about to trek into the wilderness with a baby not yet two months old.

Little Jean Baptiste cried from his place on his mother's pallet. Sacagawea immediately picked him up, cuddled him close. "Ah, Pomp, do not cry. You shall upset our honored guest."

"I assure you, he will not," Claire said, doing her best to smile.

Sacagawea smiled back and handed her the baby, as if the simple act of holding a little one could right everything wrong in the world. Claire took the boy willingly but felt no joy. The dark-haired child was half French, half Indian. *What future lies in store for him?*

Her conscience was pricked. She had left another child back in the village, a child she was supposed to be caring for during her friend's recovery.

In the midst of my personal quandary, I abandoned them. Then another thought pressed her mind. Had she abandoned her family, as well? *If their eternity is so important to me, shouldn't I have stayed with them, despite the cost? Wouldn't I have done whatever necessary, instead of seeking a way of escape?*

Claire closed her eyes. Guilt raked her soul. *I have allowed myself to become distracted by my own plight.* She told herself she had not come looking for Pierre, that *he* had found her, that *he* had brought her here, but she knew full well she had hoped he would find her.

I shamelessly threw myself into his arms. She could feel herself blush from head to toe. *He said he would take care of the situation, but how? Will he go to Run-*

ning Wolf? Will they face each other in anger? Will there be bloodshed? Will it entangle other members of the tribe?

She shuddered at the thought. The men of the expedition had weapons far more advanced than Mandan knives and arrows. If forced to use them, then the American captains' hopes of peaceful relations would forever be lost.

Those who are of like mind stay together, she thought. Surely neighboring tribes would set aside personal differences and rally against the whites. There would be all-out war. She felt light-headed at the thought, and her stomach rolled. *Oh God...please... tell me what to do and I'll do it. I'll do anything... anything...*

Sacagawea touched her on the shoulder. "Do not fret, Bright Star. All will be well in time."

Her mother's word echoed in her mind. *"Trust..."*

Claire drew in a ragged breath. *Either God loves me or He doesn't. Either He is with me or He isn't.* She knew the truth, and thinking on it, a certain peace settled over Claire. *I must return home. I am not supposed to be here. I must return home.*

There was a knock on the door. Sacagawea rose to answer it. It was Pierre. He looked sheepish and uncomfortable.

"Come. Sit by the fire," Sacagawea beckoned, but he declined. Sensing a desire for privacy on Pierre's part, the mother then reclaimed her child. Bundling little Jean Baptiste in a buffalo skin, she left the room.

Claire wished she had stayed. *What am I to say to him? I have acted so selfishly and stupidly.*

He was not happy. She could tell by the look in his

eyes. He cleared his throat and then rubbed his whiskered face. "I have just come from speaking with Captain Lewis," he said. "I asked if you might join our expedition."

Join? Had she heard him correctly?

"But he said no…for various reasons."

He did not elaborate on what those reasons were, and Claire did not question them. Her mind was still trying to process the fact that he had actually gone to the captains and asked such a thing on her behalf.

And they said no. Was that why he wasn't happy? Did he *want* to her to come with him? Did he want her to do so for reasons that went far beyond chivalrous protection? Her heart quickened. Her mouth went dry. Were her feelings for him reciprocated? She had at times thought perhaps they might be. There were times when he looked at her that way—

He was speaking again. Claire tried to process the words. "I then asked Captain Lewis if we might return to Saint Louis on the keelboat." He cleared his throat once more. "With you as…my wife. The captain agreed to that."

A surge like lightning jolted through her, but the thrill of the words *my wife* was quickly tempered by the context.

Pierre's face was stoic, not at all the expression of a young man in love. Now she understood the cause of his unhappiness. He would claim her. He would protect her. He was willing to become a dutiful, dependable husband, but to do so, he would have to give up his dream.

Laying aside a dream because it no longer fit one's frame was one thing. Being forced to put it away because of someone else, someone you could live without, was quite another. As much as she would have loved to carry his name, his children, she could not allow him to do this. She could never live with herself if she did.

I have to go home. Hadn't she just been so certain of that fact? Hadn't she just felt a peace about doing so, one that defied all reason and logic? Why didn't she feel it as strongly now?

The French side of her felt she would explode with emotions, all of them conflicting. The Mandan part of her kept them carefully contained. "You have honored me greatly with your offer," she said quietly, although she nearly choked on the words. "However, I must decline."

A look of disbelief flooded his face. At first she thought it was born of concern, and then she realized it was something else entirely. It was arrogance. "Decline?" he said. "You came to me frantic, in tears, and then, when I offer you a solution, you choose not to accept it?"

Perhaps she deserved the rebuke, but she didn't like the attitude with which it had been delivered. Her own ire was raised. What did he expect, that she should fall down on her knees and thank him? Did he think she should accept him just because he had asked? If he did, then he was little better than the men of her tribe.

"Have you nothing else to say?" he asked.

Oh, she did. She had plenty to say, but she couldn't decide if she wanted to rail at him or confess her love. *Neither is the appropriate response. God, help me... I want to follow Your path.*

She drew in a breath and spoke with the most controlled voice she could muster. "I have been weak in my faith. I was frightened. It was wrong of me to involve you in this. Please forgive me for doing so."

"That is not the issue, Claire. My forgiveness, whether needed or not, won't change your circumstances."

Why must he make this so difficult? "No, it won't, but the fact remains that I will not accept your offer of marriage. I *cannot* accept it."

"You cannot?"

"If you give up your place on the expedition, if you leave *now* and return to Saint Louis on the keelboat, you will be no better off than when you left New Orleans."

His eyes narrowed. "What are you saying, exactly?"

"You will lose your land grant."

She saw his jaw twitch. Had he not thought of that before? Had Captain Lewis failed to remind him? "You are a man who wishes to make something of himself," she said.

"I'd like to think that I already have made something of myself."

She heard the bite in his tone. He had obviously taken what she'd said in the wrong way. It wasn't that *she* would not marry a man without property. That was not what was important to her. "I do not wish to offend you, Pierre. I greatly appreciate your willingness to make such a sacrifice…but I must return to my family."

"So you can become wife to Golden Hawk? You think your life will be better with him? Or will you become a second wife to Three Horses?"

"No," she said firmly. That much, at least, she did know. "I will speak to Three Horses. I will speak to my uncle. I will press my case to Chief Black Cat if necessary."

"You have done that already," he said, "and you have failed."

"Then I will do so again,"

"And if you fail again?"

To that she said nothing.

"Why must you be so stubborn?" he asked. "Why must you insist on having your own way?"

His patience was wearing thin. So was her resolve. She had to remain steadfast or else *he* would regret it one day. The Pacific Ocean, the possibility of "what if," would haunt his thoughts. And it would be her fault. She would not allow herself to cost him his dreams.

"Why are you so intent on having your own?" she asked. "You do not offer yourself in love, but duty. Did you not leave New Orleans to escape a similar fate? How long would it be before you tired of me?"

With that he looked thoroughly confused. "What is it exactly that you want?" he asked.

Claire swallowed back the lump filling her throat. She knew she had to say goodbye. The longer she lingered, the harder it would be. "What I want most, you cannot give me."

She bolstered her resolve with formality. She could not confess her love for him, confess she would sacrifice her own happiness for the sake of his. "I thank you for your offer of marriage, Mr. Lafayette, but regretfully, I must decline."

She dared not read his expression now. With a quick curtsy, she hurried then to the door.

As Pierre stood in the hut where they had first forged their friendship, he didn't know whether to feel relieved or rebuffed, appreciative or angered. He had offered Claire his hand in marriage, something he swore he'd never do unless he was truly deeply in love.

And she refused me! Stubborn to the last! Determined to handle things on her own!

So be it, then. He had done all he could do to help her. *If she doesn't want my help, if she doesn't think I've yet made enough of myself, there are plenty of women back in lower Louisiana who do!*

And at that, he recognized the real cause of his anger. His pride was wounded. Having fallen prey to such a sin, he raked his fingers though his unruly hair. *I am better than this...or at least, I should be.* He inwardly groaned. Now self-pity was advancing. What was it about the woman that made him feel so conflicted, so addlepated, so weak in reason? He had never acted this way before. Lewis had asked if he was in love. Pierre had insisted he was not, and if scattered thoughts and wayward emotions were a precursor to such a condition, then he *never* wished to experience them further. *I will put Claire Manette from my mind once and for all. It may take me from here to the Pacific to do so, but I will do it.*

Yet he knew he was only fooling himself. He'd never forget her. He'd never be able to stop worrying about her, and every Indian woman he met as he journeyed westward would remind him of her.

Pierre sighed. *What will happen to her?* Evening Sky had once insisted that God would bring healing. Would He bring healing to Running Wolf's heart? Could a medicine man's son eventually come to exchange a lifetime of spirit worship for the worship of the true Great Spirit?

All he knew was that such things were out of his

control. "Lord, take care of her," he whispered, and with that he exited the hut.

Outside the main gate was shut tight. Claire was presumably on her way back to the village. Thinking of such, Pierre felt an unmistakable pang to his chest.

Captain Lewis stepped from his quarters. Meeting Pierre in the middle of the parade ground, he asked, "Well?"

"She said no." The pang in Pierre's chest intensified. Now it was more of a sharp pain, like the cut of a knife. Inadvertently he rubbed his ribs. *Perhaps I am growing ill*, he thought, *maybe an ague, or perhaps I've eaten tainted meat.* Whatever it was, he hoped it would soon pass.

"Then I presume you will continue westward?" Lewis inquired emotionlessly.

"Yes, sir," Pierre said, but the words nearly died on his lips.

The officer nodded curtly. Obviously he was ready to move on to other matters. "Report, then, to Captain Clark. He's in the grove, overseeing the construction of the new pirogues."

"Yes, sir." Pierre didn't hint at his oncoming illness. It was a luxury the expedition could not afford. *Whatever it is, I'll simply work through it.*

He headed for the gate. Upon its opening, he started up the hill. The wind was hard and cold today, but the ground was softening. Winter was reluctantly giving way to spring. If the weather cooperated, the expedition planned to leave in two weeks' time. *If God grants us safety and success on our journey, we'll pass this way again.*

He couldn't help but again wonder in what condition

he would find Claire. Would he find her an ostracized loner, or the unhappy wife of the medicine man's son? There was a third possibility. *One or more of the warriors could come to Christ. She may be able to seek a husband of her own liking.* A year or two from now, he might find her the happy wife of a Mandan Christian, and *with a child*.

He wasn't sure why, but that last image disturbed him as much as the others.

Determined to soldier on, he continued up the hill. His fellow expedition members were hard at work digging out the canoes. Pierre had been around boats most of his life and could tell immediately the timber they were using was not the best quality. They were making do with what they had, but the pirogues would not last long.

We'll be digging new ones again soon, he thought. The idea did not appeal to him. Even the thought of taking the canoes into the river and experiencing the vast unknown failed to lift his spirit. Work today seemed like drudgery. Nevertheless, he picked up an ax and began to chop. The illness he had previously felt gave way to determination. His comrades were by no means lazy, but it soon became apparent that Pierre was outpacing them.

"Better stay out of Lafayette's way," Colter remarked. "He's liable to take your foot or arm off, as well."

The men laughed.

"Got his anger flowing," Howard said. "What's amiss, Frenchie? You get into a fight with that pretty little squaw of yours? She refuse to give you a kiss?"

Pierre immediately stilled his ax, shot Howard a

glare for his caddish remark. It was nothing like that— *but if Howard has any idea of attempting to stake his own claim...*

Colter sensed Pierre's unspoken threat and nudged his comrade on the shoulder. Taking post at their canoe, Captain Clark issued a silent warning. Colter and Howard returned to work. After a moment, so did Pierre.

Chop. Chop. Chop... All Pierre allowed himself to focus on was that simple motion.

When Captain Clark was satisfied all was in order, he left to visit one of the chiefs in the northern village. Pierre and the rest of the men continued to work. It wasn't until twilight that they walked back to the fort. Supper was short and quiet. Pierre's arms and back were aching. He was certain he was tired enough to fall into bed and find sleep at once.

Captain Lewis had other plans for him. Whether Pierre had actually impressed the officer with the pace and quality of his work today or Lewis was simply trying to keep him occupied, he did not know, but the captain ordered him to begin crating the scientific specimens that were to be shipped to President Jefferson via the keelboat.

Among the preserved skins, pressed plants and seeds were live exhibits—a prairie chicken, a burrowing squirrel and four chattering magpies. During the transfer of the magpies to a larger crate, one escaped. As it fluttered noisily about the hut, Lewis looked up from the parchments he'd been sorting and shot Pierre a perturbed look.

He did his best to quickly fetch the bird, yet his thoughts were hardly focused on the hunt. He couldn't help but liken the darting magpie to Claire. The creature beat her wings and her beak against every wall in the room, fluttering about, refusing assistance, determined to find her own path to freedom.

Coming near enough to stir one's senses, then darting quickly away when threatened. He wondered then if that was not part of the problem. Did Claire feel threatened by his proposal? It was possible, especially given the anger he had displayed at her refusal of it. Did she think if she became his wife he would take away her freedom, her ability to make decisions for herself?

The magpie lighted on the captain's cot. Pierre stealthily reached for the man's tricorn and tossed it over the creature.

"Adroitly done," Lewis said, and then he went back to shuffling his reports.

Pierre carefully retrieved the frightened bird. He could feel her heart thumping wildly beneath her smooth black, white and iridescent feathers. For a moment he was tempted to open the door and toss her into the air. Wasn't freedom in her best interest? Reluctantly he placed the magpie with the others. The bird offered no chatter now. Neither did the rest of them. They only hopelessly beat their wings against the crate that held them.

Turning from them, Pierre continued packing. When he was finally allowed to return to his own quarters, he fell face-first onto his pallet, expecting sleep to come at once. It didn't.

He was still thinking of Claire.

Claire had cried all the way back to the village. Half of those tears fell because she knew Pierre had misunderstood her motives. His insinuation that she did not think him a worthy suitor had cut her to the core. The fact that she *had* to allow him to continue to think that was the cause of the rest. If he knew she had refused him based on what *he'd* be forced to sacrifice, he would surely try to convince her to change her mind.

He was simply that kind of man. She had seen him intervene on behalf of others regardless of the consequences to himself before. He cared for her people. He cared for *her*. He just didn't love her, at least not in the way she wanted. Her mother had left all she had known for her father because she had wanted to do so. She loved him with her whole heart and soul and he, her. Their shared loved was the bedrock of their life together. If Pierre gave up his dreams, the marriage would not stand the test and pressures of time, at least not happily.

Leaving the fort had been the hardest thing she had ever done, even harder than leaving Illinois, harder than watching her uncle and the medicine men take away her mother's body for an ancestral funeral. Were even harder times to come?

She could not be joined to an unbeliever, and she could not become a second wife to Three Horses. Still, she had been certain she was to return to this village, and that certainty grew with every step she took toward it. Yet the steps were not without fear.

God help me. Please show me that I am doing what is right.

The first thing she knew she had to do was apologize to One Who Smiles for leaving her unattended. She would then move to the difficult task of declining Three Horses's proposal. She prayed he would understand.

Thankfully the warrior was not in the lodge at the time of her arrival, and One Who Smiles bore Claire no grudge. In fact, she welcomed her with open arms, refusing Claire even the opportunity to apologize fully.

"I know you did not intend to be neglectful," she said. "You have much in your heart."

Claire greatly appreciated her friend's understanding. Yes, she did have much in her heart.

"It was actually good you left as you did," her friend said. "It gave Three Horses and me time to discuss matters."

"Has he spoken yet with Chief Black Cat?"

"No."

No? Then was he having second thoughts about his proposal? "I thought he was going to do so when Running Wolf left the lodge."

"So did I," One Who Smiles said, "but later, when Three Horses returned, he said he had not gone to speak with our great chief but with the Great Creator."

So he had gone to pray. Claire drew strength in that. "Did God give him any answers?"

Her friend nodded slowly. "Three Horses believes it is not right to take you as a wife. He believes that he should continue to try to persuade Running Wolf to allow you to remain here as my friend."

Claire heaved a sigh. *Thank You, Lord.*

"I hope this does not disappoint you," One Who Smiles said.

"No. Not at all. When your husband seeks the Great Spirit's wisdom, he does right by us all."

One Who Smiles nodded. "I told Three Horses you would say such a thing." She leaned a little closer, whispered as if the walls were listening. "I know with which man your heart truly lies."

Claire felt herself flush. "Yes," she admitted softly, "but in my heart alone he will remain."

"He does not care for you?"

"He does, but not in that way."

One Who Smiles patted Claire's hand gently. "Sometimes a man does not know his own mind. Sometimes it takes time."

Claire appreciated the comment but knew it would take much more than time. She refused to dwell on it, however. Her adopted family had welcomed her back. Claire counted that as a blessing.

Three Horses returned just as dusk was falling. When Claire handed him his tea as he took his place by the fire, he said, "Running Wolf says you may lodge with my family until the half moon…"

Which meant a week from now.

"…but I will continue to press him further."

Claire nodded. Nothing was said about the former marriage proposal. Evidently Three Horses assumed One Who Smiles had already explained his change of heart.

When nightfall came, Claire wrapped the couple's newborn son in fresh cloths, brought One Who Smiles an extra buffalo skin to keep her and her child warm and gave the fire one last stir. Rhythmic snoring drifted upward toward the center opening of the lodge like smoke toward the starlit sky.

Three Horses and Black Raven were already fast asleep. Claire couldn't help but wonder if a similar scene was taking place in Running Wolf's lodge. Was

Spotted Eagle breathing deeply? Was River Song smiling in her sleep?

Do they miss me as much as I miss them? Do they understand why I am not with them, or do they think I have abandoned them?

She thought then of the dark-haired Frenchman lying at the fort, and wondered the same of him. Did she hold any place in his thoughts?

No, she told herself. *He is probably thinking now of the Pacific, as he should be.*

With a sigh, she settled down on her own pallet, whispered a prayer for his safekeeping and another of thanks. Running Wolf would let her stay for at least another week. For that she was most grateful.

I will not think of life beyond that.

Chapter Sixteen

According to Chief Black Cat, no one in his village had a quarrel with the men of the fort except Running Wolf.

"But he would not be so foolish as to go against my hospitality toward you," Black Cat insisted by way of Charbonneau.

So tensions at the fort waned. Still the captains kept the men on premises and well-occupied. April was fast approaching. The snow was nearly gone and the ice on the river was breaking into giant chunks, drifting south.

For five days Pierre kept a most disciplined pace. There were no visits to the villages, no hunting excursions or idle time. All of the men had been doing extra duty, but Pierre especially was kept busy round the clock. Today he was digging out the last of the canoes. But despite his occupation, he couldn't help but think of Claire.

Had he misjudged her? She was an obstinate woman, an outspoken one, as well, but never in a selfish or hard-hearted way. Had she brought up the business of the land grant because she feared *he* had not thought of it? Was she concerned about the effect losing something so valuable would have on him? She knew the lure of property, and she had experienced firsthand how badly it felt to have it stolen away.

He pondered that line of thinking a little longer. *Does she think herself in the same category as Phillip Granger—if she accepted my proposal she'd be stealing the land away from me?*

If that was her motive, and he was becoming more convinced it was by the second, he felt even more ashamed for becoming angry with her. *She was acting in my best interest, and yet I accused her of thinking I wasn't good enough.*

There was something else she had said that puzzled him. He had asked her what she wanted.

"What I want most, you cannot give me..."

That sentence haunted him. What had she meant by that? And why was he so desperate to understand? Why did he want so badly to give her whatever she needed to make her happy? *Captain Lewis asked if I was in love with her. Am I?*

He knew he was definitely attracted to her. He'd been fighting it since he'd first laid eyes on her. The way she carried herself, the way she smiled, the way her nose wrinkled and the way she drew in her lips when she got angry. Even the other day when arguing with her, he'd felt the sudden impulse to draw those pert little lips back out with his own. Christian decency had kept him from doing so. *One does not go about sporting with a woman who is not one's wife.*

The conflict within him intensified. *I did ask her to marry me...but I did so for her protection...*

Protection, though, from what, exactly? Was it her uncle's anger or another man's arms?

Though he wished to deny it, Pierre was forced to admit that the thought of anyone else holding her, kissing her made him burn with jealousy. He stilled his ax, realizing at last what he felt for her went way beyond the bounds of Christian charity. He *was* in love with her, and he had been for some time.

He couldn't help but laugh at his own naïveté and unawareness. All this time he'd told himself he wasn't the marrying kind, that adventure was all he wanted. But the truth was, he had not been inclined to marry before because he had not found the right woman.

And now that I have...

His jubilation was short-lived. The fact remained that Claire had refused him. She could not come to the Pacific, and she *would not* return to Saint Louis. *The only choice left is to remain here.*

Pierre drew in a breath. Could he? Physically, yes. He'd grown accustomed to the harshness of the wilderness and was confident he could survive its challenges. The remoteness of this land did not threaten him. Chief Black Cat had already allowed another white man into his village, namely Charbonneau, and according to the chief, relations between the Mandan and whites were friendly. *Black Cat would welcome me.* Running Wolf, however, would not.

And what about Claire? He had won her friendship, but could he convince her the land grant no longer mattered to him? Could he win her heart?

The light suddenly dawned on him. *"What I want most, you cannot give me..."* Beyond the salvation of her family, of her tribe, he knew there was one thing she wanted more than anything in this life. A marriage like her parents had, one of mutual respect, faith and love.

Had he already won her heart? Had she refused him because she thought she did not have his? His mind raced over their last encounter—the looks, the way she'd come to him, clung to him, the fact that she had encouraged him not to forsake the expedition... The possibility made his heart pound. *What if she refused because she thinks more of me than she does herself? What if she thinks I proposed only out of a sense of duty?*

"How long would it be before you tired of me?" she had asked.

He hadn't understood what she meant at the time, but now he did, or at least, he hoped he did.

But was he too late? Had he missed his opportunity? Had she become the wife of Three Horses, or worse, Golden Hawk? *God forbid it*, he prayed. *Please don't punish her for my thick-headed behavior.*

"You gonna keep standing there, Frenchie?" Private Howard asked, "or are you going to help us carry her to the river?"

The last of the cottonwood dugouts had been completed and was now to be tested for its worthiness. Pierre hastily lifted his end of the pirogue, carried her to the riverbank. Captain Clark was on hand to supervise the inspection. Satisfied with the canoe's performance, Clark ordered the men be given rest for the remainder of the day. Pierre was most grateful. He couldn't wait another minute longer.

"Sir, if I may, I'd like your permission to travel to the village," Pierre said.

Clark eyed him somewhat suspiciously for a moment, waiting for further information. Pierre did not wish to divulge any more than he must. He was certain Captain Lewis had already informed him of Pierre's conflicted heart, and of his previous decision to leave the expedition. He did not wish for this man to try to dissuade him. "There is something that I need to set right, sir."

Matters might already be far beyond his control, but he knew one thing. He had to apologize to her. The blue Pacific, as beautiful as it might be could no longer hold him captive. He'd forever compare every wonder of nature to her. He wanted her to know that, even if it was too late.

"Very well, Lafayette," Clark said. "I'm headed into the village myself to dine with Chief Black Cat. You may accompany me."

"Thank you, sir."

Pierre followed Clark as far as the main village square. Then he turned for the lodge of Three Horses. Black Raven was sitting at the entrance, stringing a new bow. He welcomed Pierre with a smile and an enthusiastic, *"Bonjour, monsieur."*

So Claire is making progress in language skills, Pierre couldn't help but think with a smile. "And a good day to you, young warrior," Pierre replied in Mandan.

"Père... Mère..." Black Raven couldn't think of the words to explain that his father and mother were inside the lodge, so he simply motioned for Pierre to follow him.

Claire, however, was nowhere to be found. Pierre felt an immediate pang of disappointment followed by a surge of fear. Had she told Three Horses she would not marry him? Had she gone back to her uncle's lodge?

He did his best to offer pleasant greetings to Three Horses and One Who Smiles. The warrior bid him to join them at the fire.

"I have come to speak to Bright Star," he said in his best Mandan.

Three Horses nodded slowly.

"I have come to apologize to her. I spoke harshly to her when we last parted."

Three Horses held up his hand. "This is no matter for my ears," he said.

"It isn't?" His heart beat a little faster.

The warrior smiled. "It is but yours and hers alone."

What was the man saying? So Claire was not his betrothed? Where was she, then?

One Who Smiles must have sensed his thoughts, for she offered Pierre a comforting smile, one that held a hint of mirth. "Do not fear," she said. "All is well. Bright Star has gone to dig roots with her cousin."

"With Little Flower?"

"Yes."

That was a good sign, was it not? Then she was still lodging here. And if Running Wolf was allowing his daughter to associate with Claire again, then perhaps his heart was thawing.

"You are welcome to wait for her return," Three Horses said.

"Thank you," Pierre said with a smile. "I will do so."

Breadroot or prairie potato was an early spring delicacy in these parts. Claire would have gone already to search for them but was not certain exactly what the

plant looked like at this stage and was waiting for One
Who Smiles to be strong enough to show her. When
Little Flower had come to the lodge and asked Claire
to accompany her to the riverbank, she took it as a
wonderful, hopeful sign.

Running Wolf had permitted no contact with her
among his family since Evening Sky's death and no
real kinship since the night he'd caught Claire and
Pierre answering his grandchildren's questions about
Christ.

Mother said God would bring healing, she thought.
Was her uncle's heart beginning to soften?

Both Three Horses and One Who Smiles had taken
Little Flower's arrival in a promising way, as well.
"Go," they said to them, "and good hunting."

Claire took with her a large grass basket similar to
the one her cousin was holding. Little Flower also carried with her two sharp sticks.

"We will search among the driftwood on the riverbank," she said.

They started toward the river and followed it for
some time in the direction opposite the fort.

"We will use our sticks to poke the soft earth," Little
Flower said. "That is how we will find them."

"Are they buried deeply?"

"Not very. Do not worry. You will find many. I will
teach you."

Claire drew in a breath. The air smelled of water and
strong earth. To a Mandan it was the scent of promise,
of new life. *Perhaps this year will be different here.*
She desperately wanted to believe that. "I have missed
you, cousin," she said. "I have missed you greatly."

Little Flower offered her a look that seemed somewhat disconcerted, as though Claire's words had troubled her in some way. Claire should have read the danger right then and there, but it wasn't until she and her cousin crested a knoll and were hidden from the view of both the village and the fort that she recognized what was happening. At the bottom of the hill stood Running Wolf. He was holding several horses. Golden Hawk was with him.

An icy chill, one colder than anything she had experienced this winter, shivered down her spine. Instinct told Claire to run. Only her previous prayer kept her from doing so. *I told God I would do anything for the sake of my family's eternity*, she reminded herself. But surely this was not what the Creator had in mind for her. How could a union with the medicine man's son bring about good? What did light and darkness have in common?

"Trust..."

Reluctantly she walked forward. Golden Hawk was looking upon her with a hunger that made her nauseated. Her uncle's face bore a look of triumph. Claire cast a quick glance at Little Flower. Her cousin had fixed her eyes on the ground, refusing to look at her.

She knew. She knew what was to take place. The offer of teaching me to find roots was only a ruse. Pain cut deep, but Claire did her best to beat back the feeling of betrayal and met the men where they stood.

"You know what Golden Hawk wishes," Running Wolf said.

"I do." *God, help me.*

"He brings fine horses for your price."

The magnificent creatures stamped and whinnied as if they disliked being traded as much as she did. Still

Claire did her best to respond respectfully. It would be better if she did. "He honors you," she said to Running Wolf.

"He honors *you*. You will accept him as your husband. You will go to his lodge today."

"Trust..."

But trust did not mean silence. Conviction far outweighed the sickening feeling inside her. So did something else. Strength. "I cannot do so, uncle."

Horses' lines in one hand, Running Wolf grabbed her chin with his other and jerked her head upward. His grip was like iron. His eyes flashed fire. "You will not dishonor me," he said.

Claire swallowed hard, but her voice did not waver. "I do not wish to dishonor you, uncle, but neither can I dishonor my God."

"You cling to your white man's religion still? Even after what happened to your mother?" He struck her across the face with such force that Claire fell into the mud.

Claire heard Little Flower gasp but did not look her way. She stood to her feet slowly, straightening to full height, though she kept her chin at a respectful level as she faced her uncle once more. "Beat me if you must," she said. "But I will never willingly enter into marriage with Golden Hawk. The God of all creation forbids it."

At that, Golden Hawk shouted curses at her, claimed he called the spirits against her. She was not frightened. Despite the threats, a peace settled over her.

"I do not fear your spirits, Golden Hawk," she said, "nor anything you may seek to do to me."

Golden Hawk turned his anger then toward Running Wolf. "She is not worthy of my attention! A curse on you and your lodge!" Snatching the horses' lead lines from Running Wolf's hand, he stormed back toward the village.

Only one horse remained and that was Running Wolf's. It was laden with blankets, beads and furs and foremost, his bow. Claire recognized at once that her uncle was prepared to go trading—likely intending to sell the extra horses he had intended to acquire. That opportunity was lost now, and he looked like he was strongly considering using the bow on her.

Her strength faltered. Fear threatened to creep in. *Am I to be murdered by my mother's brother? Is my own cousin to witness the deed?*

Fear, however, wasn't the prominent emotion washing over her. Regret was. She regretted that she'd not spoken more boldly of the truth of Scripture when she had the opportunity. She regretted that she had not been brave enough to tell Pierre how she actually felt about him. *Now he will never know.*

"*Trust...*"

Apparently Little Flower had no intention of witnessing a killing. Dropping her basket and sticks, she lifted her buckskin skirt and took off up the hill. Running Wolf called after her, but she did not look back. Claire could hear her crying as she ran.

Her desertion made Running Wolf all the angrier. "You have cost me much, woman," he said, spitting the words from his lips. "If you will not bring me the price of a bride then you shall fetch that of a slave. I shall sell you to the Assiniboine tribe. They will teach you the penalty for defying the ways of one's ancestors."

To resist was futile. He would only knock her out

and then throw her over the back of his horse. So Claire stood still as he tied a length of sinew about her wrists.

God will supply my need, she thought.

Running Wolf dragged her toward his horse. Instead of growing weak with fear, Claire found her body, her voice growing stronger. God was giving her courage.

"You will do as you must," she said to her uncle. "But I will never forsake the one true God."

"We shall see about that," Running Wolf said.

Chapter Seventeen

Pierre was having a friendly cup of tea with Three Horses and his family when Little Flower suddenly burst through the door. The expression on her face was frantic. Tears streamed down her cheeks.

"I have done a terrible thing!" she confessed.

Just what horrific crime she had committed, Pierre could not determine. Little Flower was speaking so rapidly, so frantically that even One Who Smiles could barely seem to decipher her speech. Pierre was filled with a sickening fear that Claire was somehow involved. He then distinctly heard Golden Hawk's name.

Muscles tensing, Pierre's first instinct was to storm the medicine man's lodge and drag Golden Hawk out of it by his long, flowing hair, rescue Claire with no thought to the consequences to him or his fellow expedition members. "Bright Star is with Golden Hawk?" he asked, rising to his feet.

Three Horses must have sensed his plan, for he grasped Pierre by the arm. "It is not the son of the medicine man you seek," he said. "It is Running Wolf."

So she wasn't about to be wedded, but Pierre was hardly relieved. "Where is he?"

"South of the village, in the valley of the two hills. Little Flower says he intends to sell Bright Star to the Assiniboine."

A fear unlike anything Pierre had ever experienced before gripped him, but instead paralyzing him, it fueled him for action. "Go alert Captain Clark," Pierre told Black Raven. "He's visiting your chief."

Black Raven raced to find the officer. Pierre headed for the door. He had no musket, but neither did Running Wolf. He had his knife, and although he prayed it would not come to such, he would use it if need be. "I must borrow your horse, friend," he called out over his shoulder to Three Horses.

"No," the warrior replied, coming after him. "We shall take two. I shall ride with you."

"Thank you, friend."

With Little Flower still crying in One Who Smiles's arms, the men hurriedly climbed aboard their mounts. They traveled as fast as the muddy ground would allow. Pierre's heart and thoughts were racing. What he would say to Claire when he saw her was no longer foremost on his mind. What he would say to her uncle was. Three Horses reminded him of the delicate nature of his chase.

"In this land, a man does not pursue a woman unless he intends to claim her. Are you prepared to do so?"

"Yes," Pierre said firmly. "If she'll have me."

"I do not think that will be a problem."

The fact that he had no bride price did not deter him. He was prepared to do whatever necessary. *God, please...don't let me be too late...*

They crested the hill. Running Wolf's horse was already some distance from them. Claire was walking slowly behind. The sight of her tied to her uncle's horse like a slave filled him with fury. Three Horses recognized it and was prepared to use Pierre's emotion to their advantage.

"You go down," he said. "I will go this way."

Pierre realized he intended to cut Running Wolf off from behind, using the distraction of Pierre's arrival to keep Running Wolf from noticing. Nodding his agreement, Pierre kicked his horse's flanks and charged down the hill. Reaching the bottom, he thundered with breakneck speed, yelling an angry war cry of his own.

Running Wolf slowed his mount, turned in Pierre's direction. He was so focused on the screaming Frenchman approaching that he failed to notice the Mandan warrior gaining ground from behind.

By the time Pierre was near enough to notice the mud on Claire's clothing, the bruise already swelling her cheek, Three Horses was descending the hill. But Pierre barely noticed him—all of his attention was directed at the woman before him. If Pierre had any doubts of how Claire would receive him, they vanished instantly.

Relief flooded her face, that and much more. *So she did refuse me because of what I would be asked to give up,* he realized, and sighed with relief. Foolish woman. Didn't she know that the land grant and even the Pacific Ocean were no sacrifices compared to losing her?

"This is no matter of yours, white man," Running Wolf said. "Go back to where you come."

Mindful of Three Horses's silent stance and trained

arrow, Pierre quickly dismounted. "This is most definitely my concern," he said. "I love your niece. I have come to claim her as my wife." He allowed himself one split-second glance at her. Her look fueled his courage.

Running Wolf sneered at them both. "Why would I give her to a weak white man? You have nothing to offer me. I make better trade with the Assiniboines."

"Nothing to offer perhaps but myself," Pierre said, approaching slowly.

Claire gasped, realizing what he was saying. "Pierre, no! No!" A look of fright filled her face. She struggled with her bonds.

"Make me your slave if you must," he said, "but let her go free."

"You plead like a woman," Running Wolf said. "Warriors fight."

"A true warrior will lay down his life for the one he loves."

Running Wolf slid deftly from his horse, drew out his tomahawk. Claire continued to struggle futilely with her ropes.

"I've no wish to fight you," Pierre said, as Running Wolf crept forward. "I only seek Claire."

"Then you are weak," the warrior said. "And I will kill you easily."

"No!" Claire screamed.

Pierre lifted his knife, but the moment Running Wolf raised his tomahawk, he heard the distinct whoosh of Three Horses's arrow. On target, it pierced the warrior's right hand. Shocked, Running Wolf instantly dropped his weapon. Only then did he realize Pierre traveled with an ally. His arrogance had blinded him.

Wounded but undaunted, Running Wolf snapped

the arrow shaft protruding from his bleeding hand and lunged at Pierre. Claire screamed once more. Pierre charged the warrior at his knees, knocking him to the ground. They wrestled and rolled, but in the end Pierre pinned his knife at Running Wolf's throat. Three Horses had advanced and now stood over Claire's wounded uncle with his bow drawn.

Running Wolf's dark eyes reflected disbelief and fear. "I have no wish to kill you," Pierre said, "and neither does Three Horses." He lowered his knife, but for their own safety, the bow remained trained.

Breathing heavily, heart thudding, Pierre then moved to free Claire from her bonds. She was sitting in the mud. Having done her utmost to push the rope from her hands by way of her feet, her wrists were now raw and bleeding. A bruise the size of her uncle's fist was taking shape on her right cheek. Pierre had never seen a more heartbreaking sight, and yet never had he seen a more beautiful woman.

"Pierre, please…" she gasped as he quickly slit the ropes from her wrists. "Do not make yourself a slave on my account."

There were tears in her eyes. She was trembling all over. So was he. He gently ran his fingers over her swollen cheek. All he had to clean her wrists was his own handkerchief.

"In the Bible, Joseph worked for an uncle for years for his beloved Rachael. I am willing to do the same if need be. I will do whatever is necessary, because I love you."

Tears were now streaming down her face. "Then your offer of marriage was not made from a sense of duty?"

"No, it wasn't. I just didn't realize it at the time."
His fingers traveled over her jaw, lingered about her
neck. "I have loved you for quite a while."

She touched his face reverently. Her expression reflected her disbelief and wonder. "And I love you."

He smiled, surprised at how much he had wanted to
hear those words. "That's why you refused me at first,
wasn't it? You ranked my happiness above your own,
and did not want me to forgo my land grant."

"Yes."

"I'm sorry I grew so angry."

"I'm sorry I was so stubborn, but I was afraid if you
did not truly care for me, you would regret your decision. The land was important…"

Sliding his arms about her, he carefully drew her to
her feet, held her close. "Ah, Claire, you mean more to
me than any piece of land."

They were quite a pair. She bruised and muddied,
he unshaven and clad in torn elk skin. It was hardly the
setting for a man and woman confessing their love, and
yet here on the frontier, it suited perfectly.

But their love for one another was not all that needed
to be resolved. Three Horses called out to Pierre, motioned to the top of the hill. Cresting the knoll were
Captain Clark, Chief Black Cat and several of his warriors. Taking Claire by the hand, Pierre moved to re-
join Three Horses, who remained standing guard over
Running Wolf.

Claire's uncle still carried the arrow that had
wounded him. Seeing it, Claire quickly took his hand
in hers and pushed the arrow through. Using the handkerchief Pierre had given her, she began tending the

wound. Running Wolf made no sound, no sign. He simply stared at her in silence.

Coming upon the scene, Captain Clark immediately frowned at the sight of the wounded man, as did Black Cat, but both men's faces softened to a look of concern when they noticed Claire's bruised form.

Black Cat quickly commanded one of his warriors to assume guard over Running Wolf while Three Horses was told to explain. Captain Clark demanded the same of Pierre.

"Her life was in danger, sir. I could not see her sold to another tribe."

"I'm glad for that, Lafayette," Clark said. "I'd expect no less from a man of your caliber, but what are you prepared to do now? You know Captain Lewis will not change his mind about taking her west."

"Yes, sir. I know that. What I will do now will depend on Chief Back Cat." He asked Three Horses to explain his intentions to the chief.

Saint Louis was no longer an option. Pierre was now as reluctant to leave this place as Claire. The village, and particularly her family, needed to be brought to the Lord—and he thought that now, they might actually have a chance. He'd seen the flicker of relief in Running Wolf's eyes when he'd told him that he had no wish to kill him, followed by the confused but appreciative look when Claire tended to his hand. Could the man finally understand what their faith was really all about? They wielded a weapon, it was true, but that weapon was love.

With his eagle feather swaying gently in the breeze, the great dignified chief continued to listen to Three

Horses's explanation, with the translation whispered to him by Claire.

"He wishes to remain in our village, oh great one. He has no bride price to offer but will offer himself as a slave to secure my freedom."

Black Cat was silent for several seconds. Pierre heard the pounding of his own heart in his ears. What would the man say?

At last, the chief spoke slowly, resolutely. *"Slave... peace...bride..."*

Pierre held his breath, waiting for the full translation. When it came, Claire's eyes held a hint of mirth.

"The Chief says you are welcome in the village, not as a slave but as an honored guest because you wish for peace among the white men and the Mandan."

Pierre's heart quickened. "And you?"

"The Chief says Running Wolf forfeited the bride price by damaging my face. He no longer has authority over me. I now belong to *you*."

Not quite, he thought. *I belong to you.*

Pierre nodded graciously to the chief, thanked him. "What will happen to Running Wolf?" he then asked.

"Whatever you wish," Claire said. "You defeated him in battle, yet you spared his life. You now have authority over him."

The temptation to exact revenge, not for himself but for Claire, snaked through Pierre's mind for the briefest of seconds, but he knew that was not the way.

"I wish for him to go in peace," Pierre said. "I wish for him to leave me, my bride and all those around us in peace."

Chief Black Cat nodded his approval. "Then it shall be so."

Feeling ten feet tall and capable of wrestling a bear to the ground, Pierre then turned and looked at Claire. Her eyes were downcast with the modesty of a proper young maiden, but Pierre noticed she was smiling from ear to ear.

Claire could not stop trembling, but not from fear. She was overwhelmed by pure and utter joy. In a matter of moments, she had gone from being a potential slave to a fiancée, and her betrothed was not only the mightiest, wisest warrior in the village but also the man she loved. He was a man of faith, honor and compassion.

The marriage she had long dreamed of, and prayed for, was at last to take place. God had given her a man who loved her, a man who would care for her and for those most dear to her for all of his days. Her mother had been right. God had supplied her needs.

Her chief had sanctioned the match, and Captain Clark approved of it, as well. "It will be a good thing to build a family here," he told Pierre. "You will serve as an example of cooperation and mutual respect to all those who pass this way."

Only Running Wolf's eyes held doubt. Claire had watched him carefully as she tended his wound. Her uncle knew Three Horses could have shot him through the heart, but he had chosen not to do so. *Just as Pierre chose not to take advantage of him with his knife.*

"Jesus tells us to be merciful to our enemies," she had whispered.

She had dressed the wound as best she could, using the handkerchief Pierre had given her and a piece of the sinew that had previously bound her. When the treating was done, Pierre offered his hand to assist Running Wolf to his feet. Her uncle eyed Pierre still with suspicion but accepted his help.

His arrows now at rest in his quiver, Three Horses along with Black Cat and his entourage took Running Wolf back to the village.

As well as things had gone, however, Pierre still had regrets. "If only I had claimed you sooner," he said, "this could have been avoided."

Claire did not begrudge the time. She looked him full in the face. "If you had, Running Wolf would not have been ready to listen."

"You think he is?"

"Perhaps," she said. "I have hope."

"As do I."

He touched her face gently. Her cheek ached, but she welcomed his caress. She had wished for it for so long.

"How did you know where to find me?" she asked.

"Your cousin. She came to Three Horses's lodge."

"Little Flower?

Pierre nodded. "I had come to see you, to speak with you, when she burst in, confessing her betrayal. She was quite distraught. One Who Smiles is tending her."

"Then she is in good hands," Claire said. "I have hope for her, as well."

"So do I…"

He leaned toward her, ready to claim his first and rightful kiss. Claire eagerly lifted her face to him.

"Ahem." Captain Clark cleared his throat.

The two of them broke apart immediately. Pierre's ears were as red as her cheeks. They had forgotten that the officer was still there.

"Am I to assume this wedding will take place before the expedition departs?" he asked.

"Yes," Pierre said. "It must, since for lack of a priest in these parts, either you or Captain Lewis must perform the ceremony."

Clark grinned. Of all the surprise duties this expedition had produced, a wedding was surely the most unexpected. "When exactly must this ceremony be performed?"

Pierre looked at Claire, his black eyes dancing with delight. "What about today?"

She let out a laugh, partly one of joy, partly in disbelief. Surely he didn't wish for her to come to him looking like this. "As eager as I am to become your wife, Monsieur Lafayette, some time for preparation would be appreciated. I would rather be wed without bruises upon my face and wrists."

"You are beautiful to me just as you are."

Her resolve to wait wavered, but she was determined to stand firm. "Have you not duties to perform before your captains depart?"

"He does indeed," Clark said with another grin.

Pierre growled like a bear, albeit a playful one. "Have I not labored long enough for you this week? I know for certain I was assigned more duties than the others."

"Yes, you were," Clark admitted, "but it was for your own benefit. There is nothing like hard work to focus a man's mind."

In which direction Clark had wanted him to focus, westward or right in front of him, he did not say, and Pierre did not ask. "The expedition is to depart on the first, is it not?"

"It was, but Captain Lewis informed me this morning that we will most likely wait one week longer. The floating ice should be sufficiently diminished by then, making the northern Missouri much easier to navigate."

"So, the seventh of April?"

"That is the date now fixed," Clark said.

"And that," Claire added, "would be sufficient time to prepare for a wedding."

April seventh dawned bright and clear. Though Pierre might be a bridegroom, he was, at least for a few more hours, a member of the Corps of Discovery. Therefore he spent all morning and a good part of the afternoon with his comrades, loading the keelboat and pirogues. The former carried the artifacts and reports of the land previously viewed. The latter contained every article by which Lewis, Clark and the others were expected to subsist and defend themselves in the unknown.

It is a grand adventure, Pierre thought. *Like Columbus of old.* But an even grander one was about to commence for him. *I am about to become a husband and, God willing, one day a father.* With faith, love and hard work, everything he and his family would need was before him.

He and Claire were to reside temporarily at the fort until Pierre could craft a small private lodge in the village. Three Horses had offered to teach him the Mandans' building secrets, and Chief Black Cat had already chosen the spot—right next to his own lodge, as his most honored guest.

They were welcome in the village. Pierre prayed that in time, Claire's uncle would feel the same about them. Since their confrontation, Running Wolf had not spoken to either of them, but he had not resisted Claire's careful tending of his wound, nor the meat Pierre had brought from his last hunt.

"Crates accounted for!" Pierre heard Private Cruzette call.

The last of the sundries and supplies had been loaded. The boats now sat low in the rippling water.

"Hadn't you better go make yourself presentable?" Captain Clark asked Pierre. "Your young bride will be here soon."

Indeed she will, Pierre couldn't help but think with a grin. "Thank you, sir."

After a wash and a shave, Pierre donned his best elk skin breeches, linen shirt and coat, then returned to the river. There his comrades and a large group of Mandans who had gathered to witness the "curious ceremony" were assembled. Sadly, Running Wolf was nowhere to be found, but Chief Black Cat and his family, One Who Smiles, Little Flower and her children were foremost among the crowd.

A flock of geese flying overhead trumpeted the bride's arrival. Pierre drew in a breath. Claire arrived on horseback, wearing the red dress her mother had made. Her long, dark hair hung loose about her shoulders, and a crown of beads and fresh juniper shoots wreathed her head. The bruises had faded. A happy glow now graced her face. She was breathtaking.

French and Indian, he couldn't help but think, and Pierre wouldn't have wanted it any other way.

Three Horses helped her from her mount, led her to where Pierre stood eagerly waiting. With a smile, the man then placed her hand in his.

Pierre gave her fingers a light squeeze. "You are beautiful," he whispered.

She grinned, her dark eyelashes fluttering against her olive skin. "And you are most handsome," she said.

Captain Lewis stepped forward and conducted the simple ceremony. After a prayer of blessing, he looked straight at Pierre and said, "Lafayette, you may now kiss your bride."

"Yes, sir!" Amid the cheers of all those gathered, Pierre drew Claire close and pressed his lips to hers. The world around them faded for the space of a few heartbeats, until the captain invaded the moment. Duty called.

"Well, now that you have your affairs settled, I wonder if you and your wife would consider an offer of future employment."

Somewhat annoyed by the interruption, Pierre blinked. Claire, however, looked intrigued.

"I have spoken with Chief Black Cat of the possibility of traveling to Washington to meet President Jefferson upon our return," Lewis said. "We shall need interpreters, and I do believe the chief would be more comfortable traveling with members of his own tribe."

Pierre looked at his bride. He could see the eagerness in her eyes. "It would be an honor, sir."

Lewis nodded. "Very well then, Mr. Lafayette, Mrs. Lafayette...we will see you upon our return." With that the captain gave the order for the men to board the boats. Hand in hand, the couple watched them do so.

"Are you certain you don't want to go with them?" Claire asked.

Pierre turned and looked into those beautiful spring-green eyes. "I've all the adventure I need right here," he said. "I love you."

She grinned bashfully. "And I love you."

Drawing in a satisfied breath, Pierre then said, "Well, *wife*...our life together awaits."

"Indeed, *husband*."

And they turned their back on the river and walked toward the fort.

Epilogue

Washington City
December 30, 1806

"I take you by the hand of friendship…"

Claire repeated President Thomas Jefferson's words to the Mandan delegation. Since Chief Black Cat could not make the long journey, the President shook hands with his representative, Sheheke-shote, and then nodded graciously to the warrior's wife and child. The little boy flailed his arms in delight and squealed, causing Jefferson to smile.

Claire looked across the room to her own dark-haired son, Rene François, whom Pierre was holding. Anxious to exercise his newly acquired walking skills, he squirmed in his father's arms.

And soon there will be another to join our lodge, she thought happily as she laid her hand across her still-slender belly. She had not told Pierre the news yet, knowing he would be even more concerned for her than he had been on this long journey east.

Much had happened in their short time together as

husband and wife. No sooner had Captains Lewis and Clark left the village than the Sioux had come calling. Sadly, there had been thieving and loss of life. Eight warriors had died, but thankfully there was no all-out war. Committed to peace, the Mandans and several other tribes of the plains had sent their representatives to Washington in hopes of securing it.

Claire was greatly encouraged, but she did not place her faith in treaties or the men that brokered them. She placed it in God alone.

As President Jefferson turned away from the delegation to speak with Pierre, Running Wolf whispered in her ear, "You have done well, Bright Star. The White Father has honored our people. I in return honor you. Your mother would be proud."

She smiled at her uncle, so thankful that he had come on this journey, so thankful for the friendship he and Pierre were forming. "It was not my doing," she whispered.

"I know, but the Great Spirit has worked through you—" he nodded toward Pierre "—and your husband."

Running Wolf had finally come to accept the love and sacrifice of Christ. Now he walked not the path of war and superstition, but one of love and truth.

Her mother had insisted God would bring healing. *He has surely done it for my household, one member at a time. And if men and women continue to open their hearts to Him, what a world this will be...* No longer did Claire fear the future for herself or her children. God would be with them whatever came.

Inadvertently she again laid her hand across her middle.

Noticing, Pierre's eyes widened. His lips moved into a curious smile.

He knows, she thought. Try as she might, she could not hide her grin.

The moment President Jefferson turned away from him, Pierre came to where she stood. Rene François immediately dove toward Running Wolf. The tall, fearsome-looking warrior caught the child with a laugh and a smile.

Pierre pulled her aside. "Is there something you need to tell me?" he asked, a twinkle in his eye.

"Only that our children are greatly blessed."

"Children?"

She nodded. "They have a God who watches over them and a family that will love and teach them everything they need to know in order to live life well upon this earth."

He took her hand in his, squeezed it gently. Pierre's charcoal eyes told her he would like to have kissed her if not for propriety's sake. He gave her a handsome smile. "What adventures for us lay in store."

* * * * *

*Don't miss Shannon Farrington's other
sweet historical stories!*

HER REBEL HEART
AN UNLIKELY UNION
SECOND CHANCE LOVE
THE RELUCTANT BRIDEGROOM

Find more great reads at www.LoveInspired.com

Dear Reader,

Thank you for choosing my book, *Frontier Agreement*.
It was during a family vacation out west several years
ago that I first became enamored with the story of Lewis
and Clark. Returning home, I devoured the expedition
journals and any other material about the explorers that I
could locate. Soon my imagination was off and running.
In this story, Claire and Pierre are, of course, fictional
characters, as are all of her immediate family, but the
setting and events in which they find themselves are, to
the best of my ability, historically accurate.

Lewis and Clark did spend the winter of 1804–1805
among the Mandan people in present-day North Dakota,
and the medical difficulties, misunderstandings of tribal
customs, struggle for food and trouble with the Sioux actually happened. Toussaint Charbonneau and Sacagawea
did live at the fort for a time and serve as translators.
Charbonneau's disagreement with Captain Lewis, however, actually did not take place until March of 1805. I
took the liberty of moving the event forward a few months
in order to place Claire at the fort during Christmas.

While working on this project, I kept wondering
what it would have been like to have been a part of the
expedition. Would I have been able to endure the hard-
ships? Would I have been able to trust God and complete the tasks assigned to me, or would I have given
in to fear of the unknown?

I hope Claire and Pierre's story will inspire you to
forge your own frontier.

Blessings,
Shannon Farrington

THE RANCHER'S SURPRISE TRIPLETS
Lone Star Cowboy League: Multiple Blessings
by Linda Ford

After stumbling on triplet orphans abandoned at the county fair, rancher Bo Stillwater's not sure what to do with them. But when he leaves them in the care of the town doctor's lovely spinster daughter, Louisa Clark, he finds he can't stay away—from her or the babies.

COWBOY HOMECOMING
Four Stones Ranch • by Louise M. Gouge

When cowboy Tolley Northam returns home, he's determined to finally win his father's approval. Perhaps a marriage to family friend Laurie Eberly will help him earn it. But when Laurie discovers *why* he began pursuing her, can he convince her that she holds his heart?

UNDERCOVER SHERIFF
by Barbara Phinney

After a woman, a child and Zane Robinson's small-town-sheriff twin all go missing, the woman's friend Rachel Smith has a plan to find them. But for it to work, Zane must pose as his brother and draw out anyone involved in their disappearance.

FAMILY OF CONVENIENCE
by Victoria W. Austin

In need of a father for her unborn child, mail-order bride Millie Steele agrees to a marriage in name only with single father Adam Beale. But as she grows to love her new children— and falls for their handsome dad—can their convenient family become real?

Get 2 Free Books,
Plus 2 Free Gifts—
just for trying the Reader Service!

When local rancher Bo Stillwater finds abandoned triplet babies at the county fair, the first person he turns to is doctor's daughter Louisa Clark. But as they open their hearts to the children, they might discover unexpectedly tender feelings for one another taking root.

Read on for a sneak preview of
THE RANCHER'S SURPRISE TRIPLETS,
the touching beginning of the series
LONE STAR COWBOY LEAGUE:
MULTIPLE BLESSINGS.

"Doc? I need to see the doctor."

Father had been called away. Whatever the need, she would have to take care of it. She opened the door and stared at Bo in surprise until crying drew her attention to the cart beside him.

"Babies? What are you doing with babies?" All three crying and looking purely miserable.

"I think they're sick. They need to see the doctor."

"Bring them in. Father is away but I'll look at them."

"They need a doctor." He leaned to one side to glance into the house as if to make sure she wasn't hiding her father. "When will he be back?"

"I'll look at them," she repeated. "I've been my father's assistant for years. I'm perfectly capable of checking a baby. Bring them in." She threw back the door so he could push the cart inside. She bent over to look more closely at the babies. "We don't see triplets often." She read their names on their shirts. "Hello, Jasper, Eli and Theo."

They were fevered and fussy. Theo reached his arms toward her. She lifted him and cradled him to her shoulder. "There,

there, little man. We'll fix you up in no time."

Jasper, seeing his brother getting comfort, reached out his arms, too.

Louisa grabbed a kitchen chair and sat, putting Theo on one knee and lifting Jasper to the other. The babies were an armload. At first glance they appeared to be in good health. But they were fevered. She needed to speak to the mother about their age and how long they'd been sick.

Eli's wails increased at being left alone.

"Can you pick him up?" she asked Bo, hiding a smile at his hesitation. Had he never held a baby? At first he seemed uncertain what to do, but Eli knew and leaned his head against Bo's chest. Bo relaxed and held the baby comfortably enough. Louisa grinned openly as the baby's cries softened. "He's glad for someone to hold him. Where are the parents?"

"Well, that's the thing. I don't know."

"You don't know where the parents are?"

He shook his head. "I don't even know *who* they are."

"Then why do you have the babies?"

For an answer, he handed her a note and she read it. "They're abandoned?" She pulled each baby close as shock shuddered through her. He explained how he'd found them in the pie tent.

"I must find their mother before she disappears." Bo looked at Louisa, his eyes wide with appeal, the silvery color darkened with concern for these little ones. "I need to go but how are you going to manage?"

She wondered the same thing. But she would not let him think she couldn't do it. "I'll be okay. Put Eli down. I'll take care of them."

Don't miss
THE RANCHER'S SURPRISE TRIPLETS by Linda Ford,
available April 2017 wherever
Love Inspired® Historical books and ebooks are sold.

www.LoveInspired.com

LIHEXP0317

"Lie still. You may have broken something," Lizbeth instructed.

His hand moved and then his arm. Blue eyes—so like her son's—opened to slits. He blinked at her. A shaggy brow arched in question. Full, well-shaped lips moved, but no words came out.

She leaned back in surprise. The man on the ground was Fredrik Lapp, her brother's childhood friend. The last man in Pinecraft she wanted to see. "Are you all right?" she asked, bending close.

His coloring looked normal enough, but she knew nothing about broken bones or head trauma. She looked down the length of his body. His clothes were dirty but seemed intact.

The last time she'd seen him, she'd been a skinny girl of nineteen, and he'd been a wiry young man of twenty-three. Now he was a fully matured man. One who could rip her life apart if he learned about the secret she'd kept all these years.

He coughed several times and scowled as he drew in a

deep breath.

"Is the *kinner* all right?" Fredrik's voice sounded deeper and raspier than it had years ago. With a grunt, he braced himself with his arms and struggled into a sitting position.

Lizbeth glanced Benuel's way. He was looking at them, his young face pinched with concern. Her heart ached for the intense, worried child.

"*Ya*, he's fine," she assured Fredrik and tried to hold him down as he started to move about. "Please don't get up. Let me get some help first. You might have really hurt yourself."

He ignored her direction and rose to his feet, dusting off the long legs of his dark trousers. "I got the wind knocked out of me, that's all."

He peered at his bleeding arm, shrugged his broad shoulders and rotated his neck as she'd seen him do a hundred times as a boy.

"That was a foolish thing you did," he muttered, his brow arched.

"What was?" she asked, mesmerized by the way his muscles bulged along his freckled arm. It had to be wonderful to be strong and afraid of nothing.

He gestured toward the boy. "Letting your *soh* run wild like that? He could have been killed. Why didn't you hold his hand while you crossed the road?"

Don't miss
HER SECRET AMISH CHILD by Cheryl Williford,
available April 2017 wherever
Love Inspired® books and ebooks are sold.

www.LoveInspired.com